LOVE GROWS IN OMAHA

By Lola

ISBN=10: 0-9981297-0-4

ISBN-13: 978-0-9981297-0-9

DEDICATION

To my husband, Larry, as well as a long list of family and friends with love! I appreciate the loving encouragement, patience and support that I've received from them.

My beautiful daughters and grandchildren are my love and inspiration!

A Special Thanks to:

Mary W. for being my longtime extended family and prayer partner!

Sandra K. for her role in helping me bravely follow my heart. She has provided me with renewed strength to fulfill my life's journey!

Shannon C. for being my friend with encouraging words and loving support throughout this book-writing journey!

Tammy G. for being my longtime friend and my Dream Team Partner!

PREFACE

"Love grows in Omaha" is my first love and romance novel. I plan to write sequels. I'm currently writing several love stories.

This heartwarming love story is about romantic and sweet fictional characters. The names of the characters and the businesses were randomly chosen by me from my imagination.

These fictional families deal with real life issues. It's all about love, romance, family and commitment. The story takes place during the month of May in a city named Omaha. You might laugh but there's a chance you'll cry.

TABLE OF CONTENT

CHAPTER ONE
THE INTERVIEW

CLICKETY-CLACK click-click-click. That's the sound of her high heels in the hallway. She stops and walks through the open door of an office. She's there for an interview.

"Hello, my name is Amanda James. Nice to meet you."

She extends a trembling hand across the large desk. He gently reaches for her hand to acknowledge her greeting.

"My name is Jonathan Young. Please have a seat."

Amanda, or Mandy as her friends call her, notices that the huge office is furnished with a large cherry wood desk, beautiful furniture, a plush carpet and drapes. Everything in the office is really rich-looking and lovely.

She sits down on a chair in front of his desk while breathing a quiet sigh of relief. She feels comfort from the warmth of the sun shining through the windows. The sunshine adds a little extra sparkle to their eyes.

Jonathan, or Jonny as his friends call him, picks up a file from the desktop and scans it briefly. He glances up and they quickly make eye contact. They both smile in their own special way.

Mandy isn't the only one that's nervous. Jonny isn't prepared to conduct this interview. His Father, Gary Young, asked him to fill in for him at the last minute. Gary was called away on an unexpected business trip.

Mandy arrives on time filled with hope that she can land this new job with Harris and Young Modelling Agency. Her resume is impressive. She earned top scores as a business major at the Metro Business College.

Gary started this company with Ted Harris many years ago and now he's ready to retire. He wants his son, Jonny, to step up and run the business for him since Ted is already retired. Jonny, a professional photographer, has been working with his father at the modelling agency.

They've decided to hire a business assistant to aid in the transition. Even though Gary wants to be here for this interview, he believes that Jonny can handle it. He'll be working close together with the new assistant. Her job will be similar to a personal assistant on most days.

While reviewing her application and resume, he begins the interview by asking Mandy lots of questions. He's happy with what he's read. He believes that she's qualified to do this job very well!

Mandy asks questions in return regarding hours, benefits and pay. The interview goes very well and both appear to be happy. He'll share his opinion and outcome of the interview with his father before he makes a final decision.

In the meantime, he offers her a chance to take a brief tour of the building and business offices. It's approaching the dinner hour. He suggests that they walk over to a nearby restaurant for dinner after the tour.

She feels unsure but graciously accepts his offer. They both agree it's a great way to relax while getting to know the business and each other a little better. They feel confident that Gary will officially hire her because of her outstanding qualifications and her enthusiastic interest in this job.

First of all, he explains, "The office we're sitting in belongs to my father, Gary. He's the owner of this Agency."

They're ready to leave the office now. She collects her things and exits to the hallway. The clickety-clack of her heels can be heard once again. He follows her out after he turns off the lights. He locks the door for the night.

The next stop of the tour is just down the hall. He opens the door and invites her in. This room is a large portrait studio where he works as a professional photographer. He enjoys his job because he's passionate about the people he works with and has a passion for photography. Over the years, he has helped models of all ages, men, women and children create their portfolios.

He says, "This will be a quick tour. If you're officially hired, I'll show you more details soon. We should head down to the restaurant before the dinner rush. On our way, I want to show you the beautiful garden that my Mom designed."

She agrees and says, "I'm anxious to see and know more about the Agency. It'll be good to sit at the restaurant and learn more about it from you. I'm surprised to hear you talk about a garden here in the middle of a big city."

They take the elevator down from the third floor. Down in the lobby, he escorts her over to the double doors that lead out to the courtyard.

She cheerfully says, "WOW! So beautiful! Gardens in Omaha are gorgeous this time of year. Your Mom did a fantastic job of designing this garden!"

Lots of colorful flowers are in bloom and the fragrance is sweet as well as refreshing. There are flowers in hanging baskets, flower boxes and decorative round earthen pots. In one corner of the garden is a cute little sign with the words *'Butterfly Garden.'* A small tranquility fountain is centered within the area of these beautiful plants.

She spies the beautiful pink sweetheart roses along a short white stone wall. She enthusiastically says, "Pink Sweetheart Roses are my favorite!"

He responds, "Those roses were my Mom's favorite, too!

There are strings of twinkling white lights draped on the wall and a few bushes. The lights glitter like diamonds adding ambience to the patio. The area where they're now standing is just outside of the restaurant, Ted's Steakhouse.

He looks into her hazel eyes. *She appears to have both inner and outer beauty.* Although he knows that this dinner is intended for business reasons, he feels comfortable with her on a personal level.

She gazes into his dark brown eyes in return. She enjoys the personal time spent with this handsome man. She shakes her head to remind herself that this is strictly business.

They're both dressed in expensive business clothes. People might say that they make a lovely couple. He offers her the choice of sitting and talking inside the restaurant or outside on the patio. She chooses the patio because it's going to be a beautiful moonlit night. The garden patio looks and feels like paradise. He's pleased with her choice. They sit down on beautiful padded chairs next to a table covered with a white linen cloth.

The waitress strolls over with two glasses of water and hands them their menus. She asks for their drink orders.

He says, "We need a little more time to look over the menus. We'll order soft drinks with our meals. Thank you!"

There's still the question; will they want a full meal or something light? He's paying for their meals using his expense account in order to discuss business issues.

He tells Mandy, "You can order whatever you want."

She decides to eat light tonight. When the waitress returns, Mandy orders a cobb salad and a soft drink. Jonny orders a medium rare steak with baked potato, small salad and a soft drink.

While waiting for their food to be served, Jonny's cell phone rings. He tells Mandy, "I need to take this call!" He stands up and steps a few feet away from the other diners.

"Hello, Dad! How's your trip going?"

"Hello, Jon! My trip is going very well! I'm checking in about your interview with Amanda James."

Jonny gives him a good report. His Dad is pleased to hear the good news. He says, "I totally agree that she's more than qualified. It's okay with me for you to officially hire her for the job." They exchange good-byes.

He returns to the table where she's waiting. He sits down and sees a very anxious expression on her face.

The waitress is on her way to the table to serve their meals. By this time, they're both really hungry and thirsty. They take a quick sip of their soft drinks to quench their thirst. The cold drink helps to calm their nerves.

Before they eat their first bite of food, he speaks up to tell her that the phone call was from his father. Her heart is pounding. He's excited to share the good news.

He tells her, "We're officially hiring you to be our business assistant. We feel confident that you'll be a great asset to the Agency."

She feels overjoyed. They're both smiling and look forward to talking about business issues tonight.

First, they eat their delicious looking meals while they're still fresh. The waitress stops by to ask if they want to order dessert. They decline but decide to order coffee.

The coffee is served in fancy designer mugs. He drinks his coffee black while she drinks her coffee with a packet of sugar and a drop of cream. Drinking the warm coffee is relaxing while they sit and discuss Q&A's about Agency business.

They ask and answer a few questions about their personal lives. They're interested in knowing each other a little better. Since they'll work close together, they agree on the importance of clear communication between the two of them.

They enjoy this time together but it's late in the evening. He asks the waitress for the check. He leans in toward her to quietly ask her for a small to-go cup and a couple of paper napkins. She returns with the check and the requested items.

He pays the bill while asking, "Amanda, um, is it okay if I call you Mandy like your friends do?"

"Yes, of course. With all due respect Jonathan, may I call you Jonny? You know? Like your friends do?" They both smile.

"Definitely, Mandy! Can you come in to the Agency tomorrow morning around 10:00am? I'll be busy with several scheduled appointments in the afternoon."

"Yes, Jonny, but can you please tell me why?"

"I can show you your office and introduce you to my father, Gary. We can count it as your first day on the job. Friday is a business casual day so you can wear more comfortable shoes, too. Those high heels look like they need a rest." He chuckles nervously while waiting for her answer.

She begins to chuckle softly, "Yes, 10:00am will be a perfect time for me to start tomorrow. I'll be happy to dress casually because you're right about my high heels!"

"We can meet at the Agency's front office on the first floor. May I walk you to your car? I assume it's parked in front of the building. It's a lovely night for a moonlight stroll through the garden."

Jonny stops at the end of the white stone wall. Sliding one of the small flat stones reveals a storage shelf with small garden tools. He removes a small pair of clippers. At the small fountain, he moistens one of the paper napkins. He snips off several stems of pink sweetheart roses. He wraps the bottom of the stems in the moist napkin and then wraps them with the dry one.

Finally, he arranges the small bouquet in the to-go cup and hands it to Mandy with a smile. "Thank you, Mandy, for applying for the job with us at the Agency. I hope you'll enjoy working with us for a long time to come. Thank you for the enjoyable visit that I've had with you this evening."

Resisting an urge to give him a thank you hug, she says, "Thank you, Jonny, for the beautiful roses. You're very thoughtful to do this for me. I'm excited about working with you and your Dad at the Agency. I enjoyed our time together this evening. Thank you for everything!"

He stares momentarily at how beautiful she looks in the moonlight. When she smiles, her whole face lights up.

"I know my Mom would be happy for me to share the roses with you. Did you see the bench by the Butterfly Garden? It's engraved with a dedication. "In loving memory of Angela Young". She was my mother and this was her garden. She passed away a couple of years ago. She's gone but will never be forgotten. We love and miss her very much."

"Oh, Jonny, I'm so sorry for your loss. What a beautiful way to honor her memory."

"Let's walk back through the double doors to the lobby. We can exit through the front door of the building to your car."

They arrive at her car safely and say goodnight to each other. Neither one wants the evening to end but tomorrow is a new day.

CHAPTER TWO
IT'S A NEW DAY

It's Friday morning. Gary has returned from his business trip and arrives at the Agency before his son.

There's a little Deli-Bakery cafe to the right in the lobby! It's open for business early in the morning until early evening. Gary generously pays for and offers free coffee from the cafe to his employees daily. The aroma of the fresh brewed coffee draws him in for his first cup. *Always a great way to start a new day.*

He rides the elevator up to the third floor and unlocks the door to his office. The building is quiet this early in the morning. He's feeling a little tired from jet lag and the long busy week. His big comfortable chair is just what he needs to settle in and drink his coffee.

He uses this time to find out what happened while he was away. He checks his calendar and the paperwork that is stacked on his desk. Although it's good to get away, he's happy to be back! He looks forward to seeing his son and meeting Ms. James.

He hears the elevator doors open and close. The sound of the footsteps in the hallway is familiar. Glancing toward his office door, he sees his son standing there. Jon steps in and places his cup of coffee and a vase on the edge of his Dad's desk.

"Hello, Dad! Happy to see that you're back safe and sound." They greet each other with sturdy handshakes and shoulder hugs.

"How are you doing, son? I'm happy to see you this morning. I really missed you!"

Jon picks up the bud vase that's holding a beautiful single pink sweetheart rose.

His dad smiles and says, "Son, is that for me?" They grin and share a little chuckle.

"No, just a little surprise for Mandy um Amanda James. This morning, I'm planning to show her the office where she'll be working. I thought she might enjoy seeing this on her desk. Last night, I asked her to come in at 10:00am. I'll go place this vase on her desk now and I'll be right back."

His Dad smiles and says, "That was very thoughtful of you, Son. I really raised you right!" Jon smiles and heads down the hall.

He returns to his Dad's office and picks up his cup of coffee. He sits down on a chair in front of the desk for a quick visit. They enjoy their coffee together in the solitude of the early morning hours.

"I have a busy day ahead with several appointments scheduled on my calendar. What about you Dad? Will you be free around 10:00am to meet Amanda?"

"I'm looking forward to meeting Amanda James. I should be free around that time."

"She likes to be called Mandy. That's the name her friends call her. I think that you'll like her. She appears to be beautiful inside and out just like Mom. She's very excited about working here with us. I think everything will work out well with her on board. She's sure to be a big help with the transition. We can talk more about that later."

His Dad replies, "How about the three of us meet around 10:30am or 11:00am at the café for a light brunch? No need to talk about business this morning. We can just meet for some light conversation. We'll have plenty of time to get to know each other. We can talk about business another day."

"That sounds like a great idea!"

"She'll want to settle in her new office today. She'll need to fill out paperwork for the personnel office. Several legal forms are necessary to work here as an employee."

"OK, I'll have her stop in their office this morning when she first arrives."

"If there's time for another tour, you can introduce her to the people who are working here today. You two can enjoy the rest of the day. Let's enjoy the weekend, too!"

"I'll try to show her around but it'll take time to show her everything. Hopefully, she'll have time next week as well to explore and meet our employees."

"Now that Ms. James is here to sort out things, I'll seriously want to survey the business issues next week. Before Ted retired, he carried half of the burden. Now, I've acquired the full load of responsibility. Before I make major decisions about my retirement, we need to observe and consider the big picture. Owning the businesses and overseeing their operation has been a big responsibility. Although there's plenty of time before I officially retire, I really want the transition to go as smooth as possible. We can take our time to prevent stress overload."

He adds with a big grin, "I really look forward to taking a long overdue vacation this summer. I dream about taking a cruise to relax and enjoy the fun time of seeing the world."

"I agree with you, Dad. I really believe that Mandy has the best qualifications. She'll be a great asset to our Agency. Her personality impresses me. I think she'll successfully work well with both of us. You really deserve a long vacation, Dad. You've been working long hours for many years. It seems that you've been married to this job since Mom's passing. I'll do everything that I possibly can to help with your dream of retiring and a vacation cruise before the summer is over."

"Thank you, Jon!"

"I better run, I've got an appointment at our portrait studio. See you later, Dad!"

"Ok, Jon. I'll see you and Ms. James later in the morning. Thank you for the visit!"

Jon rushes out the door in a flash and quickly makes his way down the hall to the studio.

****

Buzzzzzz! BuZzZzZ! BUZZZZZ! Mandy rolls over to turn off the alarm clock. She barely slept a wink feeling the excitement of starting a new job. She jumps out of bed. *I'm grateful that I had extra time to sleep in.* After a quick shower, she gets dressed in a casual outfit and shoes. She takes time to drink a cup of tea and eat a bowl of cereal while checking her phone messages.

She arrives safely and on time at the Agency. Once again, she parks her car in front of the building. When she enters the front door, she sees Jonny. He's standing in the hallway off to the left and just outside the Agency's front office.

He smiles and says, "Good morning, Mandy! It's a beautiful Friday."

She smiles and says, "Good morning, Jonny! Yes, it is! It's supposed to be a beautiful weekend, too."

"Let's stop in the personnel office next door to pick up the forms that you'll need to complete for us today. Would you like to start your day with a cup of coffee? We can get a couple of cups in the café."

She says with a shy grin, "Okay. Filling out these forms will keep me busy. A cup of coffee sounds really great!"

As they stroll down the hall to the café, Jonny tells her the coffee at the café is free. He explains that his Dad offers the coffee free to the employees in the Agency building. They walk to the deli-bakery and everything smells delicious. He helps her find the cream and sugar for her coffee.

They walk down the hall to the elevator and ride up to the third floor. Jonny grins and says,

"Your office is ready and waiting for your arrival." They share a little laugh feeling the excitement of the new job and working together. Exiting the elevator, they turn left and walk down the hall to an office across from the studio.

He opens the door while announcing, "Welcome to your office, Mandy!"

She's very excited and stifles a little squeal. Her eyes widen with joy as she sees the bud vase sitting on her desk.

She laughs and says, "Oh, Jonny, Thank you! Is the pink sweetheart rose from the garden? It's so beautiful and smells so sweet! I love it!"

Jonny says with a smile, "You're welcome, Mandy! Yes, the pink rose is from the garden. I thought you might enjoy a little surprise. Hope you like your office. You can sit here and fill out the forms now if you want."

"Filling out the forms here at my desk will work out well. Thank you!"

"We'll make a nameplate for your desk and one for your door. They should be ready for your office next week."

"OH, I appreciate that very much!"

"I want to introduce you to my Dad this morning. We want to invite you for brunch at the café. We'll give you time to settle in and fill out the forms. I'm thinking 11:00am will be the best time for the three of us to get together. We'll meet you back here at about 10:50am. We can ride the elevator down to the lobby together. I'll leave you alone now."

Mandy is sitting happily at her desk. She says, "Thank you for everything! I look forward to meeting your Dad at the brunch. I'll see you a little later."

Although she has a pen in her purse, she searches through the desk to find a pen. She takes a mental note of the supplies stored in her desk. In the top drawer way at the back, she discovers a little photo album. *Maybe this was left behind by the person who previously used my desk.* Out of curiosity, she thumbs through it and recognizes pictures of Jonny.

Maybe this was Angela's desk when she worked here. She feels a sting of sadness in her heart. She tucks the album in a pocket of her purse. *I'll return it to Jonny and Gary during our brunch.*

She recalls seeing Angela's beautiful garden last night. She stands up and looks out the window of her office. She stands on tippy-toes and looks way down. She's able to see the butterfly garden and the pink sweetheart roses along the white stone wall.

She finds a pen and begins to fill out the forms. Filling them out isn't hard to do but proves to be time consuming. *I would like a second cup of coffee. I can enjoy another cup at the café with Jonny and Gary.*

They're standing outside her door smiling and happy. Jonny says, "Hi, Mandy. Are you ready to go to the café?"

"Yes, I'm ready. I finished filling out the forms."

"You can bring them with you. We can drop them off at the personnel office on our way."

She places the forms in a side pocket of her purse. While standing up, she says, "I didn't mean to keep you waiting."

"By the way, one of the forms is for an Employee ID. You'll need to stop in the personnel office to apply for it with a little photo of yourself. You can use your Employee ID to receive discounts on certain items and services. We also offer a few free services through our various companies. We'll talk more about that later."

Jonny looks around for his father, "Dad? I'd like to introduce you to Amanda James our new business assistant."

He glances over at Mandy, "I would like you to meet, Gary Young, my father and owner of the Agency as well as other businesses."

They reach out at the same time to shake hands. Gary gives her a warm welcome.

She smiles and says, "You can call me Mandy."

"Mandy, Jon has shared lots of great things about you. We're happy that you're on board and eager to work with us."

Jonny asks them, "Are we ready to go to the café now? We can sit down there and chat while we eat our brunch. I'm hungry!"

They laugh and his Dad says jokingly, "Ah, you're always hungry, Jon!"

They ride the elevator down to the lobby. She drops off the paperwork at the personnel office and sets up a time to create her photo ID. She's feeling a little nervous around Gary. Making a good first impression with her employer is important to her.

They choose a table in a quiet corner of the cafe. Mandy places her purse on her chair. She strolls over to the coffee counter for her second cup. Jon and his Dad also pour themselves a cup of coffee. They sip it carefully as they stand with Mandy to read the menu on the back wall.

The food is always delicious. Since this is Mandy's first time, they make suggestions about their favorite food to her. She orders a BLT sandwich which is one of her favorites. Jon and Gary order ham and Swiss cheese on rye. Their sandwiches will be delivered to their table. Gary happily pays with his business expense account.

Before their food arrives, Mandy removes the small photo album from her purse. She places it in the middle of the table for both of them to see.

She explains, "I found this album while searching through my desk for a pen. It was way in the back of the top drawer. I thought that you two would want to keep it."

Their eyes open wide with surprise. They view all the family photos. The album belonged to Angela. They recall that she kept it out on top of her desk. They wonder how it was misplaced in the back of the drawer. Father and son wipe away tears from their eyes. They love and miss her still. They're thankful that Mandy found it and returned it so quickly.

Mandy asks them, "Did the desk and office belong to Angela?"

They nod. Gary says "We hope that you'll enjoy working in there as much as she did. She really enjoyed meeting and helping the models in one way or another. She was a real beauty. Have you ever worked as a model? You're just as beautiful as she was."

She blushes and replies, "Thank you for the compliment. Evidently, Angela had a beautiful spirit and energy. They say love never dies. I'm very comfortable in her office. I love looking at her beautiful garden from the window."

With a little laughter, she continues, "No, I've never worked as a model. I remember pretending to be one while playing dress-up with my Mom's shoes, hats, dresses and makeup. It was fun to play like a fairy tale princess with her jewelry. I had my own fashion accessory toys to play with, too. As a teenager I loved reading all the fashion magazines. Although I'm not a model, I enjoy watching the runway shows."

They finish eating their sandwiches and drinking their coffee. They continue chatting while relaxing in the café.

Jonny asks Mandy, "Do you have any special plans for the weekend? If you have some free time tomorrow, we can set up a time for you to visit my portrait studio. We've hired a new photographer who will take my place on Monday morning. Saturday will be the best opportunity for taking a few portraits of you. If you're free, it could prove to be a fun time."

"I have free time tomorrow afternoon but I feel shy when I'm in front of a camera. It sounds like it might be fun. I'm free at 2:00pm, if that time works for you?"

"Yes, 2:00pm will work for me as well. We'll plan on meeting at the studio at that time. The personnel office has been instructed to give you a set of keys when your Employee ID is completed. You'll be able to enter the building and the studio if I'm running late. Speaking of the personnel office, It's probably about time to go there. You'll want to get your ID and keys before the office closes this afternoon."

"Dad? Are we ready to leave here? We should see what's happening back at the office and studio? It's been an enjoyable time visiting here. Thank you, Dad and Mandy."

Gary stands up to leave while commenting, "Yes, I've enjoyed our time together, too!" He smiles and says, "Thank you again, Mandy, for returning the photo album. It means a lot to us."

Mandy grabs her purse. She says, "Thank you for the lovely brunch and time that we've shared together! I'll walk over to the personnel office right now and take care of the ID and keys."

They walk out of the café together. Gary says, "I really enjoyed meeting you, Mandy. We'll see you again soon. Enjoy your weekend. The weather should be perfect for the next two days. Jon and I are planning to play golf at the country club. Do you have plans with your mother for Mother's Day Weekend?"

"Yes, my mother and I will share family time on her special day. I hope you both have a great evening and weekend, too. I'll see you both later!"

Directing her attention to Jonny, she tells him, "I'll see you tomorrow at 2:00pm."

CHAPTER THREE
SATURDAY AT THE MALL

Mandy went to bed last night hoping to sleep in on this Saturday morning. She awakes to the sound of a ringtone on her cell phone. Her Mom, Katherine James, is calling. They haven't spoken to each other for a few days.

Mandy answers in a sleepy voice, "Hello, Mom! How are you doing? Yes. I was still sleeping, but that's okay. I'm awake now. I'm happy to hear from you, Mom! It's been a few days since we've connected. I miss you!"

Her Mom says, "I miss you, Mandy!" then she asks, "Would you like to go shopping with me this morning and join me for a light lunch? We can go to your favorite mall. Their food court has a patio where we can relax outdoors and enjoy this beautiful sunny day."

"I have an appointment at 2:00pm this afternoon. We'll need to plan on shopping early and eat lunch around noon. I'll fill you in on the details while we're at the mall."

Katherine is hoping to catch up on the latest events of her daughter's life. She loves Mandy but they don't spend time together very often. They have busy lives and time always seems to fly by. Katherine has lonelier days and nights since her husband, Paul, passed on last year.

He would've been so proud of Mandy today. He's the one that encouraged her to earn a business degree. He was hoping that she would work with him at their family business. After her father's passing though, their business was sold to help pay off the medical bills and to provide an income for her Mom to survive. This is one reason Mandy is so excited about her new job. She'll receive a generous paycheck and great benefits. She loves her Mom and wants to help pay off the bills. She wants to provide financial support to her Mom for a happier healthier life.

Her Mom asks, "What time would you like to meet at the mall? Will an hour be enough time for you to get up and get dressed to meet me there?"

"Yes, I'm up now and sitting at the kitchen table. I just made a cup of tea. As soon as we're finished talking on the phone, I'll eat a quick breakfast. I'll be dressed and ready to leave here in a short time. I'll see you there soon. I love you, Mom!"

"I love you, too, Mandy! Thank you! See you there!"

Mandy drinks her tea, eats a breakfast bar, runs through a quick shower and gets dressed. She packs a bag with a couple of her favorite outfits and accessories. She'll take it with her to the studio. She'll go directly to her appointment after shopping at the mall and the lunch date with her Mom.

She grabs her purse and car keys. *It'll be wonderful to spend time with my Mom today. Tomorrow is Mother's Day. Although I've ordered a bouquet of pink roses, I haven't bought a gift for her yet. Now that I have a better paying job, I can buy her an extra special gift at the mall.*

She plans to pick up the flowers on Mother's Day on the way to her Mom's house in the afternoon.

Mandy pulls into the mall parking lot and recognizes her Mom standing outside the mall entrance. She parks the car and hurries over to catch up with her. They greet each other with sweet and gentle hugs. They happily enter the mall arm in arm acting like two teenage girls, smiling and having fun.

While they walk slowly down the halls, they look left and right. They enjoy window shopping and view both spring and summer fashions in the boutiques. Since their time is limited, they pay close attention to only the stores that they're most interested in.

Mandy cheerfully announces to her Mom, "Since tomorrow is Mother's Day, I would like to buy something special for you here today. I noticed that your eyes lit up when you saw the pearl necklace and earrings in the Jewelry Store window. Would you like to go in and try them on? They would make a great gift. I love to see you smile. I want you to be happy."

"Oh, Mandy sweetheart! They're lovely but too expensive. I don't want you to spend that much money on me."

"It's okay Mom. I have good news to share with you. I was hired for a new job as a business assistant on Thursday. They're paying me very well along with great benefits. I'd like to buy them for you. Let's go in and you can try them on for size."

Her Mom tries on the pearl necklace with earrings to match. They're perfect and she's thrilled that Mandy can afford to buy them. They're both smiling with light twinkling in their eyes. Mandy pays for the jewelry at the counter.

She says, "Happy Mother's Day, Mom!" While handing her the gift bag, she gives her Mom a sweet and gentle hug!

She wants to wear them right away. Using the reflection from the shop window as a mirror, she puts on the necklace and earrings.

Her Mom says, "Thank you, Mandy! I love them! They're beautiful and I'll treasure them always!"

"You're so welcome. Thank you for letting me buy them for you. Please wear them tomorrow for me especially when we go out for dinner. If there's anything that you need or want, please let me know. I'll be more than thrilled to pay for things that will make you happy."

Mandy checks her watch and sees that it's noon already.

"Mom, I think we should plan on eating lunch now. It's 12:00pm."

While walking over to the food court, they decide to order lunch at the café with the outdoor patio seating. They choose a table with padded chairs in a shaded area.

The waiter serves them glasses of cold water and places two menus on the table. They choose to eat salads and place their orders with him right away. The water is refreshing so there's no need to order a beverage.

While waiting for their salads to be served, they look at each other smiling. They're not sure who will ask the first question.

Mandy asks, "How have you been doing Mom?"

"Oh, you know how things are with me. My life is pretty much the same but I manage to keep busy. I'm just trying to hold on one day at a time. I like working in the gardens this time of year. I still keep in touch with a few of my friends. We get together to play a game of cards occasionally."

"I think it's important to keep busy. Don't give up doing the things that you love. I can come over to help you in the gardens. Just let me know when you need help. I'm glad that you're visiting with your friends, too!"

"Please tell me about your new job. Although I don't want you to be late for your appointment, I would love to hear all about it. Will you have time for our traditional Mother's Day visit tomorrow?"

"Yes, I ordered something that I'd like to hand deliver to you tomorrow. I'll share more details about my new job at that time. Actually, if you'd like, we can plan on a little outing. I can show you my new office and Angela's beautiful garden. You'll love it!"

The waiter serves the salads with the check. Mandy picks up the check to be sure that her Mom is taken care of. While they enjoy eating their salads, they continue to chat about things.

Her mom asks, "Who is Angela and where is her garden?"

"Angela was Gary's wife and Jonny's Mother. She used to work at the Agency with them. She designed a beautiful garden in the courtyard behind the building. It has lots of beautiful flowers."

Mandy adds, "Her favorite flower was pink sweetheart roses. There's a white stone wall with pink roses growing along it. I want you to see her garden in the evening. There are white twinkling lights that look like glittering diamonds."

She continues to describe Angela's garden. "She planted a butterfly garden there, too. It's amazing to see such beauty in the middle of a big city. It turns out that my office used to be Angela's office. I feel honored to work in the same office space as she did."

Her mom's eyes light up as she listens to the description of Angela's garden. "Sounds really beautiful. I think that I'll enjoy going there to see it with you."

"Jonny and I ate dinner at a restaurant located in that area on the evening of my interview. It's a steakhouse and has a beautiful garden patio as well. I think you would enjoy it. Jonny says the food is really delicious. Do you think that you'd like to eat dinner there?"

"Oh, that sounds like a wonderful fun outing. It'll be a great Mother's Day. I love spending time with you! I can dress up and wear my new pearls." She smiles with great joy!

"We can plan on going out that way late afternoon. They gave me keys to the building. I can give you a short tour. My new business assistant job is at 'Harris and Young Modelling Agency' downtown. I was hired to assist Jonny in taking over the business because Gary, the owner of the company, is ready to retire. I'll be working with both of them while they make the transition."

"I think this new job is a great opportunity for you. You've worked hard for your business degree. I'm happy to hear that you'll put your talent and knowledge to good use. I hope that everything works out for you."

"My appointment is with Jonny at his portrait studio for a fun photo shoot. He has a passion for photography and has been working there as a professional photographer. We'll probably take time for another tour of the building. I have lots of questions about what's located in the building. There's a lot to learn about the Agency. Anyway, Jonny is a nice man and I've enjoyed the time that we've spent together."

"Thank you, Sweetie, for the wonderful day. Shopping was fun. It was great to talk and laugh with you again. I guess we should say goodbye so that you're not late for your appointment."

"Thank you, Mom! I agree! It was a wonderful time spent together. I'll walk you to your car. I see that it's not too far away from here. How will you spend the rest of your afternoon?"

They exchange hugs at her Mom's car.

"After the time we spent shopping, I'll sit in my recliner and watch a few of my favorite TV shows while I rest. I might need to take a little nap. Goodbye, my darling daughter! I love you. Hope the rest of the day will be fun for you."

"Are you sure that you're going to be alright, Mom?"

"Yes, dear one. I'll be fine. Please, run along now so that you're not late for your appointment. Be careful driving in this busy Saturday traffic. I'll see you tomorrow."

"You too, Mom, I love you. See you tomorrow!"

Mandy thinks that she might be running late. She's not sure how busy the traffic is between the mall and the downtown building on a Saturday afternoon.

Mandy sits in her car feeling a little misty eyed. She loves her Mom. She worries how her Mom will make it without her Dad around. Mandy loved her Dad and misses him very much. Without a doubt, she believes that her Mom still loves and misses him, too. Losing him is still really hard on both of them.

CHAPTER FOUR
KEEP ON SMILING

Mandy arrives at the Agency just before 2:00pm. It appears that there are several employees at work today. She grabs her bag from the backseat with the outfits and accessories for the photo session. The building is unlocked.

Feeling thirsty, she stops in at the café for a soft drink. Jonny has the same idea when he arrives and heads to the café where he spies Mandy. Their eyes lock and they walk toward each other. Smiles grow bigger as they meet face to face. Their hearts are racing. Each one worries that the other can hear their heart beat.

"Hi Mandy! So happy that you made it! I want to share more about business in the Portrait Studio today. Also, we can have fun playing with the camera and the costumes that are available."

"Hi Jonny! I'm interested in learning all that I can about the Studio. I've never had a photo taken by a professional photographer. It might be fun to try on a few costumes. That'll be like playing dress-up and feeling like a kid again."

"Why don't we sit here while we finish our soft drinks and relax a little bit? I've had a busy day. What about you? How was your morning?"

"It was great! I appreciate a chance to catch my breath. I've had a busy day, too! I went shopping with my Mom at the mall. We just finished eating lunch together!"

Jennifer walks in surprised to see Jonny in the building on a Saturday. She's a receptionist that has a crush on him. They casually dated off and on before Angela's passing.

During the time Jonny was grieving the loss of his mother, he wasn't interested in doing anything. He really didn't feel up to going out and pretend that life was good. He stopped dating her and doesn't feel like returning her attention. That hasn't stopped her from flirting and wanting his attention.

Jennifer walks up to their table with a big smile and stars in her eyes. "OH, Hello Jonny!!! I'm so surprised to see you here on a Saturday. I'm so happy to see you again. How are you doing?"

She throws her arms around his neck trying to give him a hug. He gently and politely resists her touching him.

He replies, "I'm doing fine. Have you met my new assistant? I just hired her on Thursday. Jennifer, please try to make Mandy feel welcome. I'm here with Mandy to give her a tour. I'll show her around the Portrait Studio today."

Jonny turns his attention to Mandy and says, "Mandy I'd like for you to meet Jennifer. She's a receptionist here in the building."

She smiles and says, "Hello, Jennifer nice to meet you." Jennifer huffs and keeps her attention glued on Jonny.

Jonny asks, "What are you doing here on a Saturday?"

"I had a few phone calls to make and some other business issues to catch up on before Monday. It's all finished now. I thought it might be a good idea to eat a sandwich for lunch at the Deli before I leave for home." With high pitched laughter, she asks Jonny, "Do you mind if I join you?"

"Actually, we need to leave now because it's getting late. We'll see you on Monday. Have a good weekend!"

Jonny and Mandy leave the café and stroll down to the elevator. They both feel a little numb after their encounter with Jennifer. They avoid making eye contact. By the time they arrive at the third floor, they once again have a spring in their step.

Jonny is excited about spending the afternoon at the studio. He opens the door and invites her in. She's feeling a little overwhelmed by this new experience. She's also having some feelings that she doesn't quite understand. She's never had a serious boyfriend relationship before. She's trying to focus on the fact that this meeting is still business related. She's delighted to learn more about the Agency's business in a fun way!

He's wondering about feelings that he's having for her. They just met two days ago. She's a beautiful woman and he really admires her sweetness. He wants to show her around the studio and share his passion for photography with her. She'll have a chance to work on the business side of the studio soon.

Just for today, he offers her a chance to experience a photo session with him as a professional photographer. He wants her to enjoy the fun and glamourous side of the camera.

He begins to show her the camera and equipment with all the modern technology. He shares the process that's involved when a model comes to his studio for portraits. He shows her how to create a portfolio.

He gives her a quick tour around the large studio. He shows her the dressing rooms with the makeup tables and bright lights. She's excited to see all the wardrobes that are filled with a variety of outfits, dresses and costumes. There are drawers and shelves filled with beautiful and fun accessories.

"Mandy please stand here on this set? I want to start taking photos of you. You're beautiful just the way you are! It'll be fun to have you change in a variety of outfits and costumes. Would you like to keep a few prints and give one to your Mom on Mother's Day?"

She's blushing and with a little giggle says, "Okay, but I'm feeling shy and unsure about this."

"Everything will be fine if you just relax and smile!"

Jonny takes several beautiful shots of her smiling and posing in her own sweet way. He tells her, "Why don't you change into an outfit that you brought with you? I'll take the time to locate your new photos on the computer and print them. You can choose the ones that you like best."

"Okay, I'll be back in a few minutes. I brought an outfit that I'd like to change into for a portrait."

Jonny sits at the computer. He finds that the photos are superb. No need to edit any of them. Lighting is great and she's smiling with her eyes open in every photo. She's very photogenic. She'd be great at modeling.

Mandy returns smiling but still blushing. She returns wearing the same outfit that she wore for the interview on Thursday. She's dressed in a lime green dress with a short-sleeve jacket to match. She's wearing a jeweled barrette in her beautiful black hair. Her shiny high heels are white. She looks professional and gorgeous.

Jonny is surprised and pleased to see her dressed up in that outfit again. Her beautiful hazel green eyes really stand out and sparkle. She is stunning! He stands and stares at her momentarily.

"You really look beautiful, Mandy! OK, we can use the same set for these photos, too! Your face really lights up when you smile!"

"Thank you so much, Jonny, for your kind words and compliments. I want a portrait in this outfit to document the day that I was hired to work here. It's one of the happiest days of my life. My Mom will love a photo taken of me in this outfit. Will that be okay?"

"Yes, of course. I would like to keep a copy for myself if that's okay? I've taken a lot of great photos with a lot of beautiful models over the years. You're very photogenic and I feel honored to make these portraits available to you. Please see for yourself? I have the images up on the screen here."

"Thanks so much! I bet you enjoy working with this camera equipment along with the modern technology. The photos are definitely professional looking. This is a great experience. I know that my Mom will be happy to receive these prints. Yes, it's okay if you keep one for yourself. I'm not sure why you would want it but I don't see any harm in you keeping one."

"I've got a fun idea. There's a fairy tale Princess costume in one of the wardrobes. I remember a model wearing it at one of her photo shoots. She had dreams of going to Hollywood. Why don't we find it and take your photo in it? I remember your story about dressing up like a fairy tale Princess when you were a little girl."

"I saw a Cinderella type dress when I was looking around in the wardrobes. It's long enough to cover my shoes. I saw a tiara that might fit me. It looks like a kid's toy but it'll be fun to try it on." She giggles softly.

They're laughing! They're thinking how great it is to laugh again. They've been grieving over the loss of a parent. This fun time together is what they need to help with the healing process.

"OK, I'll go find the dress and tiara. I'll be back soon. I'll touch up my makeup and fluff up my hair. I'll enjoy feeling like a princess again."

He's feeling like a kid again, too. He decides to dress in a Prince Charming costume that he found in a wardrobe. He changes in one of the dressing rooms.

This will be a fun joke to play on Mandy! Hope she gets a good laugh!"

He leaves his dressing room and sees Jennifer in the studio. Mandy is still in her dressing room. He says with a frown, "Jennifer, what are you up to?"

"I finished eating my lunch. I thought you might have time for us to talk. I hope you know how much I really miss you, Jonny!"

"No, this isn't a good time to talk. Mandy and I are still busy here. We'll be finished soon and we have plans after we leave here."

"Why are you dressed in a Prince Charming costume?"

Just at that moment, Mandy opens the dressing room door. She walks out dressed in her Princess costume. Needless to say, she's gorgeous!

Jennifer looks horrified and storms from the studio in tears. She's in shock and wonders what's going on between those two?

Mandy asks, "What was that about? Why was Jennifer here? Did I interrupt something between you two?"

He's feeling sad that this scene took place. He explains, "Jennifer came in and asked if I had time to talk. I told her that it wasn't a good time. I explained that you and I would be leaving soon and that we had previous plans. I used to date her before my mother died. I guess she still has a crush on me. She certainly is acting a little more assertive now that you're here. I quit dating and going out after my Mom died. I felt depressed and didn't want to go anywhere or do too much of anything. I'm still not interested in dating her again. I guess, I'll have to make time to talk with her about it. I'm sorry that you were caught up in this scene."

"I'm sorry, too, Jonny. I can see the pain on your face. I'm sorry that you are hurting so much."

She wants to reach over and comfort him with a sweet gentle hug. She thought for a moment and decides that wouldn't be a good idea. *A personal relationship might spoil my chance to do a good job for him and his father.*

"I think you make a stunning Cinderella. I like what you've done with your hair. The tiara is a nice touch. I changed into this Prince Charming costume as a joke. I was hoping to see your beautiful smile and hear your contagious laughter."

They both laugh at the two of them standing there in the Prince and Princess costumes. They're having fun and feeling like kids again.

"Do you still feel like posing as a Princess for me? I have another set with a perfect background for a Princess. Just for fun, I can set the timer on the camera. I can capture the two of us having fun and looking like a couple of kids."

She laughs at the idea. "A photo of me dressed like a grownup fairy tale Princess would please my Mom. Posing as a princess with you dressed like Prince Charming sounds like fun."

He takes several photos of her and then sets the timer on the camera. He hurries over to stand next to her just in time. The camera flashes and they laugh.

He feels the urge to kiss her. He's caught up in the beautiful and fun moment. He resists the temptation. *Any personal relationship so soon might interfere with my need to focus on Dad's retirement.*

"Well, that's enough for today. Let's get dressed and get out of here. Would you please have dinner with me again tonight? We can take a walk through the garden patio. I can point out a few sites to you in the area."

"Sure, Jonny, that sounds great! I've had lots of fun with you here in your studio. I can understand why you have a passion for photography. I hope that you never lose it and that you can continue to have fun with it. Thank you for the prints for my Mom. She'll laugh when she sees the photo of me dressed up like a fairy tale Princess."

"Although, I won't be working here as a photographer in this studio, I still have my studio at home. I'll enjoy my photography in my spare time."

Everything is returned to its proper place in the studio. He advises her to leave the costumes on the chair. Housekeeping will pick them up tonight to be cleaned. They're ready to leave the studio.

Jonny suggests that they take her bag out to her car. They walk together to the elevator. As they wait for the door to open, they can't stop smiling at each other.

CHAPTER FIVE
HAPPY MOTHER'S DAY

Gary is up and brewing fresh coffee in his kitchen. The wonderful aroma is wafting its way up to the second floor of his large home. While walking down the steps of the large staircase, Jonny mumbles, "Good morning, Mmm, Dad, the coffee smells great. Where's Sadie?"

"Good morning, Son! I gave her the day off. I want her to enjoy Mother's Day with her children and grandchildren. Would you like to go to the Country Club and eat brunch before our game of golf this afternoon?"

Jonny and his Dad are excited about spending the afternoon playing golf. They're dressed in sporty outfits looking very handsome.

They sit together at the breakfast bar drinking their coffee looking lost in thought. Mother's Day always brings to mind bittersweet memories of Angela.

"Dad, why don't we take a few minutes to sit out on the terrace? We can enjoy Mom's flowers that are still growing out there? The gardener does a fantastic job of keeping up with both of her gardens. The bed of pink sweetheart roses in the backyard looks heavenly."

"It's a beautiful day for sitting outside with our coffee. Speaking of flowers, I ordered a bunch of her favorite flowers to take out to the cemetery today. I think it'll be meaningful to stop at the florist and then visit with your Mom before going to the Country Club."

"Aw, Dad! Thank you for suggesting that we do that again this year. I really miss Mom. Going to the cemetery with flowers will be a good way to honor her. I'm dressed and ready to go whenever you are. Do you want to drive the Cadillac? I can pack our golf clubs in the trunk."

"Sure, the Cadillac will be perfect for our outing today. Let's load them in the trunk together. We can leave now to pick up the flowers for your Mom."

"Okay, sounds like a good plan."

Mandy is already on her way to the same flower shop. She's going to pick up the flowers that she ordered for her Mom. She arrives there first. While she's paying for her bouquet, she sees a wreath made with pink sweetheart roses. 'Happy Mother's Day, Angela' is written on the banner. She feels sympathy for Jonny and his Dad. She takes the bouquet of pink roses for her Mom out to her car. She drives over to her Mom's house early. She wants time to visit before their outing today.

Jonny and Gary arrive at the flower shop missing Mandy only by a few minutes. They pick up the wreath for Angela. They also pick up another arrangement with a banner that reads, 'Happy Mother's Day, Mom'. With misty tears in their eyes, they're still smiling. They recall how much Angela (Mom) loved receiving pink sweetheart roses on Mother's Day.

They drive to the cemetery. Her headstone is easy to find with the beautiful angel statue. Gary places the wreath on the ground in front of the angel. Jonny places his flower arrangement next to it. There's a bench where they sit and reflect on past memories. They comfort each other with hands on shoulders. Angela is very loved and missed. They whisper their messages of love to her and say a prayer.

Jonny says, "Happy Mother's Day, Mom! I really miss you!"

Gary nods in agreement. He's feeling too choked up to speak. They leave there with the belief that she's resting in peace.

Mandy arrives at her Mom's house. Actually, it's her childhood home. She moved into her apartment shortly after starting classes at the business college. Her Mom is expecting her.

She knocks on the front door, opens it and calls out, "Mom? I'm here!"

"Come on in, Mandy, I'm in the kitchen making tea for us. I baked your favorite sweet roll. We can eat a little brunch while we visit. I have fresh fruit in a bowl on the table. What else would you like to eat?"

"That sounds fine to me, Mom. Don't overdo on my account. Happy Mother's Day, Mom!" She hands her the bouquet of roses in a beautiful crystal vase. She also hands her Mom a wrapped package.

"OH, Mandy, Sweetheart! Thank you for the beautiful roses. You make me happy by just being YOU. I'm so lucky to have a generous loving daughter like you. And another gift? You've already given me these beautiful pearls." They lovingly give each other a warm hug.

"I'm happy that you're wearing the pearl necklace and earrings, Mom! Yes, another gift but just for fun, okay?"

Her Mom opens the gift to find a double frame with two pictures in it. One side has the picture of Mandy dressed in her interview outfit looking very professional. The other side of the frame has a picture of Mandy looking like a beautiful grownup fairy tale Princess. Her mom is in awe as she stands looking at these two pictures. It's difficult for her to believe that her little girl is all grown up.

"Mandy, Darling! Thank you for this wonderful gift. I'm guessing these are photos from the session you had with Jonny at the studio, yesterday? They really are lovely and professional looking. He has a great talent. I guess you had fun with him at the studio. My beautiful princess daughter!" She dries tears of joy from her eyes.

She says with a giggle, "Yes, the photos are from the session with Jonny yesterday. We had a fun time! It was a very enlightening experience. I learned a lot from my visit in his studio. He says that he has a studio in his home, too. Maybe we can ask him about scheduling a family type portrait with the two of us."

They sit at the kitchen table drinking their tea and eating brunch. They chat about a variety of things.

Jonny and Gary arrive at the country club where they've made a reservation for their brunch. There's a variety of delicious foods on the breakfast buffet. They fill their plates and sit in a quiet corner. They want to visit before their game.

"How did the appointment with Mandy work out for you two, yesterday?"

"I think it worked out well. I explained a lot about the camera equipment and how it works. I gave her a quick tour. I shared what happens during a session with one of our clients. I took a few professional photos of her. She's never had photos taken by a professional photographer. She appeared to enjoy the experience both on a business and a personal level."

"It's great that you two are getting along so well."

"I suggested that she give her Mom a couple of prints for Mother's Day. Just for fun, I recommended that she dress up in a fairy tale Princess costume for a photo. I thought her Mom might like it. She's very beautiful and very photogenic."

His Dad smiles and says, "That does sound like a fun photo. I agree that she's very beautiful."

"As a joke, I dressed up in the Prince Charming costume and set the timer on the camera. We had a few laughs. That is, until Jennifer showed up unexpectedly."

"I'm glad you two had a little fun while she's learning about business at the Agency." Chuckling he says, "I would love to see that funny picture of you dressed as Prince Charming. What's happening with Jennifer?"

"I can share that photo with you. I printed a copy for myself. As for Jennifer, that's a long story."

"If you ever want to talk about it, I'm here for you, Son."

"I would like to have a heart-to-heart talk with you about Mandy. We've been spending a lot of close time together. I've only known her for a few days. When we were taking the fairy tale photos, I had to fight off the temptation to kiss her. I want to stay focused on your retirement and stay on a business level with her. We were laughing and having lots of fun. I'm definitely feeling a spark or chemistry but I don't know if she feels it."

"I'm willing to have a talk with you or at least listen later. We should leave here to go to the golf course. It's almost time for us to start playing our game. Are you ready to play golf, Jon?"

"Yes, Dad, let's go. Do you want to drive the golf cart this time? Let's plan on driving over to Mom's garden downtown afterwards. We can sit and relax there for Mother's Day on the garden patio. How about a steak dinner on the patio at Ted's Steakhouse? Dining there is like dining in paradise. It's really a beautiful place!"

"That sounds like a great idea, Jon. Yes, let's play our game of golf. We'll spend time in Angela's Garden before we eat dinner."

Mandy asks her Mom if she's ready to go downtown for their Mother's Day celebration.

She's ready to go. Mandy drives her Mom to the Agency downtown. When they arrive, she parks in front of the building. She gives her Mom a quick tour of the lobby. They ride up in the elevator to the third floor. As they walk down the hall to her office, she points out Gary's office and to Jonny's Portrait Studio.

She's surprised to see that the nameplate for her office door is in place. She reads out loud, "Amanda James, Business Assistant." She smiles and points it out to her Mom. "I wasn't expecting that until next week."

When they walk into her office, they see the new nameplate on her desk. Her Mom reads out loud, "Amanda James, Assistant Extraordinaire." She says cheerfully, "That's my girl!" They both laugh out loud.

"Mom, please come over here and look out the window and down below you can see Angela's garden. It's really beautiful even from this view."

"Yes, it's very beautiful. I can't wait to see it up close and personal. I'm so happy to see your office. I really wish you lots of luck and happiness working here."

"I want to give you a sneak peek of Jonny's studio, too. A new professional photographer will start working there tomorrow. I have the key here."

"Wow, Mandy this studio is huge. I can see why you had a good time here yesterday. I understand why Jonny loves his photographer's job here."

"Let's go down to the garden, okay, Mom? It's almost time for us to eat dinner."

They ride the elevator down and walk out through the double doors to the garden. They have a lovely surprise! The white lights are twinkling this time of the evening. The ambience is perfect for eating outdoors on the patio.

Jonny and Gary are sitting on Angela's bench in her garden. They stand up quickly to greet Mandy and her Mom.

Mandy asks, "OH, are we intruding?"

Gary replies, "No, It's good to see you here. We thought it would be a good idea to spend time in Angela's garden reflecting on Mother's Day. We're planning to eat a steak dinner over at the restaurant."

"I brought my Mom out to have dinner at the restaurant, too. I thought it would be a fun Mother's Day celebration. I wanted to show her my new office and Angela's beautiful garden before eating dinner. I hope you don't mind?"

Gary says, "Not at all." Jonny nods in agreement.

"I'd like to introduce my Mom, Katherine James, to you two. Mom this is Gary and his son Jonny."

Gary greets Katherine with a gentle handshake. "Hello, Katherine, it's very nice to meet you. You have a lovely daughter. We look forward to working with her as our assistant."

Jonny greets Katherine with a gentle handshake, also. "It's nice to meet you,

Katherine. I agree with Dad. You have a lovely daughter. Happy Mother's Day to you!"

They enjoy chatting while standing in the beautiful garden. There's a slight refreshing breeze. Gary invites Mandy and Katherine to join them for dinner. Mandy and her Mom look a bit surprised. They accept the invitation. It might be fun to have dinner with these two handsome men.

The restaurant's garden patio is a perfect setting for a happy Mother's Day celebration.

CHAPTER SIX
HIS STORY

The atmosphere is energized with excitement on this Monday morning. Everyone at the Agency appears eager to start a new day as well as a new week.

Gary is excited about his future retirement. He dreams of travelling and seeing the world.

Jonny is excited for him and wants to help his Dad in any way that he can.

Mandy is excited to assist the two of them with their business issues. She believes this job will make her future bright as well as contribute to a brighter future for her Mom.

In the last few days, she's grown to care about Gary and Jonny. She's willing to complete a job that allows Gary to retire happily. What she needs to do to help them is still a mystery. Jonny will take over his Dad's responsibility of overseeing their businesses. She'll find out more about this at their first official meeting this morning.

The new photographer, Frank Collins, was hired to take Jonny's place at the portrait studio. He'll arrive this morning. Jonny will help him settle in at the studio. He'll be there to answer any questions that Frank might have about the camera equipment as well as his role for the Agency.

Mandy arrives at her office with a cup of coffee in hand. She finds a stack of brochures on her desk. Gary left a note that reads, *'It'll be helpful if you take time to read through these brochures before our meeting this morning.'*

The colorful brochures are like the ads you see at travel agencies or visitor centers. They're for the Modelling Agency, the Imperial Inn (hotel), Ted's Restaurant, the Regal Limousine Service and a Travel Agency all located in Omaha. She picks up the pamphlet on top and begins to read it.

She hears Jonny's voice out in the hall. He's talking to someone she doesn't recognize. She assumes that he's the new photographer. They're talking about business issues and, of course, photography.

She looks up to see Gary standing in her doorway. He says, "Good Morning, Mandy! I see you found the brochures that I left for you. Reading those will give you a little introduction to my businesses. Our meeting this morning will be about that."

"Good morning, Gary! Yes, I scanned through the brochures and read the descriptive information. They're lovely with all the colorful photos. Thank you for being so thoughtful."

"My pleasure."

"Thank you for this beautiful office and for everything that you've done for me here. Also, my Mom and I had a memorable time at the restaurant last night. Thank you for treating us to a delicious steak dinner."

"You're welcome, Mandy. I enjoyed meeting your Mother. She's a lovely lady. I would like to see her again sometime. The time spent on the garden patio with the four of us was just delightful."

"Mom enjoyed the evening and she might like to see you again, too."

"Are you ready to go with me to my office for our meeting with Jonny? I just saw him in the hallway talking to Frank, our new photographer. Jonny is on his way to my office now."

"Yes, I'm ready to go."

"If you would like to get a fresh cup of coffee, you can come with me down to the break room on this floor. I'm going to refill my cup as well."

"Sure! I didn't know about the break room. I haven't explored this end of the hallway."

They continue chatting while walking down the hall. Gary explains, "The coffee in the break room is made fresh by one of our Deli-Bakery employees. They usually make their rounds to the break rooms mid-morning. We routinely stop in their café for our first cup of coffee."

"This is a lovely room. It has a peaceful and relaxing atmosphere. Thank you for showing it to me."

"Jonny mentioned that you drink your coffee with sugar and cream. You can find those little to-go packs of cream from the cafe in the refrigerator. Just help yourself to what you need. Sugar packets are on the counter by the coffee urn. Okay, let's go down to my office. I'm sure Jonny is waiting for us."

"Thank you again for your kindness. I'm ready and excited about our first business meeting."

They chat quietly as they walk down the hall to Gary's office. Jonny is waiting in a chair with a cup of coffee in hand but stands when Mandy and Gary walk into the room. Mandy and Jonny smile as their eyes meet.

"Hello, Jonny!" and "Hello, Mandy!" are spoken simultaneously. No surprise to anyone by the electrical charge that's filling the air.

Gary says, "Hello, Jonny!"

He motions to Mandy, "Please have a seat."

She sits down in the same comfy chair that she sat in during her interview. The office may be huge but sitting so close to Jonny has her heart racing.

Gary notices that Mandy is looking a little pale. He asks her, "Mandy? Are you okay? Did you eat breakfast?"

"Yes, I ate a light breakfast. I think that I'm feeling a little jittery due to the excitement of working here at your Agency. I'm sorry to cause any inconvenience."

"No, you're fine! I think it's perfectly normal for you to feel jittery. I've felt that way before when I'm meeting new people or going into a new place. It feels similar to stage fright. What do you think, Mandy?"

"Yes, I agree. I'll be okay but I think that I need a glass of water."

Gary says, "I can call down to the café and ask them to bring us a pitcher with three glasses. Would you like something to eat from the café? We can order sandwiches and have them delivered? If not now, then maybe later."

Jonny replies, "No thank you, I'm not hungry. I'm feeling too nervous to eat anything right now. Maybe later!"

Mandy replies, "Maybe later is my vote too." She smiles and says, "Thank you!"

There's a knock on the door. Jonny gets up to answer it. He assumes that it's a person from the café. A lady is delivering the water that his Dad ordered for Mandy. He takes the tray from her hands. The water is free but he chooses to tip her for the delivery service."

Gary quickly asks, "Why don't we spread out over at the conference table? We might be a little more comfortable over there."

Jonny sets down the tray at the end of the conference table. He pours three glasses of crystal clear chilled water. He thinks to himself, *"This is just what I need, too."* They settle in at the conference table. They're feeling refreshed and a lot more relaxed.

Gary says, "I think this will work out better for all of us. We all have a little more breathing space. Mandy, I see that you brought your journal and pen. This is a good time to take notes. I'm going to share my story from the beginning."

He looks at Jon and says, "'You can take notes too if you want, Son. You know most of the story about our business but mostly from a family perspective. Mandy's notes will be sufficient to help you out later on. Please feel free to ask any questions."

Gary is sitting at the end of the conference table. Jonny is sitting on Gary's left. Mandy is seated across the table from Jonny. Gary takes a sip of the cool water and begins to share his story.

"When I was a young man earning my business degree, I met Ted Harris. We were roommates living in a dorm. We became best of friends because we shared a lot in common. We both had a passion for photography, sport cars, sports and dating beautiful women.

We shared a dream of owning our own business. After we earned our degrees, we discussed what kind of business we would own. Because of mutual interests, we decided to find a way to use our talents together. We wanted to become partners in a photography business.

We did some research and started shopping around for a location. The building that we're sitting in today is the same building we started our business in many years ago. It's been upgraded over the years to keep up with all the modern conveniences. We remodeled it as the business grew. The entire second floor is the 'Harris and Young Modelling Agency'.

The administration offices are on the third floor. There are several rooms and offices on the first floor that are used for modelling classes. We also have an office with a travel agent. They assist the models that need to travel to various locations for their modelling jobs.

Ted and I have been successful with the modeling agency. We started up several other businesses in this location. Mandy, did you know that the Deli-Bakery café and the steakhouse restaurant was Ted's idea? Yes, we own both of those businesses. Ted had some great ideas.

Between the two of us, we started up a hotel (The Imperial Inn) and Regal Limousine Service to assist our models and their agents. Whether they come to Omaha on business or for a vacation, we do all that we can to accommodate them. The hotel, located across the street, is luxurious and offers lots of amenities. Riding in one of our limousines to and from the airport is a memorable experience. Speaking of memorable experiences, I want to back up for a few minutes. When Ted and I first started our photography studio, we didn't have a receptionist. We took care of business on our own merits. But when we started the Modelling Agency, we decided to hire a receptionist. We needed help with this new business. We researched and figured out how to make our business successful.

We hired a talented and beautiful young lady by the name of Angela Wright. We fell in love and were wed a short time later. Angela Young as you know, Mandy, used your office before you. When she passed on, I didn't have the heart to hire anyone to take her place. Until now that is because we need your assistance. Just like she helped make our business successful many years ago.

Ted Harris retired earlier this year. I would like to retire this summer. When he retired, I bought out his half of our businesses. I wanted him to retire happily as well as be financially secure. Ted and I were very successful in owning and running the businesses together. Now that he's retired and I have full ownership, I need to take on these new issues in a serious way. That's why Jonny and I hired you to be our Assistant Extraordinaire.

I've been meeting with our attorney to prepare contracts for Jonny and I to become business partners. He'll own half now and will inherit everything as set forth in my will."

Gary's glass is empty. He reaches over for the water pitcher to refill his glass. Mandy is busy writing out her notes. She's grateful for the brochures on her desk for further information.

Jonny says, "Dad, would this be a good time to take a break? I'd like to get a sandwich now and stretch my legs."

His Dad agrees, "Yes, this is a good time for it." Mandy nods in agreement.

"Thanks for sharing your story, Dad. You opened my eyes to see how dedicated you've been to Ted, Mom and the businesses. You've really been a great Dad and I really appreciate you. Your businesses are very successful. You've invested long hours and hard work. Thank you, Dad!"

Gary dries his eyes. "You're welcome, Son. I sure do miss your Mom helping us out here, but I'm glad we have Mandy with us, today." They exchange a quick hug.

Gary and Jonny look at Mandy with welcoming smiles. Gary asks her, "How about you, Mandy? Would you like to eat a sandwich? We can take a break and order sandwiches at the Deli. We can eat out on the garden patio and take in a breath of fresh air."

Jonny nods in agreement. Mandy replies, "That's a great idea. I'm hungry and I definitely need fresh air. Thank you, Gary for sharing your history. I think this is a great beginning. There's more to your business than meets the eye."

Jonny suggests, "I can call the café and place the order for our sandwiches. When we go down to pick them up, we can buy the beverages."

Gary and Mandy simultaneously say, "The usual!"

Their eyes light up and laughter fills the room. Gary tells them that the meeting is over for today. He feels choked up thinking about Angela and a little frayed from telling his story.

CHAPTER SEVEN
ASSISTANT EXTRAORDINAIRE
AT WORK

Gary, Jonny and Mandy ate their sandwiches and drank their soft drinks outside at a table close to Angela's garden.

Jonny says, "The weather is beautiful today. Perfect for a picnic on the garden patio."

With a concerned look on his face, he asks, "Are you feeling okay, Dad? You look a little tired and flushed today."

His Dad replies, "Yes, I'll be okay. I'm a little more tired than usual. I'm feeling too warm sitting out here in the sunshine. I'll go back to my office and check on how things are going there. I might take a little rest on my sofa. If things are going okay, I'll take the rest of the day off."

"You really look very tired. I agree that you should take a rest."

"I hope that I'll feel better tomorrow. No need to worry, Son. Why don't you and Mandy spend time talking about our businesses or make some plans to tour the hotel. We'll have another meeting soon to discuss a plan of action.

Just take your time and enjoy the day. I'll check in on Frank in the studio on the way back to my office."

"Okay, Dad, you should take the rest of the day off to rest and relax. Frank has my cell phone number. He can call me if he needs help or has a question. He should be doing okay. He worked as a professional photographer before coming to work here. We had a good talk about things this morning. He seems happy and he's fitting right in."

"Good to hear that Frank is doing well at the Studio. Giving him your cell phone number was a good idea."

Jonny says, "I'd like to visit with Mandy out here. We'll return to her office soon to talk about things."

"Is that okay with you, Mandy? Or would you like to move on and chat in your office? It's really a lovely day. Wherever you want to sit and talk is fine with me."

"I would like to get up and walk through the garden again. We can walk around the buildings. I would like to explore this area. We can walk and talk at the same time. Will that work for you? I'll be more than ready to return to the office after a walk in the sunshine."

"Yes, where would you like to walk to first? You sound serious like someone on a mission."

"I want to see the hotel and limousine service as well as the inside of the restaurant. I want to walk through the second floor to observe the modelling agency. Your Dad left brochures on my desk this morning. I'm impressed by what I read. I want to see the buildings for myself and learn more about the businesses. I want to be ready for whatever action or plan that you and your Dad have in mind for me. It's my intention to be successful at this job."

Jonny chuckles, "You are on a mission! Glad you're taking all of this so seriously. We really appreciate that you're willing to assist us with these business issues. You don't have to see all of those buildings in one day. We can take our time to enjoy the day, too."

He adds, "If Dad is feeling better tomorrow, he and I will sit down together in his office. He and I will work together on his current scheduled appointments."

Mandy says, "Okay, time is getting away this afternoon. We'll walk around and observe as much as we can. Tomorrow, I'll take the brochures with me while I walk through each of those buildings. The more details that I can learn from the description of these businesses the easier my job will be."

"Ted's Steakhouse is the restaurant that we own. We ate at the restaurant last night and last Thursday. Thank you by the way for joining us for dinner last night. Dad and I enjoyed meeting your Mom and visiting with you two."

"Yes, I saw the brochure with the name of the restaurant. Mom and I enjoyed the dinner with you and your Dad."

You haven't been inside of the restaurant yet. The décor is designed for relaxing and a pleasurable dining experience. Maybe we can dine inside one night this week."

"Are you okay, Jonny?"

"I'm feeling a little tired and too warm. I think I'll leave when Dad does. I'm a little concerned about him. I have my cell phone if anyone has a question or a problem. I can work from home in my office. You can take off early, too. I can give you my cell phone number, also!"

"I'll give you my cell phone number just in case you need to reach me while I'm out of the office. I sure hope that your Dad gets the rest that he needs to feel better. I told Mom a lot about you two and my new job before our encounter in the garden last night. She enjoyed meeting your Dad. It was a fun time for Mom and I."

"You're welcome. I'm feeling a little thirsty. I think I'll go to the café for a cold beverage to-go. Would you like one, too?"

"Yes, I think I'll have a cup of water to-go. I'll go in with you. I'll get a cup for myself at the water fountain."

Mandy feels an attraction to Jonny. She enjoys seeing his smile, hearing his voice and just being with him. She's trying hard not to let it show. It's important to her to do an outstanding and professional job.

Jonny is feeling the chemistry more each day. He's struggling with his feelings. He doesn't want to be involved on a personal level. At least not until his Dad is officially retired this summer. He finds Mandy's laughter to be contagious. He admires her sweet disposition and determination to do a good job for him and his Dad.

The desire to hold hands, hug or kiss is strong. They make themselves stop thinking about it.

They take the to-go drinks with them for their walk through the garden. Mandy takes a brief look inside the restaurant. It's already busy with an early dinner crowd.

"Jonny, I would like to walk across the street to the Hotel and Limo Service. I want to take a look around that area. Do you think your dad is doing okay? Should you call him to see what time you two might leave here?"

"No, I believe that he'll give me a call when he's ready to leave. He's good about keeping in touch with me on a personal level like that. He might be resting or busy so I'd rather not disturb him. We can walk across the street together. When he calls, we can make plans to leave here at that time."

The Hotel is huge with lots of amenities. Mandy definitely plans on exploring the inside tomorrow. They walk around the outside of the Hotel building. In the back corner of the lot, they see limousines as well as the garage and office building for this service.

"Wow, Jonny! I've never seen a limousine up close before. I've seen them on the road from a distance. They are much bigger and longer than I imagined. Black limousines look professional for business purposes. White ones remind me of prom nights and celebrations. Have you ever ridden in one?"

Jonny chuckles, then says, "Yes, many times. Last week I rode in one to the airport with my Dad. When he took his last business trip, I rode with him to see him take off. Did you know we have our own company plane at the airport?"

"No, I don't think that was mentioned in our conversations. Do you like to fly? I've only flown twice and didn't really enjoy it. I was a little girl so I might feel different about flying now that I'm older."

"You never know; the occasion may arise for us to ride in a limo out to our plane. Maybe we can take the plane out for a flyover of the city." He's joking but wants to see how she'll react to the possibility.

She looks a bit stunned. In reality though, she thinks that it might be a fun thing to do, especially with Jonny.

"I'm getting tired and a little overheated from our walk and exploration. Are you ready to go back to the Agency? I'll take you up on your offer. I'm going to leave early today. I'll take the brochures from my desk. I'll study them more at home while I rest. I'll enjoy tomorrow's exploration of the buildings, when I'm feeling a little more energized."

"Yes, let's walk back to the Agency. I'll go check on Dad and Frank. If everything is going well, Dad and I can plan to go home together. He really does need a rest. The last business trip took a lot out of him and we had a busy weekend."

She tells Jonny, "Thanks for the walk in the garden and walking across the street with me.

Thank you for a happy Monday." She smiles! She walks into her office and puts the brochures in her purse.

Jonny checks in with Frank at the studio for an update. Everything is going well. No problems that Frank couldn't handle which is a good sign. Jonny introduces Mandy to Frank and vice versa.

They walk down the hall together to Gary's office. Jonny peeks in and finds his Dad sitting on the sofa with his head back and resting with his eyes closed. Mandy whispers, "Please say goodbye to your Dad for me. Give him my best and my wish that he feels better soon. Thanks! Have a good evening."

Jonny says, "I also enjoyed our walk and exploring the area together. See you tomorrow."

Mandy goes out to her car and drives home to her apartment.

Jonny walks quietly over to his Dad so that he's not startled awake. He says gently and softly, "Dad are you okay? Are you ready to go home now?"

His Dad opens his eyes and appears to be a little disoriented. "Yes, Son, I'm ready to go home. I really didn't mean to fall asleep. I just meant to rest my eyes then I dozed off. I'm feeling more tired than usual. Maybe Sadie will make some of her homemade chicken soup for me. That should give me a lift."

"I checked in on Frank and everything is going well at the studio. Mandy and I had fun taking a walk in the garden. We walked over to the restaurant, hotel and limousine service buildings, too. I suggested that she take off early. We should leave now. I want to take you home for some much needed rest."

They arrive at home to see Sadie in the kitchen preparing their supper. She's a gourmet cook. Everything that Sadie cooks is delicious and smells out of this world. When she sees Gary, she realizes that something is not quite right. She offers, "Would you like for me to cook my homemade chicken soup for you, Gary?"

Gary laughs, "Yes, please, sounds wonderful! How did you know?"

"You're looking tired and a little down. Usually my soup builds you back up and gives you a lift."

Jonny greets Sadie and then adds, "We'll go change into more comfortable clothes and clean up for dinner. We'll return soon. I'll be ready to eat the food that you're cooking for us. Thank you, Sadie!"

Mandy arrives at her apartment glad to be home. She goes to the refrigerator for a soft drink and sits down to rest on her couch. She puts her feet up and feels relieved to be home after a long emotional and stressful day. It was a good day overall but she still feels exhausted. She pulls out the brochures from her purse and sets them on the coffee table in front of her. She'll study each photo and every word on them before she goes to bed tonight. She learned a lot today. She knows that there's still a lot to learn in order to do her job successfully.

CHAPTER EIGHT
DAD'S DAY OF REST

Jonny is up, dressed and ready to go to work. He walks down the stairs to the kitchen. Sadie is cooking a big breakfast. The aroma of fresh coffee as well as the bacon and eggs frying in the pan is a great way to start his day. He notices that his Dad isn't sitting at the table. His Dad's usual routine is to drink a cup of coffee while Sadie is cooking.

"Sadie, where's Dad? Is he up yet? He's usually down here before me."

"I think your Dad might still be in bed. He wasn't feeling well last night. Maybe he's not feeling any better this morning."

"I'll go upstairs and check in with him. I'll be back to eat your delicious breakfast soon."

Jonny walks upstairs to his Dad's bedroom. He listens for any sign that his Dad is up and moving around. He knocks on the bedroom door quietly. He hears a moan and a hoarse, "Come on in, Jonny."

He opens the door and walks in. He sees that his Dad is still covered up in bed looking very sleepy. "Dad? Are you feeling okay? Is there anything I can do for you?"

"I'm not feeling very well, Son. I think that I'll need to take the day off and rest in bed. I feel like I'm coming down with something. If I'm not feeling better by tomorrow, I'll call our doctor for a checkup."

"Okay, Dad. I think it's a good idea for you to rest. Is there anything in particular that I can do for you at your office today? I can try to handle your business appointments for the day. I'll try to learn what I can about your office routine on my own. I hope you're back on your feet soon. The office won't be the same without you there."

"Yes, Jon, that'll be very helpful. It won't be too long before it'll be your office. Please check my calendar. You can call me on the cell phone if you have any questions. Thanks, Son."

His Dad props up the pillows and sits up. "Would you mind bringing me up a cup of hot coffee? I'm feeling chilled like I have a fever."

"Sure, Dad? Sadie is cooking breakfast. Would you like something to eat, too?"

"No, thank you. I'm not hungry. Maybe Sadie can warm up a bowl of her chicken soup for lunch. I don't feel up to anything but a cup of coffee right now."

"I'll be right back with your hot coffee, Dad."

Jonny hurries down the stairs to the kitchen. He tells Sadie, "Dad isn't feeling well. He's decided to stay home from work to rest in bed today. He asked me to bring a cup of hot coffee to him upstairs."

"Do you know if he wants to eat breakfast?"

He said that he doesn't want anything to eat right now. He mentioned that he might like some of your chicken soup around lunchtime."

Jonny pours a cup of coffee for his Dad and carries it upstairs on a serving tray. He sets the tray down on a table in the hall while he knocks on the door.

He opens it and asks, "Dad? I've got your coffee for you right here. Can I come in?"

"Yes, Jon, please come on in. Mmmm!!! Thank you very much for serving coffee to me this morning. Good luck, Jon. I wish you a great day at the office."

"You're welcome! Please rest well. Are you doing okay? I need to eat breakfast before I leave for the office."

"Yes, I'll drink my coffee and try to fall asleep again. I feel weak and tired. I'll call Sadie on the intercom, if I need urgent help."

"I'll call you around noon and see how you're doing. Call me at any time, Dad. I'll be here for you, if you need me. See you later."

Jonny returns to the kitchen. Sadie has his breakfast ready and waiting for him. He pours a cup of coffee for himself and offers one to Sadie. They talk about their concern for His Dad. He hardly ever gets sick. They've never seen him looking so run down. Sadie reassures Jonny that she'll serve him a bowl of soup upstairs, if his Dad doesn't come down to the kitchen before lunchtime.

Jonny ate his breakfast and then he went upstairs to freshen up. He leaves for the office feeling very concerned about his Dad.

Mandy arrives at her office a little earlier than usual. She's anxious to explore and learn all that she can. She's surprised to see that Jonny and Gary aren't in their office. She wonders if everything is okay. She didn't see them in the café or anywhere on the third floor. She'll wait to see if Jonny arrives before she leaves to walk over to the hotel. If he's not in by that time, she'll call him on the cell phone. She's concerned for Gary's welfare.

She looks over the hotel (Imperial Inn) brochure once more while drinking her coffee. The sound of the elevator door opening makes her heart race again. She steps out into the hallway. She sees Jonny but his Dad is nowhere in sight. Jonny walks down the hall toward her.

She says, "Hello, Jonny! How is your Dad feeling today?"

"Hello, Mandy! Dad isn't feeling well today. He's taking the day off. He has chills, feels weak and very tired. I think the day of rest will do him a world of good."

"Is there anything that I can do? My Mom has a nursing degree. She was a registered nurse before she retired. If he needs a good nurse, I know where he can find one."

"That's kind of you, Mandy. Dad says that he'll call his doctor tomorrow if he's not feeling better."

"If he needs a friend to talk to, my Mom is a good listener. She cares about people and good at ministering TLC (Tender Loving Care). They can talk on the phone."

"I'll let Dad know about her nursing and TLC experience. Her friendship might be an encouragement to slow down and take better care."

"Are you going to cover his office today?"

"Yes, I'm going to check his calendar and contact any clients that need his immediate attention. I think that he has an appointment with the attorney sometime this week. We'll have to wait and see if Dad will feel up to that meeting."

"If you need any assistance, that's why I'm here, Jonny. Just let me know please? My plan for the day is to explore the Imperial Inn like an undercover agent. I want a first-hand account to add to my final reports. I have the brochure and my journal so that I can observe and take notes."

"I'm sure that Dad will want you to do that. It's part of our plan to "sort things out" before he retires. He needs to make a major decision about the hotel. There are several issues to consider regarding his businesses. We need you to paint the big picture for us."

"I'll follow through with my plan to explore the hotel. You can call me on my cell phone if you need my assistance in your Dad's office. Good luck! See you later!"

"Good luck to you, too. The Imperial Inn is huge. You'll probably need the whole week to finish everything that Dad wants you to do. It'll take time to survey the hotel issues."

"I'll do my best."

"Oh, be sure to check out the exercise room and the spa. You can get an employee discount when you use their services. Sounds like fun, doesn't it? Did you get a list of employee benefits from the personnel office?"

"I received a benefit package but I haven't taken time to read everything in it, yet. Thanks for letting me know. It does sound like fun. It'll be another opportunity to experience something new in my life."

"I'm going to work in Dad's office now. You can call me on my cell phone if you need me. I'll be there to help you out in any way that I can. See you later."

Jonny settles in at the desk in Gary's office. It's all a little overwhelming. He sits trembling inside as he thinks about trying to fill his Dad's shoes. He focuses on his Dad's health and retirement. He thinks his Dad will be healthier and happier living free from stress. *It'll be great to work out the business issues so that I'm not overstressed. I'm still young with my whole life ahead of me. I have dreams of meeting the right lady to marry and have a family. Mandy is on my mind once again. She's someone that I think is amazing.*

He uses his cell phone to check in with his Dad. Gary's cell phone is vibrating on his nightstand. He woke up shortly before noon with an improved appetite. Sadie served him chicken soup and a few crackers upstairs on a bed table. The extended rest and the soup is giving him a lift. Gary answers his cell phone thinking that it must be his son, Jon.

"Good afternoon!"

"Good afternoon, Dad!" How are you feeling?"

"I'm sitting up and drinking a cup of Sadie's chicken soup. I'm feeling slightly better than last night. I'm still feeling run down and feel like I need more rest. I'll stay in bed until I've slept long enough to restore my energy."

"That's great, Dad! We all care about you here. Hope you feel better soon. Speaking of people caring, Mandy told me that her Mom is a retired Nurse. You know Katherine likes you. She'll be a good friend to talk to about things. She's a very caring person. I can get her number from Mandy if you want to give her a call."

His Dad chuckles, "I know she's a caring person. I got that much from our dinner together. We exchanged cell phone numbers that night. We both agreed it might be fun to get together again sometime. We haven't had time yet to call and make plans. There's no reason for us to rush things. We'll take our time. We both have other things going on in our lives right now."

Jonny is surprised and shares a little chuckle. "I agree Dad. I'm glad you have her number in case you want to talk to a friend."

"If I'm feeling better, I might call her this evening. I really don't want to be a burden to anyone. How are things going for you at my office? Or should I say our office?"

"I checked your calendar. I can handle your appointments for today. I noticed that you have an appointment with our attorney later this week. Do you think you'll be able to keep that one? Should I call and reschedule it?"

"Let's wait and see how I feel by then. He's drawing up important contracts and changes in my will. I have other important business to discuss with him as well."

"That's a great idea. We'll just take it one day at a time. I'll let you finish drinking your soup. Call me if you need anything please. We'll talk soon. Rest well."

They exchange good-byes. Gary finishes his soup and sets the cup on the tray. He gets up out of bed and freshens up. He returns to his bed and curls up under the covers. He closes his eyes and quickly falls asleep.

CHAPTER NINE
TAKING CARE OF BUSINESS

Mandy is waiting for the elevator on the third floor to ride it down to the lobby. The bell dings and the elevator doors open. To her surprise, Jennifer steps out of the elevator glaring at her.

With a scowl, Jennifer says, "It's you! Jonny's new assistant! I want to have a chat with you."

Mandy doesn't really have time for Jennifer right now. She responds, "Hi Jennifer, I'd be happy to chat with you. I can see that you're really upset. Please try to calm down first."

"You bet, I'm upset. I've seen the way you look at MY Jonny. I'm in love with him. I don't appreciate you acting so sweet toward him. I've known and cared for him for years. We used to date before his Mom died. I've been waiting for him to feel better about going out with me again. I know that it'll take time but I'm patient."

"I don't think that this is the best place for us to talk about Jonny. He's close by in his Dad's office today."

"Maybe you're right but I really need to set you straight."

Mandy sighs, "I can take a few minutes to chat with you if you can stay calm. How about going with me to the Deli and we can chat quietly over a soft drink or tea. I've got a busy afternoon ahead of me. I'm sure you have work to do here, too."

"Okay, I appreciate you sitting down and chatting with me. Let's go down to the Deli for a quick break."

They ride the elevator down to the lobby without saying a word to each other. The tension is thick. They arrive at the Deli and Mandy buys iced tea for two. Mandy hopes the cold drink will help them to cool down and relax through this chat. They sit in a quiet corner.

Mandy tells Jennifer, "I'll be working close with Jonny. It's my job as an assistant to help Jonny takeover for his Dad when he retires. We've become friends over the past few days. We're just friends! Jonny and I want the business to be successful. We want his Dad to retire happily this summer."

"I saw the two of you in the studio dressed in those ridiculous costumes. That didn't look like business to me. I came in to talk to Jonny because I've really missed him. There you were dressed like a Princess and Jonny like a Prince. What was I to think about you two? I left heartbroken and angry at you for trying to lure my Jonny away."

"We were talking about studio business but Jonny offered to make a couple of fun photos for my Mom for Mother's Day. It turned out to be a few laughs but there's nothing between us."

"I still feel upset and angry when I recall that moment. I'm trying to stay calm but I can't help but to warn you not to take my Jonny away from me."

"I really need to get back to work, Jennifer. I suggest you do the same. There's still several hours of work ahead of me today. Just stay calm and go back to work. I have to leave here now."

Mandy stands up and tells Jennifer goodbye. Jennifer is still scowling as she takes a long look at Mandy from head to toe. She huffs and hurries out the door with tears pooling in her eyes.

Mandy walks out of the café door over to the front entrance of the building. She pauses for a quick chat with the security guard on duty. He doesn't know any reason why Mandy should feel concern about Jennifer's behavior.

She crosses the street to the hotel, known as the Imperial Inn. She's glad it's a chilly spring day. The cool breeze helps her to calm down. The chat with Jennifer definitely made her feel uptight. *I'll deal with my feelings later. I really need to make my way through the hotel today.* If necessary, she'll use the rest of the week to finalize her report. Today, she wants to walk through the hotel, observe and take notes.

The first thing she notices is that Valet Parking is underground. The parking attendants are sharp looking in their uniforms. They appear to perform their job with speed and accuracy.

When she walks up to the front doors, she's cheerfully greeted by the doorman. Although she's not sure about tipping, she pulls out a couple of bills from her purse. She securely places the bills in his hand. *If only Jonny were here to guide me. I'm not experienced at tipping. I'm sure Jonny has experience in this kind of thing.*

Mandy walks into the lobby of the Imperial Inn. Looking up and all the way around, she feels frozen in time by what she sees. The beauty and electrical charge in the air is like a fairy tale scene. She feels like a Princess. The luxury in this place is far more than she ever imagined.

She wants a first-hand account of how the staff are treating their guests. She wants to know if the guests are satisfied with their stay there. She'll meet with the administrative staff soon. She needs to obtain a clear understanding of how the hotel is operating. This information will be important for her report to Gary and Jonny. A first-hand observation and experience will give her clarity on how the business is faring at this moment in time. Gary wants the businesses to be in top shape before Jonny takes over.

She's feeling a little dizzy over the excitement of being in the hotel and taking part in this adventure. She has the brochure in her hand. While checking out the photos, she's trying to determine the location of everything available in the hotel. She walks over to the concierge and asks a few questions. The concierge believes that Mandy is a potential guest.

She thinks, *First things first.* Exploring each one of the floors is foremost on her mind. She asks at the check-in desk about taking a tour. *Hopefully, someone will be able to answer my questions.* The assistant manager on duty, Betty, offers to guide her through a quick tour.

Betty answers Mandy's questions willingly and shows her the interior of the conference rooms. She explains that catering is available from their restaurant for meetings and large parties.

Most of the large suites are occupied but Betty describes them to Mandy. Betty shares details as though Mandy is planning to stay overnight. The honeymoon suite is unoccupied. Betty gives her a sneak peek inside. It's definitely a fantasy suite for newlyweds.

Mandy is thinking seriously about registering for an overnight stay in one of the smaller suites. As a guest she'll have more freedom and feel more relaxed about walking in the halls. After the tour, she explores on her own. She locates the indoor pool, exercise room, spa, boutiques, restaurant and other places described in the brochure.

She's feeling hungry and thirsty. She notices that the restaurant is very crowded and busy. There's a little café available for small meals and snacks. She decides to order a sandwich and sits down for a rest. *This is a good time to write out my observations and experiences in my journal.*

She hears her cell phone ringing in her purse. It's Jonny. He's calling to see how she's doing at the hotel.

Mandy answers, "Hello, Jonny. Is everything alright with your Dad? Are you doing okay?"

"Hello Mandy, yes, everything is going as well as can be expected. I spoke with Dad on the phone earlier. He said he was feeling a little better. He plans to sleep for the rest of the day. He admits that he's extremely exhausted."

"I'm still at the hotel. I'm taking a break after exploring and a guided tour. I'm ready to eat a sandwich here in the café. Do you have time for a break? You can join me here. I'll wait."

Although the idea sounds great, Jonny says, "No, I don't think that I'll have time to join you. I'm going to be in a meeting here in Dad's office soon. I'm not sure how long it will last."

"I'm thinking of staying in one of the small suites here overnight. I read in our employee pamphlet that I can get a discount with my employee ID. It'll be to my advantage to experience the quality care that's offered here. This will be another first time experience. As a registered guest, I can wake up in the morning and do my undercover work." She laughs sweetly!

"That's a wonderful idea Mandy! Perhaps tomorrow, if Dad is feeling better, he'll return to his office. Maybe, we can meet tomorrow at the café in the hotel and have a business chat. We can make plans to explore together. I've got to go for now. We'll talk more later."

"Okay, talk to you later."

Mandy is glad that he likes her idea about an overnight stay. She goes to the counter to register for a small suite for the night. After she receives her room key, she locates the room and takes a look around. It's luxurious. She thought that her apartment was big before she saw the size of her suite.

She realizes that she needs to go home to pack an overnight bag. She walks out of the hotel, crosses the street, gets into her car and drives to her apartment.

She proceeds to pack her bag with necessary items. Because she's feeling a little playful, she packs a change of clothes for the exercise room and her swimsuit. She thinks to herself, *Just in case there's a little time for fun. The pool and exercise room are for the guests. Perhaps, I can visit the spa another time. It all sounds like a dream.*

She takes a shower and changes her clothes at her apartment. She takes the overnight bag out to her car and drives back to the hotel. She settles in at her luxurious suite. It's still early in the evening. The thought of exploring still appeals to her. While studying over the brochure again, she wants to check out the boutiques with their fine clothing.

First, she calls Jonny to give him an update. He doesn't answer his phone. It goes straight to voicemail. She tells him the room number in case he's unable to reach her by phone. She's feeling concern for Jonny's Dad.

Next, she calls her Mom to let her know where she's staying overnight. She tells her Mom that they should plan on a mini-vacation at the hotel soon. Her Mom is excited about the possibility. Mandy implies that her Mom will receive the royalty treatment. Mandy is willing to do that for her Mom!

She steps out into the hallway to take the elevator down to the lobby. As she steps out of the elevator, she sees Jonny walking toward her. She gasps in surprise. He's smiling which makes her heart race faster.

"Jonny? Is everything okay? Why are you here?"

"Yes, everything is fine. After my meeting, I listened to my voicemail. I thought it might be fun to surprise you with an invitation to eat dinner here at the restaurant. Would you like to have dinner here with me tonight?"

"That sounds like fun! We can have a little business chat, too. But, Jonny, if it's okay with you, I'd prefer eating somewhere not so fancy. I'm not very hungry due to all of the excitement of the day. Can we dine where I can eat a light meal?"

"Sure, would you like to come over to my house? I want to check-in on Dad, too. Sadie, our cook, can fix you a light meal. I'm hungry for steak and potatoes. I'll call her to let her know. If you say yes, I promise to drive you back here early."

"I feel nervous thinking about it. It's a lovely invitation. Are you sure it won't be a problem for your cook, Sadie? I'll say yes if she's okay with the unexpected company."

"I'll give her a quick call right now."

"I came down here to check out the boutiques. I'll just be right over here. You can find me again when you're done talking on the phone."

Mandy opens the door to the boutique and walks down the aisles looking at all of the beautiful dresses, hats and shoes. There's also a jewelry counter with lovely barrettes, necklaces, bracelets and earrings. With all of the models that travel to this area, it's understandable that the clothing in this boutique is world class.

She leaves the boutique and sees that Jonny is still talking on the phone. She finds a little settee in the lobby and sits down to rest her tired feet. She's walked around a lot today.

Finally, Jonny is finished talking on the phone. He walks over and sits down beside her on the settee. They both feel the energy change between them and their hearts are racing once again.

"I talked to Sadie and she's happy to prepare the meals for us. I also talked to Dad. He feels rested and in fact called your Mom this evening. He invited her over for a visit with him. They're drinking coffee and eating apple pie." Jonny and Mandy smile and feel happy for their parents to find a new friendship.

"Oh?! Are you sure you want to eat at home, Jonny? Maybe we should give your Dad more time to rest. Maybe we should let your Dad and my Mom enjoy their visit. It would be good for them to talk freely about things."

"You're right, Mandy, I didn't think about that. Will you please plan on coming home with me for a meal soon? It would be good for us to talk freely about things, too. Would you like to go to Ted's Steakhouse and eat out on their patio again? It's a beautiful evening and the twinkle lights will be on. We can enjoy the fresh air in the garden. I'll call Sadie and Dad to update them on our plans."

"Yes, Jonny, I'll agree to eat dinner at your house soon. Eating out on the garden patio sounds like the perfect place for another business meeting."

CHAPTER TEN
COULD THIS BE LOVE?

Jonny and Mandy enjoy their dinner at Ted's Steakhouse. They enjoy it more this time than on other occasions. It's a beautiful evening with a cool gentle breeze caressing the flowers in the garden. The fresh air is sweet with the fragrance of flowers. Once again, the twinkle lights are glistening like diamonds.

They finish eating their meals. It's time for their chat about business. They order cups of hot coffee. She wants to relax and feel the comfort of the warm cup in her hands. She needs to share her encounter with Jennifer.

"Jonny, I need to tell you about my encounter with Jennifer today. She wanted to chat with me. She was visibly upset. In order to help her calm down, I invited her to the café and bought iced tea for us. She thinks that I'm trying to take you away from her. I felt slightly threatened. I chatted with the security guard on duty. He made me feel a little safer."

"Oh no, Mandy, I'm very sorry that she verbally attacked you in that way. I'll definitely sit down and have a long talk with her. I really didn't want to push things and cause her any pain. I also don't want her to cause you any pain. I'll need to set the record straight as gently as I possibly can. I know that she's very sensitive. She thinks that she's in love with me. I haven't told her that I'm not in love with her. I was really out of it after my Mom died. Thank you for sharing this information with me, Mandy."

"You're welcome. I thought you should know what's happening with her. She seems fragile and hurting deeply by my presence with you."

He reaches over and gently picks up her hand. He gives it a sweet gentle kiss and says, "I'm sorry that you're caught up in my personal problems like this."

She feels shock watching him kiss her hand. She's also surprised by the fact that she likes it.

"It's okay for now. I hope that you'll talk to her and help her to heal. I can see why she's in love with you. You're a very handsome, fun, talented and passionate man."

"Thank you for the compliments. I think you're pretty amazing. It would be easy for me to fall head over heels in love with you. You're the sweetest, caring and talented lady that I've ever known."

"Thank you for the compliments. We really need to talk about business. It's getting late and I'm feeling very tired. Maybe we can meet tomorrow and I can share my notes. I want to ask you a few questions after my time of exploring."

"Okay! Actually today has been really stressful trying to fill in for Dad. My head feels like it's swimming with all the new information that I've learned today. I'll escort you back to the hotel and to your suite. I want you to be safe."

He pays for their dinner. They walk back through the garden and across the street to the hotel. Jonny escorts her with his hand on the small of her back. It's chilly outside. His touch helps her to feel warm.

Jonny walks her to the door of her suite. She unlocks it and turns back to tell him good night. Their eyes lock. There are stars in their eyes. They quickly look away from each other. They're lost in a daze. Their hearts are racing and pounding. They can barely breathe.

They gently and sweetly embrace saying, "Good Night."

Mandy quickly says, "Thank you for a lovely evening. I'll see you tomorrow."

She opens her suite door and walks in. She's ready to close the door when she hears Jonny speaking.

"I enjoyed the evening, too. Thank you for letting me take you out for dinner. Sleep well. See you tomorrow."

Although they're still in a daze, they smile directly at each other. She slowly closes the door as she watches him turn and walk toward the elevator.

She stays in for the rest of the evening. She reads over the notes in her journal. She takes time to edit and write additional information. It's a struggle to stay focused. Thoughts about Jonny creep in and try to take over.

She calls her Mom on her cell phone. Her Mom answers on the second ring. There's laughter in the background. She hears Jonny and his Dad talking in muffled voices. The lady's voice might be Sadie's but she doesn't know for sure.

"Hello, Mom! Are you still visiting with Gary? Is he doing okay? How are things going with you?"

"Hello, Mandy! Yes, I was ready to leave through the front door when Jonny arrived. We stopped long enough to greet each other and say goodnight. I'm on my way out the door again. Gary is feeling better. He called me and we had a nice chat. He invited me over for apple pie and coffee. I enjoyed my time visiting with him and Sadie."

"That's great news, Mom! I'm going to take a long relaxing bath and go to sleep. I want to be up bright and early to finish exploring. I'm just calling to see how you're doing and to say good night. Drive safe, Mom! We'll talk soon."

"Good night my darling daughter. Talk soon!"

She looks out the window, while closing the drapes. The view is breathtaking! She didn't take time to look out earlier. With the city lights, the area is lit up like Christmas. She can see the lights reflecting off the river in the distance. There are lights on the boats that are drifting by. She pulls the cord and closes the drapes.

Mandy takes advantage of the whirlpool bath that's in her room. This is another new experience for her. She looks forward to relaxing before falling asleep. It was a long stressful day. She enjoys her bubble bath, pulls the plug, gets out and dries off. The hotel provides a beautiful plush robe. She totally feels pampered and like royalty. She's thankful for this new luxurious experience.

She changes into her nightgown and follows her usual bedtime routine. First, she brushes her hair and then her teeth. The hotel provides a variety of small bottles of lotion, creams, and makeup remover. After she puts the night cream on her face, she's ready to turn off the light and fall asleep.

She sets an alarm on her cell phone and sets it on the nightstand. She curls up on the large queen size bed. She falls asleep and dreams about the beauty that surrounds her. Jonny is in her dream looking like a handsome Prince.

Jonny is at home talking with his Dad. He shares how his day was spent at his Dad's office. He listens while his Dad updates him on how he's feeling rested and ready to go to the office in the morning. He wants to ask his Dad about his visit with Katherine but decides not to pry. Earlier, he overheard him mention to Katherine that he enjoyed their visit. Knowing that his Dad is feeling better and that he enjoyed Katherine's company is enough information for now.

Jonny can't stop thinking about Mandy. He's trying hard to keep things on a business level with her. The love attraction he feels for her is strong. He follows his nightly routine and curls up on his bed. He's having a hard time falling asleep with memories of Mandy floating through his mind. He's tempted to call her but decides not to. He knows that Mandy plans to be up early in the morning. He tries to shake it off. *Could this be love?* He shakes his head and closes his eyes. He falls asleep within minutes and dreams about Mandy being a Princess.

They sleep through the whole night and wake up surprised by their funny dreams.

Mandy's phone alarm rings. She presses the snooze button while she tries to wake up. Her sleep was deep and she doesn't want to get out of bed. The bed is comfortable and warm. She gets up with determination to enjoy the day. She made plans last night with Jonny to talk about business issues today. Her personal feelings are confusing and she's having a difficult time staying focused.

She tries to keep her mind off of Jonny. She relives the memory of him kissing her hand and the warmth of his hand on her back as they crossed the street. The memory of the "good night" embrace is the most unsettling feeling of all. She has mixed emotions and she tries to sort them out. *Could this be love?*

She calls her Mom on her cell phone to invite her to eat lunch with her. *It'll be a nice experience for us to eat lunch here at the hotel's cafe.* Mandy leaves a voicemail message for her Mom to call her back.

She gets dressed in a business outfit and goes to the café for breakfast. She orders coffee, eggs, bacon and toast. She needs the extra energy for the activities that she has planned for the day. After eating breakfast, she returns to her room to freshen up.

After she freshens up, she sits at the desk in her room. She opens her journal and reads it to be sure of its accuracy. Last night felt like a dream. She takes her cell phone out of her purse to check for messages. She hopes that her Mom will return her call. She wants to have a mother-daughter talk to seek her advice regarding her feelings for Jonny.

She decides to finish exploring in the hotel. She wants to listen, observe and take notes about what's happening there. Her first thought is to check out the basement where the exercise room is located. Now that she's a validated guest, she has no insecurity about walking in the halls and looking around.

The exercise room has a variety of equipment. It's partitioned off to accommodate both men and women. Both sections are maintained by instructors. It appears to be both clean and safe for the guests. She hopes to use the exercise room on a different day. As an employee at the Agency, she's allowed free access to this room.

Her next stop is to check out the indoor pool. It's in a room separate from the main area of the hotel. The only swimmers are guests using it for exercise first thing in the morning. There's no one playing around like you would see at a family pool.

The sign for the spa has an arrow pointing across the other side of the floor. She walks to the door and opens it. She sees a receptionist and hears her ask if she has an appointment. There are all sorts of wonderful new things to try out in this spa. She reads the list of services. She thinks about her Mom. *Wouldn't it be wonderful to treat my Mom to a massage? I would love to pamper myself with a massage and a facial. I'm glad that I get a discount with my employee ID.*

Her next stop is in the lobby where she saw the boutiques last night. The very back of the lobby looks like a mini-mall. There are little shops that line the back wall. There are a few padded benches around a medium tranquility fountain.

She visited the ladies clothing store last night. She enters the shop for men. There are fine business suits, shiny shoes, belts, belt buckles and hats. There's also a counter with men's jewelry including fancy watches.

There's a clothing store for children which includes shoes as well as a few toys for both girls and boys. Next door is a general purpose store with a variety of miscellaneous items. The stores are stocked with things to accommodate the hotel guests. It's all very impressive.

Mandy takes a little break on a settee in the lobby. She checks her phone for messages again. Her Mom hasn't returned her call. She calls her Mom but there's no answer. She's thinking about Gary and Jonny and how they're doing today. *This would be a good time to walk across the street and check in with them. I don't have to check out until 1:00 this afternoon. There's plenty of time for me to come back for my bag and personal items.*

She gets up and walks across the street to the Agency. When she arrives on the third floor, she hears Gary and Jonny talking. Their voices are coming from Gary's office. She slowly walks up to the door and stops just outside of it. Jonny sees her and stands up quickly. Their eyes lock and Mandy can barely speak.

She catches her breath and finally says, "Good morning. I'm sorry. I didn't mean to interrupt anything. I'm just checking in to see how you're feeling today, Gary."

"Good Morning, Mandy dear. I'm feeling much better today. Jonny and I were trying to catch up on the events of yesterday. Also, we're discussing our plans for the day."

Jonny's heart is racing once again but he manages to speak, "Good Morning, Mandy. Happy to see you. How was your overnight stay at the hotel? I hope you slept well."

"I slept just fine. I've been up and exploring for a few hours now. I took a little break from the hotel to check on your Dad. I guess I should have called him instead." She directs her attention to his Dad. "I'm glad to see that you're feeling better and back in your office today."

Jonny asks, "Mandy, do you have time to take a walk and talk with me?"

"Sure, as long as you and your Dad are through with your meeting."

Gary says, "Yes, go ahead, Jonny, we can talk more later."

"OK, Dad, I'll see you later."

He walks over to Mandy and places his hand on the small of her back while ushering her away from the door and into the hallway.

Gary is left alone, shaking his head and wondering what's going on with those two? *Could it be love?*

CHAPTER ELEVEN
IT'S COMPLICATED

"What do you want to talk about, Jonny? I have to return to the hotel before the 1:00pm checkout time. I need to collect and pack my personal items. I can't afford to waste any time here. I'm trying to reach my Mom, also. I want to invite her to eat lunch in the café. Then, I can show her my suite during my lunch hour. It'll give her great joy to see the luxury first-hand."

"We have a lot to talk about. We agreed last night to talk about business issues, if Dad returns to his office. We shouldn't talk about these things in the hallway. Will you talk with me in your office?"

"I need to share my notes with you from my journal. It's back at the hotel on the desk in my suite. It has a beautiful office area where we can talk about business. Is that okay with you?"

"Yes, I've worked in one of their office suites before. It was quiet and comfortable. Let me check in with Dad to let him know. My discussion with him can wait but he should be kept in the loop. He can call if he needs me to return to the office."

"I'll wait for you here and we can walk over together."

Mandy checks her phone messages once again while she's waiting for Jonny. Her mom hasn't returned her call. Jonny returns from sharing their plan with his Dad. She shares with him that she's worried about her Mom.

He says, "Just a minute while I check with Dad. Maybe he's heard from her today."

"Ok."

"Yes, Dad says he spoke with her briefly. She plans to work outdoors in the yard and in the gardens today. She probably left her phone indoors to protect it."

"Aha, well that would explain why she hasn't answered her phone or returned my call. I'll plan on eating lunch with her another day."

"Are you ready to go so that we can talk about things? Dad doesn't have a problem with continuing our discussion later. He said that he will call on the cell phone if he needs my help."

"Yes, I'm ready to go."

They walk out of the Agency building, cross the street and arrive at Mandy's suite without speaking to each other. She opens the door and suddenly realizes that she needs to repack her bag. It would be best if her bag is ready to carry out to her car before 1:00pm rolls around.

"Jonny, make yourself comfortable in the office area while I collect and repack my personal items. Will you please open the drapes so that it's bright and cheery in here?"

"Sure, I like bright and cheery. You have a gorgeous view from this window. I'm thirsty. Would you like a cold beverage? Better yet, I can order lunch for us from room service. My treat!

Since your lunch plan didn't work out with your Mom, would you like to eat lunch here?"

"I'm very thirsty, too. I would appreciate restoring my energy. I've walked around a lot this morning. Thank you for being so thoughtful and caring. I would like a glass of sweet iced tea. Hmm?! I haven't seen their menu. If they can prepare a fresh fruit dish, that's what I would like to eat. Thanks."

"I'll place the order now. I see that your bag is sitting by the door and ready to go. Please try to relax because you deserve a break."

"I'll find my journal and pen. We can chat while we wait for our lunch order. I'll try to take it easy during our lunch break."

Jonny calls room service and orders their meals. He orders two sandwiches and two glasses of iced tea. They tell him that it'll be delivered in fifteen minutes. He hangs up the phone.

He says, "We can chat for fifteen minutes before the food arrives."

"Thank you. I don't need my journal to share that the Imperial Inn is an awesome place. I've enjoyed exploring here and staying overnight. It's great to get a first-hand experience before I meet with the administrative staff. My observations of the employees, the beautiful building and the guests have given me a clearer understanding about this business."

"Ted and my Dad made a wise and valuable investment in this hotel. It was their effort to provide for the people connected with the

Agency. It's my understanding that Ted was in charge of keeping up with the business end of the hotel. It was his baby so to speak. Now that Ted is retired and Dad has full ownership, we want to get an up-to-date report on how it's being run. We want to know that the guests and employees are treated right and happy. You're the perfect candidate to give us a report before Dad retires. He plans to sell it if it isn't prospering or if it doesn't have a promising future."

"I haven't read any past financial reports, yet. They'll be important for my presentation to you and your Dad. I've seen and heard a lot that's very positive during my stay here. I believe the staff is doing a great job. They're taking good care of the guests. I never heard any complaints by employees or guests. It appears that all of the employees and the staff appreciate and respect your Dad. They perform their duties with passion. I believe that the guests are grateful for their caring attitude. I've had a peaceful feeling here since I first arrived yesterday."

There's a knock on the door. Jonny gets up to answer it. He hears a lady in the hall announce, "Room Service." He opens the door and she pushes a cart with wheels into the room. Their food arrives earlier than expected. That's okay because they're really hungry and thirsty.

"Everything looks and smells delicious, Jonny! Thank you!"

Jonny tips the delivery lady and says, "Thank you very much! Have a good day."

Mandy is busy in the kitchen area taking plates out of the cupboard and setting them on a small round table. She finds silverware and napkins in a drawer. Jonny starts laughing. She doesn't realize that room service provides everything they need. He points to the cart to show her what's on it. They share laughter as she puts the plates back in the cupboard

Jonny sets the table with the items on the cart. They both take a seat at the table with smiles and a sigh of relief.

"Let's not talk about business while we eat. Please try to relax for the next few minutes. Okay?"

"Sounds great to me. I enjoy being pampered. Thank you!" She giggles and blushes. "We'll have to leave here after we eat. I just noticed the time. We can finish our business chat back at my office if that works for you?"

"We'll figure that out when the time comes. Please just relax and enjoy the moment." He smiles. *There's probably not going to be another moment like this one.*

With a deep sigh she says, "Okay!"

"I've thought about you often since last night. I hope that you're not upset about our goodnight hug at your door."

"I was stunned after it happened but I'm over it now." Mandy thinks, *I really don't want him to know how much I enjoyed him kissing my hand, touching my back and hugging me good night. I don't want him to know how it made me feel.*

Jonny thinks, *I really don't want her to know how I feel. I don't think we should talk about our personal feelings in this setting.* "I'm glad that you're not upset. I guess it was impulsive of me. I really enjoy your company."

Mandy thinks, *I really enjoy being with you, too. I'm confused by my feelings and need more time. We shouldn't talk about our personal feelings.* "I'm finished eating and ready to leave the hotel. Are you ready to go?"

They sit gazing into each other's eyes. There's something special between them but they won't acknowledge their feelings for each other.

"Yes, I'm going to wash my hands. I'll carry your suitcase down for you."

"Okay, thank you, you're a real gentleman." They share a little laughter and big smiles.

She opens her purse and leaves a tip for the maid. She puts her journal and pen in her purse while looking around. She doesn't want to forget any of her personal items in the room.

They ride the elevator to the lobby. She checks out and turns in her key. They exit and walk across the street to her car. He helps her stow her bag in the backseat.

"Thank you for carrying my bag. I appreciate your help. I'm going to take a few minutes to call my Mom again. I need to speak with her about something important. I'll meet you in my office."

"It's my pleasure. I'll see you there."

She calls her Mom and this time her Mom answers. She says, "Hello, Mom! How are you doing? I tried to call you earlier to invite you to lunch. Did you get my messages?"

"No, I haven't checked my phone messages yet. I've been working in the yard and in both gardens. It's a big job but I love doing it. The vegetables and the flowers are growing very well. I'm sorry I missed your calls. I left my phone in the house."

"Is it okay if we meet for a mother-daughter chat tonight? I know that I'm a big girl and can make my own decisions. There's something important that I want to talk to you about. I can bring dinner over to you or we can eat and chat at my place. Which do you prefer?"

"I'm tired from the yardwork so I prefer staying here. I'm resting in my recliner right now."

"I'll call you before I leave work. You can let me know at that time what you want to eat for supper. I love you, Mom! Please, rest well."

"I look forward to seeing you. I love you!"

Mandy leaves her car and walks into the building. As she passes the glass double doors to the garden, she sees Jonny and Jennifer sitting on a bench together. Jennifer is crying and Jonny has his arm around her trying to comfort her.

She doesn't want to disturb them. She walks on by and rides the elevator to her office. She stops in to see how Gary is doing. He's not in his office. Feeling weary, she sits in her office alone. *This is a good time to type my notes and begin to prepare my report about the hotel.* She removes her journal from her purse and types her notes on the computer. It's very quiet and she's alone. She hasn't heard from Jonny. She hasn't heard any voices from Gary's office.

She's thirsty for a glass of sweet iced tea from the deli. She picks up her purse and goes down to the lobby. When she walks into the deli, she sees Gary and Jonny sitting at a table with glasses of tea. They're having a serious talk. They don't notice her when she walks in. Each one appears to be lost in thought while the other one is speaking. She buys the glass of iced tea and takes it up to her office.

While drinking her tea, she scans over the remaining brochures. *What should I do next? I think I'll wait until after my presentation to Jonny and his Dad.* There are lots of changes in the works for them. She wants to work for them and not against them.

She stands and walks over to the window. Jennifer isn't out there now. The garden is very beautiful. Seeing the beautiful flowers gives her a lift.

The elevator is sounding off and she hears footsteps in the hallway. There are two pair of heavy footsteps. She looks out hoping to see Jonny and his Dad. His Dad walks into his office while Jonny walks toward her.

Jonny greets her with a smile and leans in to give her a hug but quickly backs away. "Did you get in touch with your Mom? Is she okay?"

"Yes, she was working in the yard and now she's resting. We made plans to eat dinner together tonight. We're going to have a mother-daughter talk."

"I'm glad to hear that she's okay. You two are really close. My Mom and I were really close, too. Standing here in her office still feels a bit awkward. But I'm glad you're here."

"I saw you talking to Jennifer out in the garden. And then I saw you and your Dad talking in the Deli. I hope you're doing okay, Jonny!" She leans in to give him a comforting hug but she stops. They look at each other with questioning eyes.

"Yes, Jennifer saw us walking out of the hotel together. She assumed too much. She confronted me. I convinced her to talk with me outside in the garden. I explained everything to her the best that I can. She really didn't want to hear what I had to say. I want you to be safe and not feel threatened by her."

They look at each other in a serious way. Simultaneously, they shake their heads and say, "It's complicated!"

CHAPTER TWELVE
LET'S HAVE A PICNIC

It's casual Friday. Business seems to be going well. It's time to put business aside. It's time for a little rest and relaxation.

Everyone is excited about the weekend and the perfect weather. You can feel the buzz in the air and hear the chatter about their plans to get out and about. There's lots of talk about fun outdoor activities.

Mandy's presentation to Jonny and his Dad was impressive. She's breathing a little easier and excited about the next adventure.

Gary rescheduled his appointment with his attorney for next week.

Jonny asked Mandy to go out on a date over the weekend. They're taking time to discuss their options. They can't seem to decide on where, when and what they want to do for fun.

Mandy had a meaningful mother-daughter talk over dinner. She's feels better about her feelings toward Jonny. Her Mom offered her loving advice and support.

Jonny had a long talk with his Dad about his sad feelings regarding Jennifer and his happy feelings about Mandy. His dad also offered his support with loving advice.

After a long stressful week, Gary is home relaxing in the family room. He's reminiscing about the fun time that he shared with his family in the past. Spring and summer outings are on the top of the list. He recalls how much he enjoyed fishing at the lake house. He misses the days when he took his son fishing on their boat. He remembers Angela's laughter when Jonny caught his first fish. He's feeling lonely.

He thinks about his sweet new friend Katherine. He enjoyed the time he spent with her the night they met at the restaurant. He recalls sitting in his kitchen, eating apple pie and drinking coffee with her. Their visit was very comforting. He hasn't talked and laughed with a beautiful lady since Angela passed on. He enjoys their phone conversations, too!

Maybe I can talk Katherine into going on a picnic with me at my lake house? I think it would do us a world of good to have some fun in the sun. It'll be refreshing to get away from the city for a day. He calls her on the cell phone.

"Good evening, Katherine. How are you doing this fine evening?"

"Good evening, Gary. I'm doing fine and you?"

"Pretty good. I'm glad it's the weekend. I'm calling to ask you to go out with me on a picnic tomorrow. It's supposed to be a beautiful sunny day. Sadie knows how to pack a delicious meal in a picnic basket." He chuckles.

"That sounds lovely Gary. What time will you pick me up? Where do you want to go for a picnic?"

She laughs with excitement. She's feeling lonely, too! *It's been awhile since I've gone out with a handsome gentleman.*

"What time works for you? I was thinking mid-morning. That'll give us enough time to drive my convertible to my lake house. We'll take the scenic route. By the time we arrive there, it'll be time to eat lunch. Let's say about 10 o'clock? Will that work for you?"

"Ahem! Gary, did you say "convertible" and "lake house"? Sounds exciting! Yes, I can be ready to go by 10:00am. I'll give you my address."

"Yes, that would be helpful. OH! And do you like to swim? You might want to pack a swimsuit. If there's time, we might take the boat out for a ride." He adds with a chuckle, "And one more thing—do you like to fish?"

"Whoa, Gary?! I thought you were asking me to join you for a picnic? You're offering me a full day of fun things to do. Yes, I'd like to swim, fish and ride in a boat as well as eat a picnic lunch with you tomorrow." She laughs with great joy.

"Thank you, Katherine for agreeing to go out with me. I've been feeling lonely. I enjoy your company and our conversations. I hope you'll have a fun time tomorrow."

"Thank you, Gary! I enjoy spending time with you, too! I hope that we'll both have a fun filled day."

"I'll see you tomorrow at 10:00am. Have a good night!"

"Good night, Gary!"

They're both smiling and thinking about the conversation they just had. They look forward to a day away from the city. A day of fun in the sun will surely diminish their feelings of loneliness.

She calls Mandy to share the exciting news. Mandy answers but she's not at home. There's a lot of noise in the background. Her Mom can't understand what Mandy is saying. Her Mom says that she'll try to call back later.

Mandy and Jonny decide to watch a comedy at the movie theater. They're standing in line to buy popcorn and soft drinks. It's very noisy which explains why her Mom couldn't hear her clearly on the phone.

Gary hasn't been at the lake house since the end of last summer. He finally had the emotional strength to pack up Angela's personal items. He donated some of her not-so-personal items to charity. Her personal items are packed in boxes and stored in a closet at home.

He talks to Sadie about packing a picnic lunch for tomorrow. He requests finger food and some fresh fruit. There isn't any food at the cabin. Sadie offers to pack up some food as well as other supplies. *They might need more than picnic food if they spend the day out there.* He accepts her offer.

"Thank you, Sadie, for your help. I appreciate the food and supplies for the lake house. I look forward to spending fun time out there again."

"You're welcome. Katherine is a sweet lady. I like her. Hope you have a wonderful time together."

"I'm going to drive out there tonight and pick up the place a bit. I'll need to remove the dust covers from the furniture. The dust is probably an inch thick." He laughs.

"I'm willing to give you a hand if you need it. It does my heart good to see you smiling and happy again."

"Thanks Sadie. I appreciate your support. Yes, if you don't mind. I would appreciate your help in setting up the lake house. There won't be time in the morning to clean it before I pick up Katherine. We plan to arrive there before noon. I'll take these boxes of supplies out to the car. Do you want to ride with me or would you prefer meeting me there in your car?"

"I'll take my car because I need to stop at the store. I need to pick up a few items for your picnic basket." She smiles.

Sadie has been working for the Young family for many years. She's a great friend and they treat her like family. She had a great relationship with little Jonny when he was growing up. There's still lots of love and respect between her and the family.

They arrive at the lake house just a few minutes apart. He unlocks the door and turns on the lights. Sadie follows him in and starts opening up all the windows to air out the rooms. She moves fast pulling off the dust covers from the furniture. She folds them up and collects them to be laundered.

Gary unpacks the boxes and puts away the food in the pantry and in the refrigerator. He finds supplies for both the kitchen and for the bathroom. He puts them away in their proper places. He hangs up a clean hand towel and places the liquid soap on the sink top. Sadie fills in by adding items from her female perspective.

Gary and Sadie work together gathering the dust bunnies. He sweeps the floor while she dusts the tops of tables, chairs, dressers and the mantel on the fireplace, etc.

Sadie mops the floor. Gary carries the dust covers and miscellaneous items out to pack in the trunk of his car. He's really happy that Sadie is there to support him. It's really difficult for him to be in the lake house. It's filled with so many fun memories of Angela and Jonny. The energy of her sweet loving spirit still lingers there.

Gary and Sadie close the windows and look around at a job well done. Everything is fresh and clean and ready for Katherine's outing with him tomorrow. It's time to leave the lake house.

Gary notices the pink roses in bloom in a flower bed alongside of the house. He finds the clippers and cuts a few stems. Sadie finds a vase under the sink. They arrange the roses and add water. He places the vase on the table inside the screen porch. The beautiful roses are a nice final touch!

"I think I'm ready to leave here and return home. Thank you so much Sadie for your help. It looks great and it feels good to be back here. Don't go overboard on the basket, okay, Sadie? Katherine doesn't eat a lot. I'll see you later at home."

"I'm planning to pack a traditional picnic basket with your favorites. Hopefully, she'll enjoy what I prepare for you. I'll see you later."

Gary arrives at home and unpacks the trunk. Since Sadie is out of the house, he takes the dust covers to the laundry room and starts the washing machine. It's been a long time since he's started a load of laundry. He's feeling a little extra energy that he wants to burn before bedtime.

He goes to the garage and checks out the convertible. He wants it to be clean and ready to pick up Katherine in the morning. Everything looks great. His auto service takes good care of his garage and cars. He stands for a minute imagining Katherine in the passenger seat. He pictures the breeze blowing through her beautiful hair with the top down. He recalls the beautiful scenic route to the lake.

He thinks of Jon and calls him on the cell phone. Jon answers, "Hello, Dad. How are you doing? Is everything okay?"

"Hello, Son! I'm doing great. I'm calling to let you know that I'm going to bed a bit early tonight. It's going to be a beautiful weekend. I was reminiscing about our fun time at the lake house when I began to feel lonely."

"I understand, Dad! I've been thinking a lot about the lake house, too. The weather is warming up again. There are lots of great memories there. We had lots of fun and laughter."

"You know, Katherine and I talk on the phone often. I enjoy spending time with her. Her laughter is contagious and I enjoy our conversations. I thought it would be fun to ask her out. I called to invite her out on a picnic with me. Then, I remembered the lake house and offered her a chance to go swimming, boating and fishing. She accepted my invitation. Sadie and I went out there tonight to prepare the house for visitors."

"That sounds great Dad! I'm dropping Mandy off at her apartment. We went to the movie theater on a date tonight. I'll be home soon. If you're still up, we can talk more about it. I'll see you later."

"Hope you two had a fun evening out. If I don't see you tonight, I'll see you in the morning."

He finds Sadie and says, "Thank you again for everything! Your help made me very happy. I'm going to bed early. I want to be fully rested in the morning for the fun activities with Katherine. I'll be ready to start the day at my usual time. Good night!"

"It's my pleasure. See you in the morning! Sleep well."

CHAPTER THIRTEEN
LOVE IS REVEALED

Jonny drives Mandy to her apartment from the movie theater. *It was lots of fun watching the movie but I really felt nervous about holding her hand. I want to kiss her good night but she seems nervous about being close to me. Maybe she doesn't like me the same way that I like her.*

She had a fun time with him at the theater. The movie made them laugh out loud. *I really like him a lot and I wish our date didn't have to end so early. Maybe I should invite him in. We didn't talk in the theater or while he was behind the wheel driving. Better yet, we can sit out on the patio and drink a glass of iced tea together. It's a beautiful night to sit outside and visit.*

"Would you like to come in for a short time? It's a beautiful night. We can sit outside on the backyard patio. It isn't very fancy. The apartment complex doesn't provide a big yard or a front porch. I have some sweet iced tea and soft drinks in the refrigerator."

He unbuckles his seat belt and gets out of the car. He walks around and opens her door.

"Thank you for the invitation. Sounds wonderful. It's a beautiful night to sit out under the stars. I would love to drink a glass of iced tea with you."

She unlocks the door to her apartment. He likes her apartment because it has a comfortable and peaceful atmosphere. She goes to the cupboard and sets two glasses on the countertop. She opens the freezer and places several ice cubes in each glass. While pouring the tea, she asks, "Would you like fresh lemon in your tea?" She squeezes a slice of lemon into her glass.

"No thank you. I'm not very fond of lemon or anything with a sour taste." He chuckles.

She leads the way through the patio doors. He sets his glass down on a table and sets the chairs upright. She opens a little storage closet and pulls out two comfy chair pads. They sit down at the table across from each other.

"I had a phone chat with Dad tonight while in the parking lot of the theater. He shared the news that he invited your Mom on a picnic tomorrow. Maybe that's why your Mom was trying to call you while we stood in line at the concession stand. Maybe she called to share the news with you."

"Hm?! Maybe?! It's too late to call her now. I'll try calling her in the morning. What else did your Dad have to say? Did Mom accept the invitation?"

"According to Dad, she accepted the invitation for the picnic as well as a chance to go fishing, boating and swimming."

Her jaw drops. Yes. *Way to go Mom!* "That sounds like a lot of fun. How will they do all of that in one day?"

"Dad invited her to our lake house. Would you like to drive over and see it? It's still early on a Friday night." He smiles.

She smiles, "Sure. My mom and I love the outdoors. I didn't know that you had a lake house. Do you really want to drive over there right now?"

"Yes, it'll be fun driving over there at night. It's really a beautiful house on a beautiful lake. It's usually peaceful and relaxing there at night. Dad said that Sadie helped him clean it up and stock it for their outing tomorrow."

"OK, let's go! I'm excited for Mom and anxious to see the house, too."

They put their glasses in the sink. She grabs a sweater and he gently helps her put it on. She leaves a lamp on and locks the door behind them.

He opens her car door and walks back around to the driver's side feeling happy as a lark. He drives the scenic route and arrives at the lake house in a short amount of time. She really loves the view of the lake and the house. The whole area is beautiful and serene.

She gets out of the car before he has time to open her door. She's mesmerized by the beauty surrounding her. She walks over to the lake's edge. Strolls over to the boat dock and fishing pier. Checks out the boat and walks to the end of the pier to check out the lake. *So beautiful!*

He joins her and gingerly puts his arm around her. She gets a chill and feels a bit of an electrical charge run through her. *It must be from the night air by the water.* She steps back and turns around to walk toward the house. He walks with her holding the house key in his hand.

He unlocks and opens the door. He invites her in. Her first thrill is the pink roses in a vase on the table. She knows that'll make her Mom happy. He gives her a quick tour. He's happy to be at the lake and inside the house again. He hasn't been there since he and his Dad packed up his Mom's things. *Sadie and Dad certainly did a great job cleaning up this place. I'm glad he plans to use the house for a fun time again. I know that he's been sad and lonely. It's great to see him smile again.*

"The lake and the house are so beautiful! Thank you for driving me out here. I'm even more excited for my Mom now that I see what she has to look forward to. She's going to love it! I think we should go. I don't want to disturb anything for them."

"Yes, but we can sit out on the patio and relax under the stars here for a few minutes."

"Okay, maybe for a few minutes. I'm tired and want to go to bed before midnight."

He locks up the house. He's wishing that he could do something special for his Dad. He thinks about it but nothing comes to mind. It appears that Sadie and his Dad have taken care of everything.

He points out a little two seater yard swing that he and his Mom used to share. He walks toward it and feels lost in the memory of those days. She walks over to him because she sees his sadness. She places her hand on his shoulder to comfort him. They look at each other once again with questioning eyes. They kind of melt down and settle on the swing. Side by side, lost in thought and swaying the swing ever so gently back and forth.

"The one thing that we should talk about is the one thing that we can't seem to talk about."

"What's that Jonny?"

"I've known you for a short period of time but I have feelings for you that I don't understand. I've never been in love with anyone before. From the first day I met you, I felt like it was love at first sight. I've tried hard to avoid these feelings. They don't go away. I don't know if its love, Mandy, but I know I have extraordinary feelings for you. I really respect and admire you. You're amazing. I've tried hard to keep it strictly business but I have to face the fact that I'm crazy about you. I think about you all the time. I want to be around you and hold your hand like this."

He slips his hand over the top of hers while looking into her eyes. She lets him hold her hand.

Jonny adds, "I think about the good night embrace we shared in the hallway by your suite's door. I want to hold you and hug you every time I see you. I know that it's not proper behavior in a workplace. I don't know how you feel."

She's trying to catch her breath so that she can speak. She blinks to break the hold that he seems to have on her with his eyes. She's very surprised that he shared his feelings with her. She's been trying to keep her feelings in check and on a business level.

She tries to speak but she's short on air to breathe. She clears her throat and tries again. "Ahem. Jonny? I didn't know that you felt that way. I haven't been in love before. I'm not sure what love is but I have feelings for you. I care very much about you and think about you often. I often relive the moment when you held and kissed my hand. I really liked the good night embrace. I had a dream about you being my Prince Charming." She laughs.

"I had a dream about you being my Princess." They both laugh. Their eyes lock once again.

He asks, "Is it okay if I kiss you?" He leans in toward her lips. She leans up toward his lips. They share a sweet and gentle kiss. Their hearts are beating very fast and they each gasp for air as their lips part.

Mandy says, "I think, I might be falling in love with you, too. But no need to rush into anything. It's like the seeds of love are planted in our hearts. We should take it slow and give them time to grow. If it's true love, we'll surely know it."

"I agree. I'm glad we had this talk. I've been really nervous around you because I didn't want to upset you. I never want to do or say anything that will hurt you. That thought alone makes me think that I really love you."

"I think that we can hide it while in the workplace. Don't you? It'll be difficult but we still have an important job to do in order for your Dad to retire happily."

"Yes, I agree. We'll need to hide our feelings while we're at work. I've been hiding my feelings for days."

They look at each other and smile. Then they share another sweet and gentle kiss. When their lips part, they each take a deep breath. They sway quietly on the swing lost in thought for a few minutes.

Sitting out under the stars is very pleasant. A slight cool breeze drifts in off the lake. It's quiet and peaceful. They almost fall asleep on the swing. They're feeling relaxed and very happy together. They're also feeling joy for their Mom and Dad. It's a good feeling to see them smile. They don't want them to feel lonely.

She checks her watch and asks, "Will you please take me home now?"

"Yes, I can imagine the look on their faces, if they show up in the morning and we're asleep on the swing." He laughs!

"Oh, no, very funny!" She laughs!

"You look very sleepy. I'm sleepy, too!"

They stroll back to the car hand in hand. He drives her back to her apartment. He walks her to the door with his arm around her waist. She unlocks and opens the front door. They share a good night hug and kiss. She opens her door and walks in while waving goodbye to him. She blows a kiss to him and he catches it in the air. He blows a kiss to her and he watches as she catches it in the air, too!

They both smile and he returns to his car. He drives home and finds that everything is quiet. He assumes that his Dad is sleeping. He turns off the lights and locks the door. He slowly tiptoes up the stairs. After following his nightly routine, he goes to bed. He dreams once again about the one he loves.

She picks up her apartment half-dazed. She gets ready for bed. She can't seem to get that sweet and gentle kiss out of her mind. Finally, as soon as her head rests on the pillow, she falls asleep and dreams once again about the one she loves.

CHAPTER FOURTEEN
PICNIC IN PARADISE

Morning comes early for Katherine. She wakes up to the sound of her alarm. She showers, gets dressed and packs a bag. She takes an extra change of clothes just in case she gets wet on the boat or while fishing. She packs her swimsuit. *Even if I don't swim in the lake, it'll be great to get a suntan.* She packs suntan lotion and a sun hat.

She goes to the kitchen and brews a pot of coffee. She drinks a cup of coffee with her breakfast. She has time to spare before Gary arrives. She walks out in her gardens to water the plants and check on their growth.

It's a beautiful spring day and she's really looking forward to her outing. *What a wonderful day for a picnic and other outdoor activities.*

She sits in her recliner and drinks another cup of coffee. She's nervous but also very excited!

Gary is in the kitchen while Sadie is cooking his breakfast. One of his favorite morning meals is ham, eggs, hash browns and orange juice. He's drinking his first cup of coffee.

Jonny wakes up to the aroma of breakfast cooking. He hears his Dad and Sadie talking and laughing. He gets up and dresses in a pair of sweat pants and a t-shirt. He wants to talk to his Dad before he leaves the house for the day. He hurries down the stairs to the kitchen.

"Good morning, Dad and Sadie. How are you doing today?"

Dad says, "I'm doing great, Son. How about you? Did you sleep okay last night?"

"Sure, I'm feeling very well, thank you!"

Sadie says to Jonny, "There's something different about you this morning. You look different. Hm?! I'm not sure what it is. What happened to you last night?"

Jonny replies, "Nothing happened. Everything is fine. How are you feeling this morning? It's going to be a beautiful day."

"Do you want to eat ham and eggs for your breakfast like your Dad?"

"Yes, it smells so good. I'll have what he's having, if you've prepared enough for me, too."

"Yes, I had a feeling that you might like the same meal. I already have a place set at the table for you."

"I'll pour myself a cup of coffee. Do you want a cup, Sadie?"

"Maybe later after I put the food on the table."

"What about you, Dad? Would you like another cup of coffee?"

"Sure, fill 'er up!" He chuckles.

Sadie serves the food on the plates. Everything is on the table that they need to enjoy their meal.

Sadie prepared the food for the picnic. The lunch is ready to be packed in the basket. She'll pack it for him just before he's ready to leave to pick up Katherine.

Sadie has a little surprise for him. She's a romantic at heart. She watches lots of romance movies. She likes the movies where couples have picnics sitting on a blanket under a shade tree. When she stopped at the store last night, she picked up another little basket, a bottle of champagne, two champagne glasses, gourmet cheese, crackers, fresh strawberries and chocolate sauce.

She thinks, *I loved Angela, may she rest in peace. I believe she would want Gary to be happy with a little romance in his life again.*

She pours a cup of coffee and tells them, "I'm going to drink my coffee on the terrace. I know that you two need to have a private talk. If you need me for anything, please let me know."

Gary replies by saying, "Thank you, Sadie. I'll be ready to leave soon. I'll let you know."

While they're eating their breakfast, Jonny talks with his Dad about last night. They share things in general about their relationships with their new friends.

"Do you have any special plans for today?"

"No, not yet. I hope to get out and enjoy this beautiful weather. I'm so glad that you'll spend time out at the lake house. I hope you'll make some happy memories with Katherine there. She's a very loving and caring person. I'm glad you two are good friends. I hope you really enjoy your time together. I like seeing you smile. I'm glad that you won't feel so lonely anymore."

"I hope you find something fun to do outdoors today. I don't want to be late. I need to get ready to leave. Keep in touch, okay? See you later."

"Ok, I'll keep in touch. I hope the reception for the phone signal will be strong out by the lake. Have fun, Dad!"

Gary gets up and walks to the door of the terrace. "Sadie, I need to leave now. Will you please give me a hand packing the picnic basket?"

"Sure. I have two baskets for your outing. One for lunch and one for later in the day."

She packs the food from the refrigerator in the baskets and offers to carry one out to the car for him. He gets in the white convertible with the top down and places his basket in the back seat. She sets her basket down on the floor next to his.

"What's in the second basket, Sadie?"

"It's a surprise! You two can enjoy it when the stars come out tonight." She giggles with her hand over her mouth. "Bye! I wish you both a wonderful time at the lake."

Jonny is standing at the garage door watching. He gives his Dad a slight wave and says, "Goodbye, see you later."

"I'll be going then. Thank you for everything. Hope you enjoy your day, Sadie. Please take the rest of the day off. Jonny will be out and about I'm sure. He's looking for a little fun in the sun, too. Bye!"

He waves as he drives out of the garage. *What a gorgeous day! I'm really nervous. Hopefully, I'll be okay once I arrive at Katherine's house.*

He arrives at her house right at 10:00am. He gets out and walks up the sidewalk to her front door. He admires the beautiful flowers and bushes that are in the front yard. *I hope that I'll have a chance to see her backyard.*

He rings the doorbell. She opens it and invites him in.

"Good morning, Gary."

"Good morning to you, too. Would it be a problem for me to take a look at your backyard? I had an idea the other day and I want to see if It'll work out for you."

"Not a problem at all. Let's go through the kitchen and right out the back door."

"Oh, yes, you have a nice big backyard. Your gardens are growing nicely. I'll talk to you later about my idea if that's okay?"

"Yes, later! I'm ready to go when you are. I made a thermos of sweet iced tea to take on our picnic. It's my favorite picnic drink. Do you like iced tea?"

"Iced tea sounds great. Thank you for making it. That was thoughtful. Yes, if you're ready to go, we can leave now. Is that your bag by the door? I'll carry it for you."

"Yes, I brought a few things that I might need for our outing. Thank you for carrying it for me."

They step out the front door and she locks it behind them. He carries her bag and places it on the backseat. He wedges the thermos between the two baskets.

He drives off and follows the scenic route to the lake. Just as he imagined, the scenery is awesome. *It's refreshing to breathe in fresh air and witness the beauty of nature around us.* She's a little nervous. She's still not sure what to expect. She watches him while he drives on the country road. The road is hilly and narrow like an old cow trail.

They arrive at the lake house. Her jaw drops and her eyes grow big. The lake and the house are breathtaking. She feels like she's in a dream. He goes around and opens the door for her. She gets out and just stares in disbelief that she'll spend the day with him at this lake. She feels great joy.

He picks up her bag and the heavier picnic basket. "I'll make a second trip to carry the other basket and thermos in."

"Oh, no, that's okay, I can carry those just fine, no problem."

He unlocks the door and opens it wide. He invites her in. He places the basket on the counter and her bag on a chair. She places the thermos on the counter by the refrigerator along with the second basket.

Directing her attention to the roses on the table, he says, "I picked those for you last night. Thank you for agreeing to spend the day with me.

I hope that we both have lots of fun in the sun today."

He smiles and sees that she's smiling back with a tear in her eye. She feels very touched by his thoughtfulness. She walks over and picks up the vase leaning in to smell the roses.

He says, "You look so beautiful standing there with those pink roses. Is it okay if I take your picture?" He pulls out his cell phone. She nods and smiles. He smiles and says, "Thank you!"

"Thank you for the compliment. I want to take a few photos, too. I have a feeling our picnic will be special. I want to capture that moment in time as a memento."

"Maybe later we'll have time for taking more photos. Let's take care of the food and enjoy our picnic lunch. I'm hungry. Are you?"

"Yes, I'm ready for lunch. What's in the little basket? Is there food in there that needs to be stored in the refrigerator?"

"I really don't know what's in the basket. Sadie placed it in the car at the last minute and told me it's a surprise for us to enjoy later. It must be something special because she was giggling about it. Let's open it together and look inside."

They open the basket and look at the goodies inside. They're laughing as they enjoy removing the items. They set the champagne on the counter along with the two glasses.

Gary says, "The cheese, strawberries and chocolate sauce need to be chilled in the refrigerator until later. I have an ice bucket and ice for the champagne. I don't drink anything with alcohol. Sadie was very thoughtful to give us this gift."

"Yes, very thoughtful! It's a very romantic gift. I take it then that she approves of our friendship and our outing today?"

"Of course, she likes you. She thinks it's great to see me smile again because of our friendship."

"Are we going to eat our lunch inside or outdoors?"

"We have several options. We can either eat here in the kitchen area or at the table in the screen porch. OR there is a gazebo with a table in the garden alongside the house. OR" he laughs "we can sit at a table down by the lake. I bet Sadie packed a tablecloth. We haven't opened that basket yet. She probably packed everything that we'll need for our picnic including salt and pepper."

Katherine asks, "Where would you like to eat our picnic lunch?"

"If you don't want to choose one of those places, I'll choose the gazebo."

"That was going to be my first choice with the weather and scenery being so perfect. Thank you so much for inviting me here to spend the day with you. I'm already having a great time and we haven't started our picnic yet."

They smile with very loving eyes. They truly enjoy each other's company very much! He picks up the basket and she grabs the thermos of tea. He escorts her out to the gazebo. He sets the basket down on a bench and opens the lid.

She picks up the tablecloth that is right on top and spreads it out on the table. *Perfect!* He sets the table with the napkins, plates, silverware and glasses. She pours the tea into the glasses.

He sets out plastic containers filled with a variety of his favorite foods. Sadie packed a variety of sandwiches cut in triangles with the crust trimmed off. There's egg salad, turkey, chicken salad, ham and Swiss cheese.

In one of the containers there's potato salad. In another there's a vegetable platter with carrot sticks, celery, and sliced cucumber. The last container holds two pieces of apple pie. Last but not least, Sadie packed the salt and pepper shakers.

They look at each other with delight. Their eyes are sparkling with happiness.

He says, "Sadie packed all of my favorite picnic foods. I hope that you'll like them, too."

"What's not to like? She was generous to prepare a variety of food to choose from. I already know that I like her apple pie. That's a great dessert."

"Okay, let's sit down and please relax. I'm ready to enjoy this wonderful feast. How about you?"

"Yes! Thank you." She fills her plate and waits for him to fill his. They enjoy their time together talking about things in general. The weather is perfect as well as the view of the lake. The gazebo in the garden is the perfect spot for their picnic.

CHAPTER FIFTEEN
A FAMILIES GET-TOGETHER

Gary and Katherine clear the table in the gazebo. They place the leftover food and items in the basket. They carry the basket and thermos to the kitchen. They store the leftover food and tea in the refrigerator.

He washes the plates, silverware and glasses. He leaves them to air dry on the countertop on a dish mat. He'll pack them in the basket when it's time to return home.

She picks up her bag from the chair and heads toward the bathroom. She tells him that she wants to wash her hands and freshen up. When she looks in the mirror, she notices that her face is really red. She applies more sunscreen. She didn't think that she would need a sun hat while sitting in the gazebo. *I'll wear my sun hat when we're out on the lake fishing in the boat.*

He's waiting in a chair on the screen porch. He's sitting back resting with his hands clasped behind his head. He stands up when he sees her walk toward him.

She walks up and stands looking into his eyes. She says, "Thank you again for a delicious meal and showing me a wonderful time here."

"Thank you, too. It was my pleasure. The day isn't over yet unless you want it to be?"

"I've had a great time. What else do you want to do?"

"I think we should relax before we take on any outdoor activities. Would you like to take a boat ride?"

"Sure, that sounds like fun."

"Great. Let's just sit here and talk until the time feels right. I want to share my ideas about your yard with you. Is that okay?"

They turn two chairs around to see the view of the lake while they talk. They watch a flock of geese fly by.

"The other day you told me on the phone that you were working out in the yard and in your gardens. I know that's really hard work for you. Trying to keep up with the yard work is a big responsibility. Gardens can be double trouble."

"Yes, it's very hard work. I just have to work on it a little bit each day. I love gardening. The time I spend working in my gardens is more like playing. It's very rewarding to watch my flowers and vegetables grow. Eating the fresh food from the garden is a real treat. Before Paul passed, he did a lot of the hard work. I always felt free to "play" in the gardens."

"Angela loved working in both of her flower gardens. After Angela passed, I hired a gardener to maintain her garden at home as well as her garden where we met. She really loved growing pink sweetheart roses. Our gardener's family has a lawn care service. I can give you their contact information."

"Thank you. I'd appreciate having the extra time to do other things. I thought about a lawn service but I'm not sure who I can trust."

"I noticed that you have a good-sized backyard. Angela loved the greenhouse that I built for her. I'm thinking that might work well for you. It would be less back breaking if you set your flowers and plants in planter boxes on tables. If you're interested, we can work on that project together.

My gardener would be willing to volunteer his time to help me build the greenhouse. That's his passion. I could hire his family to help us if necessary. You can supervise the whole project to be sure that it's the way you like it."

She stands up cheerfully saying, "That sounds like a dream come true. Thank you!" She gives him a "thank you" hug.

They feel comfort and healing with the gentle embrace. They let out a soft quiet sigh as they feel the release of tension between them. A huge burden of heartache is lifting from within.

They sit down in the chairs while holding hands. They talk about their kids. Then, like a light bulb turning on, they turn and look at each other.

Katherine comments, "You know, it might add to our fun in the sun by inviting the kids out here. The four of us might have a good time fishing on the boat. Mandy used to go fishing with her Dad. When I was a little girl, I used to go fishing with my Dad."

"I was thinking the same thing. I didn't want to spoil a chance for us to have fun together. It was emotionally difficult for me to leave Jon behind. He's struggling with his decision about what and where he might go for fun in the sun today. There are so many memorable moments for him here at the lake house. Thank you for suggesting that we include the kids in our outing. He leaned in with a smile and gave her a little kiss on her cheek."

"I assumed your Jonny and my Mandy would figure out something else to do today. I think this would be fun for them. I know it'll be fun for me to watch the kids enjoying the outdoors. I'd like to hear them share a few laughs. They're going through a lot of changes in their lives."

"We can plan an outing for the two of us on a different day. I'll call Jon and see what he's up to. Do you want to call Mandy?"

"Yes. I'll call her from the living area so that we can hear without talking over each other."

He calls Jon and invites him to join them at the lake house. She calls Mandy and invites her to join them at the lake house, too. Just as expected, Jonny and Mandy are together. They're sitting out on the back patio at her apartment complex. They had plans to swim in the pool there. They changed into their swimming attire and walked over to the pool. It was way too crowded.

Jonny and Mandy are sitting in chairs at the table. They both jump up in excitement.

Mandy tells her Mom, "I'll talk to Jonny and I'll call you back."

Jonny tells his Dad, "I'll check with Mandy and then I'll call you back."

They're smiling and excited like school children out on a holiday vacation.

"I'm so glad that you drove us to the lake house last night. I'm thrilled to go there again for a little fun in the sun. What about you, Jonny? Would you like to spend some time with your Dad and my Mom?"

"Yes, the lake house is a fun place. We can go swimming on the beach, fishing on the boat and maybe we can have a picnic. Are you sure you want to go there?"

"Yes, it's a beautiful day! We can sit in the swing again. Are you okay? I know you love and miss your Mom. Will it be a problem for you to spend the day out there?"

"No, I'm sure my Mom would want Dad to move on with someone as great as your Mom. I really miss her very much. It's hard to face the family-time memories when I'm there. I'll be okay."

She gives him a comforting hug. He kisses her sweetly on the forehead and holds her lovingly.

"We better hurry. Are you ready to go? We're losing daylight. Do you have a fishing license? I'm going to stop at the bait shop and buy one on the way."

"No, I don't have a current fishing license. The last time I went fishing was with my Dad."

"Do you have sunscreen and a sun hat? I don't want your beautiful face to be sunburned. If you don't have what you need, I'll pick it up for you at the store on the way."

"Okay, I'll go pack a bag with a change of clothes and a sun dress to wear on top of my swimsuit. It'll just take a minute or two."

After a minute passes, they quickly walk out the front door to Jonny's car. While he's driving, Mandy calls her Mom back.

She tells her, "We're on the way to the lake house." She also adds, "We're stopping at the bait shop for fishing licenses and bait."

Her Mom says, "That's great. I'll tell Gary about your plans. We'll need to purchase fishing licenses for ourselves as well."

As soon as they end the call, Katherine walks over to share the news with Gary.

"Mandy called and said that they're on their way. They plan to stop for bait and fishing licenses. We'll each need a license as well. How do you want to handle this little problem?"

"OH, yes, the bait shop is close by. We can take the car and purchase them really quick. We can return here before the kids arrive. Are you ready to go?"

"Yes, of course, let's go!" They both laugh with delight. "Do you have fishing poles for Mandy and I to use? Are there enough life preservers for us to wear on the boat?"

Gary laughs at her enthusiasm. "Yes, I have extra fishing equipment in my storage shed. I believe that we have enough fishing poles and tackle for all of us. We'll look in the shed after we return from the bait shop. I think our life jackets are still in good shape. I'll check them out later, too."

They arrive at the bait shop. Purchasing the fishing license is quick and easy.

Gary takes a few minutes to look at the new fishing equipment. *I haven't used my old fishing equipment for a couple of years. I want to buy new fishing gear for this summer season. It's great to enjoy fun time at the lake house again.*

Katherine admires a woman's fishing hat. She buys it and places it on top of her head. It has a drawstring that'll prevent it from flying off while riding in the boat.

They leave the store and hurry back to the lake house.

"Jonny stops at the bait shop and buys a fishing license for Mandy and one for himself. They walk through the store to shop for other things that they might need. She's wearing a sun hat. He asks her if she would like a new fishing hat. Her eyes light up! She chooses one that's similar to the hat her Mom bought there. He pays for her hat and bait for fishing on the boat.

Jonny and Mandy actually arrive at the lake house a short time after their parents. He parks his car in the driveway next to his Dad's car. Great timing!

Everyone is excited and greet each other with smiles. Mandy walks over to greet her Mom with a hug. Jonny and Gary focus their attention on the beautiful ladies.

"Hey, Dad, do we have anything to eat in the house? I told Mandy that we can have a picnic."

"Yes, Jon, please help yourself to whatever is there. Sadie packed a great lunch for our picnic. There are plenty of delicious leftovers that you two can eat. I'll help you sort it out."

Mandy and her Mom stroll arm in arm to look at the lake. Watching the ripples in the water is relaxing. They're both very excited about being there. There's a level of comfort that's felt by the four them acting like a whole family.

Mandy and her Mom walk into the kitchen. They see that Jonny found the paper plates and picnic supplies. He was planning to surprise Mandy by bringing the picnic basket outside. He doesn't want her to do any of the work. He wants her to relax and enjoy her time there. *I'm having a difficult time trying to hide my love for her. I think Dad knows. He smiles at us like he knows our secret. I wonder if Mandy has shared her feelings for me with her Mom.*

"Would you like to have a picnic outside or do you prefer eating indoors? What would you like to drink? Your Mom brought tea and we have soft drinks in the refrigerator."

"I would enjoy eating down by the lake. I saw a table with benches close to the water. Tea would be great. Is there anything that I can do?"

"I've got everything we need packed in the basket. I can carry it down there. You can help me set the table to save some time."

"Ok!" She smiles. *It's really difficult to keep my love for him hidden away from his Dad. I talked to Mom about the way I feel about him. I wonder if he shared his feelings for me with his Dad.*

They walk down to the table at the edge of the lake. Jonny packed a red checkered tablecloth that he found in a drawer in the kitchen. He covers the table with it first. Mandy pours tea in the glasses.

"They start unpacking the containers of food from the basket. They sit down and fill their plates. They enjoy their picnic while surrounded by the beauty of nature. It's a perfect picnic except for the fact that they're unable to relax. They're unsure about revealing their secret to their parents.

Gary and Katherine are on the dock uncovering the boat. They prepare it to ride out on the lake where the two families will go fishing together.

CHAPTER SIXTEEN
FAMILY FUN TIME

Mandy and Jonny ate their picnic lunch by the lake. They clear the table and pack everything back into the basket. In the kitchen they unpack and take care of all the items in the basket. They're alone in the house. They share a gentle hug and a sweet kiss.

"I'm really nervous around our parents now. Do you think that we should reveal our secret to them? I want to feel more relaxed and enjoy the fun time with them."

"Yes, I've been thinking the same thing. I think my Dad knows already. I feel nervous about how your Mom will react to the news. I really didn't expect to feel so uptight about spending time out here. I want us to relax and join in the fun time, too."

"Why don't we go sit on the swing and talk for a few minutes? I had a pleasant time swaying on the swing with you last night."

"I enjoyed our visit out here last night. Your Mom and my Dad are prepping the boat for us to take it out. When they're finished, we'll need to check out the storage shed for the fishing gear. Your new fishing hat looks really cute on you."

He gently takes her into his arms and gives her a little squeeze with a big smile. She smiles back and giggles while trying to keep her feelings under control.

"Speaking of hats, I wonder if my fishing hat is still around here somewhere? Let's go look in my bedroom closet. That's the last place I saw it on a hook."

"Aw! Jonny, this room is so cute. It's fun seeing things from your childhood."

"Ah, good I found it. How does it look?"

"Looks great! Maybe you can add a hook and lure to my hat so that we can match." They both laugh and feel like kids at heart.

"It'll be fun to help you decorate your hat but the fishing tackle is in a box in the storage shed. Let's go out and take a look at what's out there."

"Okay!"

"It's locked and I'm not sure where the key is. Let's go ask Dad if he has it."

They walk out to the boat dock and are distracted by the appearance of the boat. The four life jackets are placed on the benches two by two. There's a cooler for cold drinks. A little basket with plastic cups. A couple of fishing tackle boxes are stowed on board with a couple of fishing poles. Gary and Katherine went to the shed to find their fishing gear.

His Dad laughs and says, "Aw, Jonny, where did you find your fishing hat?" He wipes away teardrops from his eyes. *Sweet and precious memories.*

"I found my hat in my bedroom closet? Still hanging on a hook. Where's your old fishing hat, Dad?"

"I don't remember for sure. Will you check in my bedroom closet? You might find it there."

"Okay, I'll be right back. Can I have the key to the storage shed? Mandy and I want to find what we need to go fishing on the lake, too."

"Oh, yea!" He hands his son the key with a smile.

Jonny takes the key and heads toward the house. He goes into his Dad's bedroom and checks in the closet. There on a hook, he sees his Dad's old fishing hat. It's also decorated with a fishing hook and a lure. He laughs but he also wipes away tears from his eyes. He recalls his Mom and Dad sharing love and laughter in this lake house. It seems like a lifetime ago. He takes the hat out to his Dad beside the boat.

"Aha, thank you Jonny. I'll wear it today. It's been a long time. Why don't you help Mandy find a pole and tackle in the shed?"

He looks around for her and then asks, "Where is she?"

He starts walking around the area looking for her. He spies her sitting in the swing with her feet firmly planted and her head hanging low.

"He walks over to her and asks, "What's wrong? Are you feeling okay? You look so sad."

"I think we should tell our parents. I really dread spending time on the boat while trying to keep my feelings so bottled up inside."

Jonny sat down beside her and wanted to put his arm around her. He resisted the temptation. "I know what you mean. If we tell them, then we can relax and really enjoy ourselves with them. Boating and fishing is a fun family experience. It's a chance to be close and share laughter. I want to tell them. We should tell them together before we get in the boat and go out on the lake."

"How are we going to do it? How can we tell them in a way that is comfortable for all of us?"

"Let's think about it while we go to the shed together and choose our fishing gear."

They look over at the boat dock. Their parents are not there. They look around for them on the way to the shed. They can see them inside the lake house trying to cool off and rest a bit.

"He unlocks the storage shed door. Everything is organized with the fishing poles hanging up on hooks on one of the walls. Tackle boxes are placed neatly on shelves. He picks up his old tackle box. He opens it and searches for a lure to decorate Mandy's hat. She's watching his every move. He remembers a girlie lure that his Mom had just for fun. It has a sparkly rhinestone and something pink dangling off of it. He finds it in his Mom's old tackle box. He gives it to Mandy with a smile and a tear in his eye.

"This belonged to my Mom. I can help you pin it to your fishing hat. I also found a fake hook that'll look cute on it, too."

She also wipes away a tear but smiles at him. She says, "You're always so thoughtful. I know that your Mom's lure and the memory of her means a lot to you. Thank you! This is fun!" She kisses him on the cheek. She gives her fishing hat to him.

He decorates her hat with the lure and hook. He places it on top of her head. "Yes, the lure and memories of my Mom mean a lot to me. YOU mean a lot to me, too. It's time to make new happy memories here." He leans in and gives her a kiss on the lips.

They hear voices behind them. Turning around, they see their parents standing there and smiling.

"We were wondering where you two were hiding?" They laugh.

"We're not hiding, Dad!"

"Did you find the gear that you need to take out on the lake? Oh, I see Mandy's hat is decorated with your Mom's pink lure. Very sweet idea! I believe she's smiling down us right now. What about the poles and tackle?"

"I have my old tackle box that Mandy and I can share. Which pole do you think would be best for her?"

"Let's take your pole off the wall. We have several spare rods and reels that she can choose from." He looks at Mandy and asks her, "Which pole looks right for you?"

"I really don't know. It's been a long time since I've held a fishing pole in my hands. Will you please choose one for me?"

Jonny reaches over to the wall. He removes his fishing pole and one for Mandy. He hands a fishing pole to Mandy and asks her, "How does that feel in your hands? Does it feel too big and heavy? If it's okay, let's get out of this shed. It's getting too warm in here?"

"I think you made a good choice, thank you! It feels light enough for me to handle out on the boat."

Jonny carries two fishing poles and his tackle box out of the shed. They load them into the boat. The four of them are gathered beside the boat that's packed and ready to go.

Mandy says, "Mom?" and Jonny says, "Dad?"

They look and listen to their children intently.

"Can we go sit at the gazebo where it's cool? We want to have a little chat with you two?"

His Dad says, "Yes." Her Mom nods in agreement.

Gary and Katherine stroll over to the gazebo with their hearts pounding unsure about what's going to happen. They sit down at the table. Mandy and Jonny sit on one side while Katherine and Gary sit across from them.

"Is everything okay, Son?"

"Yes, well I hope so. Mandy and I are happy to be here with you for a fun day but we can't relax. In order for us to relax and really enjoy our time together, we need to reveal a secret to both of you."

Her Mom, looks at her daughter. "A secret?"

"Yes, Mom. We've been keeping a secret about our feelings toward each other. We felt an immediate attraction toward each other on the day of the interview at the Agency. We've tried to keep our feelings in check at the office. We didn't want to cause any problems that would interfere with business."

The four of them look around trying to read facial expressions. They're smiling and their eyes are wide with wonder.

Jonny explains, "We finally admitted our feelings to each other last night out there on the swing. We've been trying to hide our feelings of love for each other. Last night, we shared our feelings but want to hide them at the office."

"You know, Jon, I already suspected that you two might be falling in love. I've seen the way you smile and look at each other. I'm okay with that. The look. is the same as when I met your Mom." He laughs and smiles so big that his face lights up.

Katherine says, "I don't get to see you two together very often. I've seen the change in my daughter. She's smiling and happier than she's been for a long time. It crossed my mind that she might be falling in love. My only hope is that you don't rush it. Take your time to really know each other. Love is a beautiful thing. Give it time to grow to increase chances of your love lasting ever after."

Jonny adds, "We want our love to grow freely and really get to know each other. We're hoping that it'll be okay to show affection around the two of you. We like holding hands and sharing an embrace but don't want to upset you. We want to laugh and talk on the boat without worry."

Gary says, "I think that you two are mature enough to make the right decisions. Just relax and be yourself is my vote."

Katherine says, "Yes, that's my vote, too!"

"This is a little awkward but as long as we're clearing the air, I really like being with your Mom, Mandy! I like holding her hand and sharing an embrace with her, too!"

"I know that she likes you and I'm definitely okay with that! I'm very happy for the two of you to find a close caring friendship."

Jon says, "I'm okay with you and Katherine being friends, too! I'm very happy for you two."

They look around at each other again and everyone is looking more relaxed. They stand up and hugs with best wishes are heard and received by all four of them. They truly feel like one big happy family.

Gary cheerfully says, "Are we ready to take the boat out and have some fun on the lake?"

Jonny asks, "Do we have everything we need packed in the boat? If so, I'm ready to go. What about you Mandy?"

"I'm definitely ready. Let's go!"

Katherine says, "As far as I know, everything is in the boat ready and waiting for us."

Gary says, "Katherine's right!" He takes Katherine's hand and walks down to the boat dock.

Jonny and Mandy follow behind while holding hands. They glance up at each other feeling relieved and relaxed ready to enjoy family fun time in the sun.

CHAPTER SEVENTEEN
FUN IN THE SUN

The four of them look great in their fishing hats and life jackets. Gary unties the ropes from the dock and starts up the motor on the boat. He successfully pulls away from the dock and drives toward the middle of the lake. There's a slight breeze and the spray of water feels refreshing. He stops at his favorite fishing spot and drops the anchor. His favorite fishing spot is off to the right hand side of the lake.

Jonny is so excited! He baits his hook and then Mandy's. Gary baits Katherine's hook as well as the hook on his pole. Jonny lets Mandy cast her line out first on their side of the boat. He carefully casts out his line so it doesn't tangle with hers.

"How does everyone feel about eating fresh fish cooked on the grill for supper tonight?" He's serious but laughs anyway. Katherine says, "That really sounds great. I haven't eaten fresh fish for a really long time. What would you like to eat with the grilled fish?"

"Just about anything that tastes good cooked on a grill. We can wrap up potatoes in foil as well as corn on the cob. Wedges of zucchini sprayed with butter and sprinkled with seasoning is a real treat cooked on the grill, too. What would you like to eat with fish?"

"Dad, that all sounds perfectly delicious. What about you Mandy?"

She laughs, "Well, I think we better catch a fish before we plan on grilling it." They all laugh!

Katherine says, "That's true but I think the food you suggested will be just fine with grilled fish."

Mandy innocently asks, "What about the strawberries and chocolate sauce that I saw in the refrigerator? Is it okay to eat that with supper tonight, too?"

Katherine and Gary look at each other and burst out laughing. Her Mom says, "Yes, Mandy, we can eat the strawberries and chocolate for dessert. Sadie packed those as a surprise gift for fun. It's perfectly alright to share them with you, too."

Mandy blushes and says, "Oh, sorry, I didn't know. They sure look delicious."

Her Mom says, "It's fine! No need to say sorry about anything!"

By this time Gary and Katherine have cast out their lines on their side of the boat. Mandy stifles a squeal of excitement as she feels a nibble on her line. She starts reeling it in. Jonny gets the net and scoops up the fish into the boat. It's a catfish and the perfect size.

Jonny says, "Woohoo! That one is big enough to keep for our supper tonight! Good Job, Mandy!" In their excitement they share a quick hug!

He pulls his cell phone out of his pocket and takes her picture with the fish for a memento. He laughs and says, "How about a selfie? Let's make funny fish lips faces!" They all laugh at the fun time while celebrating Mandy's success.

"Way to Go, Mandy! That's my girl!" Katherine pulls her phone out of her pocket and asks, Please, may I take a picture of you two smiling with your fish lips? So funny! It's so good to see you two having a good time.

"Do you have your phone, Mandy?"

"No, I left it back at the house."

They're laughing hard but they smile for her camera. She takes this funny photo for her memento.

Jonny helps take the hook out of the fish's mouth. He puts it in the cooler to keep it fresh until they go to the cleaning station. It's located close to the lake and near the bait shop.

They continue to fish for another hour. Each one is lucky enough to catch several fish. They're happy that they're big enough to keep. Everyone is excited by their successful catch. Jonny hasn't caught a fish in the lake since last summer. Lots of smiles and laughter is shared by the four of them. They all have a really good time together.

The thermos of cold tea is empty. Everyone is thirsty and hungry. They all agree that it's time to take the boat back to the dock. Gary pulls up the anchor after everyone stows their gear safely away under the benches. He starts the motor and they enjoy their ride back to the lake house. Jonny helps his Dad tie the boat to the dock with the big heavy ropes.

Gary helps Katherine out of the boat by giving her his hand. Jonny helps Mandy out in the same manner. They all unload the fishing gear and stow it back in the storage shed.

Gary mentions that the ladies can freshen up and change their clothes while he and Jonny take the fish down to the cleaning station. They need to prepare the fish to be grilled.

They walk back to the house with the clean and fileted fish in the cooler. They chat along the way. They're happy and having a wonderful day.

Gary carries the fish to an outdoor table by the grill. He places them on a platter. He sprinkles them with seasoning and wraps them in foil. He finds the grill that was stored away in the shed. He cleans it and builds a fire with charcoal. The smell of the smoke sets his heart racing as he recalls the memories from the past. *It's time to make new memories.*

He sees Jonny standing down by the beach and looking up at a tree where a long thick rope is tied on a branch. The tree has grown a lot in two years. He reaches out to it and discovers the rope is frayed and falling apart. He turns and walks to the house. *Maybe later! It would be fun to swing over and splash into the lake again!*

Gary walks into the house while the charcoal heats to the right temperature. He calls out to Katherine and Mandy! They answer from the kitchen. They plan ahead by prepping the food for the grill.

Katherine says, "I hope you don't mind if Mandy and I work here in the kitchen. We kind of made ourselves at home. We found a few of the items we need but haven't found everything. We found the food that you mentioned."

Gary says, "I really don't mind it at all. I'm happy that you're making yourselves feel at home. Thank you for helping to cook supper. I started a fire in the grill and it should be ready to cook the fish and the side dishes soon. I'll help you find the things you need."

"I found the foil and the olive oil as well as a few spices."

"Great! I'll need those for the fish, too, as well as lemon juice and butter."

Jonny walks in and calls out to Mandy. She's excited to see him. He wants to clean up and change his clothes before they get too close. He freshens up in the hall bathroom and walks back to his bedroom. He returns to the kitchen feeing fresh and clean. He gives Mandy a big smile and a gentle squeeze around her waist.

Gary's bedroom has an attached bath. He cleans up and changes his clothes. Now, they're all clean and ready to work in the kitchen together.

The kitchen isn't really big enough for the four of them. Jonny wants to show Mandy the beach and the rope swing. He just wants to have some alone time with her. He asks his Dad and her Mom and they both agree it's a good idea for them to go out. They can enjoy the outdoors while their parents prepare supper. The kids offer to set the table when the time comes.

Gary goes outside and places the foil wrapped fish on the grill. Katherine brings out a platter with the foil wrapped potatoes and corn on the cob. She sets it down on the table for Gary to cook it according to his expertise. She returns to the kitchen for the zucchini.

She asks him, "Would you like to have a glass of iced tea? It's pretty warm out here, especially by the grill."

"That sounds really great, thank you." Do you want to sit outside and watch the kids have fun while the food is cooking on the grill? I want to stay close by to make sure it doesn't burn."

"Yes, I'll bring out a glass of tea for me, too. We can sit under a shade tree in these lounge chairs. Everything sure smells good. Thank you so much for everything. I've really had a wonderful day! I can't stop smiling."

She returns with the glasses of tea. The kids are standing by the grill oohing and aahing at how great the food smells. They're hungry and thirsty.

Mandy says, "Jonny, would you like a glass of iced tea? I'm going to get one for myself and I can bring one out for you, too."

Yes, iced tea would be perfect right now but I'll come in with you. I think Dad wants us to set the table."

He turns and gets his Dad's attention. "Where do you want to eat supper tonight? How about the screen porch? We can still enjoy the outdoors in there without being exposed to the sun and the bugs."

"Perfect idea!" Mandy and Katherine nod their heads in agreement.

Mandy pours the tea in two glasses. Jonny finds the checkered table cloth. They fill a basket with everything they need to set the table on the screen porch. They take their tea outside to wait for the food.

The sun is starting to set and the sky is filled with beautiful colors. The temperature is starting to cool down slightly.

"Well, I guess we won't have enough time to go swimming today. The water will be too cold this late in the evening. It's been a wonderful day. Thank you, Dad, Katherine and my Mandy! Hope we can get-together and have another fun day at the lake house soon."

Gary says, "The weather is supposed to be warm tomorrow. Maybe you two can swim out here. I've really enjoyed my time here and would love to drive out again. What about you Katherine? Would you like to swim in the lake and eat another picnic?"

"Oh, Gary, I don't know! I'll think about it and let you know."

"What about you Mandy? Would you like to come out here tomorrow so that we can have a chance to swim and play on the beach? We can plan to eat another picnic, too."

"Maybe in the afternoon when it's cooler. I look and feel like I've had too much sun today. It has been a wonderful day though. I hate to see it end. I'll think about it and let you know later, okay?"

Gary checks the food carefully peeking into the foil and testing it with a fork. Everything looks and smells done. He tells everyone that the food is ready to eat. He removes it from the grill and places it on a platter. He takes it into the kitchen and removes the foil. He places the food on serving platters. Everyone pitches in to help carry the dishes. They place them in the center of the table. Jonny finds serving spoons in a drawer and places them on the table.

Everyone is hungry and grateful to sit down to eat this feast. The four of them feel happy and like a family again. They enjoy their meal. Jonny and Mandy clear the table and place the dirty dishes in the sink. Mandy finds the containers with the strawberries and chocolate sauce in the refrigerator. She sets them on the table with serving spoons. Jonny has located four small bowls and four forks. Sadie cleaned the strawberries and quartered them.

They enjoy the strawberries with chocolate. It's the perfect dessert. The four of them sit at the table for a chat about this and that.

Although, they're feeling tired, they clean the kitchen together. Katherine washes the dishes and Gary dries them. Jonny puts the dishes away in the cabinet. Mandy returns the silverware to the drawer.

They go outside for fresh air and take in the beauty of the lake once more. Gary takes care of the grill and makes sure the fire is out. He carries the tongs and fork to the kitchen. *I'll take care of that later.*

The ladies gather up their personal belongings. Gary offers to take Katherine home when she's ready. Jonny offers the same to Mandy. It's late and they're ready to return home.

They enjoyed sitting on the screen porch while watching the beautiful sunset. They had fun in the sun! The sunset is a perfect ending to a perfect day.

CHAPTER EIGHTEEN
RAINY SUNDAY AT THE LAKE

Gary drives Katherine home from their outing at the lake house. They have a brief chat in the car before he walks her to the door. They share a hug and a good night kiss.

When he arrives home late, he discovers that his son is asleep. He sits in the living room thinking things over. Although he's feeling tired, he's not sleepy yet. He can't seem to unwind and relax.

There are lots of decisions that I need to make regarding family, business, retirement and a dream vacation. I'll go back to the lake house and sleep there for the night. It'll be a great escape and a good place to deal with the stress I'm feeling right now.

He walks to the kitchen and writes a note to Sadie:

'Sadie, I'm going to sleep at the lake house tonight. I have decisions to make that are weighing heavy on my mind right now. There are a few chores I can work on at the house tomorrow. I don't know what Jonny's plans are for the day. The coffee pot is set on auto-brew for in the morning. Enjoy your Sunday! I'll see you later!'

He packs a bag and drives over to the lake house. While listening to a radio forecast, he hears that there's a chance of rain showers on

Sunday. *I guess we won't have another family get-together today.*

He arrives at the lake house and breathes a sigh of relief. The beauty of nature that surrounds him is very comforting. He sits in a lounge chair out by the lake breathing in the fresh air. Twinkling stars fill the sky overhead. He misses Angela and tears begin to fill his eyes.

He stands up and carries his bag in the house. He's missing her too much to sleep in the bedroom. He opens up the fold-out couch by the fireplace in the den and sleeps there.

Morning comes with sunlight shining through the window at the lake house. Gary wakes up to hear the pitter-patter of rain on the roof. He stays in bed to rest a little longer.

Katherine wakes up in her bed feeling sore from the outdoor activities. She's still sleepy. She rolls over and falls asleep.

Sadie is up and in the kitchen ready for her usual routine. She finds the note from Gary. She reads it and turns on the coffee pot. She looks around to see if there's a note from Jonny.

She pours a cup of coffee for herself and steps out on the terrace. The sound of the gentle spring rain is comforting like music. She watches the rain fall gently on the flower garden. The sweet smell of rain is very refreshing.

She hears noise in the kitchen. When she goes in to check, she sees Jonny pouring a cup of coffee. She asks, "Are you ready for breakfast, Jonny?"

She hands him the note that his Dad left for her and he reads it. "Yes, I'll just have a bowl of cereal and orange juice today. I can do that for myself. Please sit with me Sadie."

"That's okay, Jonny, I like caring for you. I'll be happy to sit with you and drink my coffee. It's raining outside and feels a little chilly even with the sun shining."

"Thanks for sharing this note about Dad, Sadie. I hope he's going to be okay. He sounds troubled. I wonder, maybe I should go out there and give him a hand. We had a great time at the lake house yesterday. I'll tell you more about it when we have more time."

"I would love to hear about your day at the lake house. I hope everyone had a good time."

He eats his breakfast and tells Sadie that he's going to drive out to see how his Dad is doing. He wants to give him a hand with the chores.

He drives out to the lake house and finds his Dad up and eating breakfast and drinking coffee. His Dad is surprised to see him but also very happy to spend time with his son. They're both smiling but showing signs of stress and concern. His Dad pours him a cup of coffee and they sit on the screen porch looking out over the lake.

They watch the drops of rain as they ripple in the water over the lake. The sun adds a sparkle to each drop as it falls. When the rain stops, they see a big beautiful rainbow in the sky. Its beautiful prismatic colors are shining down across the lake.

They marvel at the beauty and express their joy at experiencing this moment together. They recall the many times similar moments were shared with Jonny's Mom. They both really miss her and are struggling with moving on.

Now that the rain has stopped, they sit and talk about the chores that need to be done there. Jonny shares, "I'd like to replace the rope swing. The tree has grown a lot. The rope is frayed and falling apart. I'll have to climb up the tree with a new rope."

His dad tells him, "I need to clean up the grill from our cookout last night and store it in the shed. I plan to take inventory of the shed. We can go shopping at the big Sporting Goods Store. It'll be great to have new fishing gear and other items around here during this summer season."

His Dad adds, "It'll be fun to have another outing on Memorial Day Weekend. Hopefully the weather will be warm for swimming and playing in the lake. I want to invite Katherine and you can invite Mandy."

"Another great idea, Dad. I really enjoyed the day with them here yesterday. That weekend will be a great one for us to relax out here again."

"I'm ready to work outside. I'm going to take it slow and easy. There's no hurry, Jon. We've got the whole day free to enjoy our time here."

Then he adds, "I can't stop thinking about your well-being, things at work, our meeting with the attorney, retirement and a vacation. Angela and Katherine are also on my mind. Maybe we can sit down later and we can talk freely about things. A lot of my decisions concern you and will affect your life."

"I really understand, Dad! You're feeling stressed about the future changes in our lives. I'm here for you when you're ready to share your thoughts and feelings. I'll do whatever I can to help us get through this stage of our lives. I know it won't be easy."

He continues, "I think I saw some thick rope out in the shed that I can use to replace the rope swing. I might need your help tying the knots in it."

"If you want my help, we can do that together first. I can take care of the grill later."

Jonny changes into older clothes that are suited for climbing the tree. Gary finds the rope and they determine the length that he needs for the new swing. The rope appears to be just the right size.

They go out to the tree by the lake. They work together tying strategically placed knots in the rope. He winds up the rope into a circle and places his left hand through it. His Dad helps him secure it over his shoulder.

Jonny climbs up the tree and onto a branch that is sturdy enough to hold his weight.

His Dad is watching carefully. He asks him, "Do you think that branch is strong enough for the weight of an adult to swing out on the rope? I think it'll work fine. What's your opinion?"

"I believe it will be fine, too. I certainly don't want anyone to be hurt out here. I remember how much fun I had when I was younger."

He successfully secures the rope to the sturdy branch. He's ready to climb down. His foot slips on a slippery lower branch. He takes a fall down to the ground and hits the edge of the lake. He tumbles and splashes into the water.

The water is shallow there but his Dad is struggling with his footing trying to get down the bank to help his son. There are several large stones at the edge of the lake. The ground is slippery and muddy from the recent rain showers.

"Son? Are you okay? Please answer me!" He's worried that he may be seriously injured.

He's unable to answer his Dad because he fell down so hard that he's struggling to catch his breath again.

His Dad finally makes his way down to where his son is in the water. Jonny is moaning and struggling to sit up. He's in a lot of pain. His Dad takes out his cell phone and calls for the paramedics to help him.

They arrive with sirens blaring. They rush over to care for his needs all within 10 minutes. They check him out and carefully lay him on the stretcher. He needs to be examined at the hospital. They'll check for broken bones and internal injuries. Gary rides with him in the ambulance to the nearest hospital.

Jonny speaks in a low raspy voice, "Thanks, Dad for being here with me and taking care of me. Can you please call Mandy and let her know what's going on?"

"Yes, but I can't use my cell phone here inside the ambulance. We'll have to wait until we arrive at the hospital. I have her number in my phone for business purposes."

They arrive at the hospital and the paramedics wheel Jonny in to the Emergency Room. His Dad signs forms and provides necessary information for his son. He wants his son to receive the best care possible. The ER staff wheels him into a room where they're checking his vital signs and calling up to Radiology to take X-rays. The medical personnel also draw blood and talk to him about what happened. The nurse cleans up the cuts and abrasions on various areas of his body. His knee and ankle are very swollen and need ice packs.

Gary takes a moment to step outside the hospital doors to call Mandy. She answers, "Hello, Gary? I'm so surprised to hear from you on a Sunday. Is everything okay?"

"Mandy, dear? Jonny asked me to call you. He had an accident and is at the Omaha Community Hospital. Do you know where that's located? He's in the emergency room and they're running tests on him to determine the extent of his injuries."

"Oh, no? Yes, I know where it's located. It'll take me a minute to change my clothes and I'll be right there. Please tell Jonny that I love him and that I'll see him soon."

Mandy changes her clothes and makes a quick call to her Mom. She wants to let her know what's going on with Jonny. She knows her Mom cares about Gary, too. She drives anxiously to the hospital and finds his Dad in the waiting room.

"What happened? What kind of accident? How is he doing? Is he going to be okay?"

"What happened is that he fell out of a tree at the lake. He hit the ground then tumbled into the shallow water. He had the wind knocked out of him and he was unable to get up on his own. I called the paramedics for help in case he had injuries that I couldn't see."

"Why was he in a tree?" Shaking her head, she says, "Never mind. He can share the story with me later."

"They're taking X-rays and running other tests. I watched a nurse clean up the cuts and abrasions. He has ice packs on his swollen knee and ankle. That's all I know right now. It's better to be patient and wait than to get in their way."

The doctor finally walks out with a report about Jonny. The doctor tells Gary and Mandy, "We want to keep him overnight for observation. Can you sign the forms to have him admitted? After he's settled in his room, you can visit with him for a short period of time.'

"Yes, I can sign his admission papers. I want only the best for him. How is he feeling? Tells us please? What did the tests reveal?"

"His X-rays and scans revealed that there are no broken bones. He's badly bruised with cuts and abrasions. My concern is his level of pain. He'll need some strong pain meds for him to sleep through the night. He has a slightly sprained ankle. His ankle and knee are very swollen. He won't be able to walk on his own. Our nurses will take good care of him. He has a swollen bump on his head. I would like to see the swelling in his body go down before he's released to go home. I think a good night's rest here will be the best thing for him."

Mandy asks, "What is his room number? When can we go in to see him?"

The doctor replies, "After the nurses have done all that they can for him, they'll come out and let you know where he is? You'll be able to visit with him at that time." He walks away leaving Mandy and Gary standing there stunned and tears in their eyes. They exchange a quick comforting hug.

The hospital doors open and they look in that direction. Katherine is closing her dripping wet umbrella and drying her wet shoes off on the mat. Gary and Mandy rush over to greet her. They tell her that they're happy she's here.

The nurse is looking for Gary. The three of them notice her and gather around her. She tells them that they can visit with Jonny now for a short period of time. He may be sleepy due to the medication. His body was beaten up by the fall.

They locate his room and go in to see him. He appears to be asleep. Quietly, they tiptoe in and stand by his bedside.

Mandy kisses him on the forehead and says, "I love you, Jonny. I hope you heal and get well soon."

Gary takes his hand and whispers, "Jon, I love you, son. Rest well and we'll see you tomorrow."

Katherine walks up to Gary and places her hand on his back offering comfort to him.

The nurse comes in to check his vital signs. She says, "He's really out of it right now. It would be best if you let him rest now and visit with him tomorrow."

The three of them say goodbye to him. They assure him that they'll be back tomorrow. They leave his room.

Gary asks Katherine if she can give him a ride home. He explains that he rode over in the ambulance with Jon. She agrees to drive him home.

At the hospital door, they notice that it's still raining. Katherine opens up her umbrella. The three of them huddle under it while they dash out to the parking lot. She holds the umbrella while they walk Mandy to her car and they say their goodbyes.

Katherine walks arm in arm with Gary to her car. He's feeling and looking a little lost. She drives him home safely. He feels really alone without Jonny there. He's constantly on his mind.

Katherine stays for a few minutes with Gary. She hopes that the rain will stop. They go to the kitchen and Gary makes a pot of coffee. Sadie walks in and offers to help.

They update her on Jonny's accident and his overnight stay in the hospital. Sadie's eyes are overflowing with tears.

CHAPTER NINETEEN
JONNY RECEIVES TLC

It's 10:15am Monday Morning. Jonny wakes up in a hospital bed feeling the effects of the pain medication. He vaguely recalls why he's there. His doctor is in the room examining him. He's checking out cuts, bumps, bruises and abrasions on Jonny's body as well as the swelling in his knee and ankle. He's still very swollen and in a lot of pain.

The doctor asks, "How are you feeling Jonny?"

Jonny replies, "I'm in a lot of pain and it's difficult to move even the slightest bit. How am I doing, Doctor?"

The doctor tells Jonny, "You have a lot of soft tissue injury. I want you to stay in bed at least another 24 hours. You'd take a big risk, if you try to make a trip home in your car. You could cause more harm to yourself. Rest assured that we'll take good care of you here."

"Have you talked with my Dad this morning?"

"Yes and your girlfriend called to check on you, too. Your family and friends really care about you. Your Dad will be here again in the afternoon."

"Again?"

"Yes, he was here this morning but you were in a deep sleep because of the pain medication. He thought it would be best to let you sleep. I agreed."

"Is it okay to use my cell phone here? I'd like to talk to him as well as my girlfriend."

"Yes, but please limit your time on the phone. I want you to rest over the next 24 hours. I'll see you tomorrow."

"Okay, Thank you!"

"Hope you feel better soon. I know you're anxious to go home. Your Dad is anxious for you to return home again. Try to rest for now, Jonny. There's plenty of time for visiting this afternoon."

"Can you give me another dose of pain medication before you leave? My head, knee and ankle are throbbing with pain."

"I'll send the nurse in to give you something. Have you eaten breakfast?"

"No, not yet. I'm hungry though!"

"That's a good sign. The nurse can help you with your meal if you need it."

"Thank you for everything, Doctor. I really appreciate it. I really want to get out of here as soon as possible. I have a lot of things to do in a short period of time."

"You're welcome! We want to see you up on your feet and doing well, too. One day at a time. You took a nasty fall and it'll take time for all of your injuries to heal."

"I'll ask the nurse to check on your meal and your pain medication."

Jonny checks on his nightstand but doesn't see his phone. He's in too much pain to get out of bed. He wants to call his Dad and Mandy. It's a few hours before visiting hours.

The nurse comes in with a breakfast tray for Jonny. Soft scrambled eggs, toast, coffee and juice. She sets it on his bed table. She tries to adjust the bed high enough for him to comfortably eat the food. He's uncomfortable and asks her for more pain medication.

She checks his chart and leaves the room. When she returns, she has a tray with a syringe. She uses it to inject a pain medication into his IV line. She writes down the information in his chart.

She offers to feed him but he says he can handle it. She assists him in picking up the cup of hot coffee. He takes a couple of sips and places it on the bed table.

He's getting sleepy again. She removes his tray of dishes from the bed table. She slides the table out of the way, puts up the bed rails and lowers the head of the bed. He tries to adjust the pillows but he can't move them. She helps him settle in and he falls asleep for a couple of hours.

In the meantime, Gary and Mandy are at work. They sit in his office and talk about Monday morning business. They had a long talk about Jonny. They plan to visit him this afternoon. Mandy will go to the hospital after work. She wants his Dad to visit with him first.

Back at home, Sadie is cleaning and preparing the downstairs guest room for Jonny's return from the hospital. Years ago, the downstairs guest room was designed for Angela's parents when they came for a visit. They were unable to climb the stairs. Now that Jonny can't climb the stairs, this room will be perfect for him to recuperate in.

Katherine is waiting to hear how she can help out. She's a licensed registered nurse with years of experience. She's willing to volunteer to care for Jonny as needed. Between her and Sadie, she believes he'll receive great care.

There's also talk about a male nurse that will visit him daily to care for him. They all love Jonny and want the best of care for him. They want to give him lots of TLC (Tender Loving Care). They want him to return to his good health as soon as possible.

Gary leaves the office and goes home to change his clothes. He drives to the hospital from there. When he arrives, Jonny is awake. He's hungry and thirsty. Two nurses are trying to get him propped up by raising the bed and adjusting his pillows. They offer to help him eat his dinner. He's finally able to sip and swallow water without too much pain.

When the nurses leave the room, his Dad pulls up a chair beside Jonny's bed. They finally have time to visit. He's very happy to see his Dad and tries to smile. His attempt to smile hurts right now. His Dad tries to comfort his son and tells him it'll take time for the injuries to heal.

At Jonny's request, his Dad looks for his cell phone. They come to the conclusion that he left it at the lake house. When he changed to climb the tree, he didn't put in his pocket. His Dad says, "Do you need to make a call? You can use my phone."

"I miss Mandy. I want to ask her if she'll stop by for a visit. The doctor said that I need to stay overnight again."

"Yes, we know. We came in to see you this morning and called the doctor to ask how you're doing. You were still sleeping when we came in and decided not to wake you. We spoke with the doctor after his visit with you at 10:00am. He told us that he believed you should stay at least for another 24 hours. He told us that we can visit with you during visiting hours."

"Is she okay?"

"Yes, Mandy and I spent the day talking about business issues. She's planning to visit you in about an hour. She wanted me to visit with you first. She really misses you. She's anxious to see you."

"It would be best if I don't call her then. I'll be patient. It's very hard to stay awake with pain medicine. I really need it because my whole body hurts."

"I'm really sorry that this happened to you, Son. I'm relieved that you are doing so well. I had imagined that your injuries were a lot worse based on how hard you fell."

"It really was a bad accident. I climbed that tree dozens of times when I was a kid. The fresh rain and mud made the tree and my shoes slippery. I'm sorry it happened, Dad. This is taking time away from the office and sorting out things for your retirement."

"It's okay, Son. We still have time and Mandy is a go-getter. She's catching on and learning things that she can help you with after I retire. And you know, I'll be able to help out. You can ask questions on the phone. I can spend a day or two at the office until everything is in your competent hands. Mandy will be there as your assistant to help you just like your Mom assisted me."

"Thanks Dad for your caring and loving attitude. Your patience with me means a lot. I didn't want to let you down. I love you, Dad! Thanks for visiting me here. My eyelids feel heavy. I think that I need a nap before Mandy arrives."

"Get the rest you need and feel better, Son. I love you, Jon! I'll return later tonight and I'll bring your phone. Can you tell me what you need for tomorrow?"

"I'm sorry, Dad. I'm just too sleepy now. I'll see you tonight. Thank you for visiting with me."

Gary leaves after his son falls asleep. He thanks the nurses on the way out for taking good care of him. He drives back to the lake house. He locates Jonny's personal items and packs them in a bag to take to the hospital. Then, he drives home for a light supper. He rests in his recliner before driving to the hospital again.

He shares an update with Sadie and thanks her for preparing the spare room. He calls Katherine to ask her if she'd accompany him to visit with Jonny. She says yes of course. He makes plans to pick her up around seven.

Jonny is sleeping when Mandy first walks in his room. She walks over quietly and kisses him on the forehead and gently picks up his hand to hold it. She quietly pulls up a chair to sit with him by his bed.

She whispers, "I love you, Jonny! I'm so happy to be here with you. Please get well soon. We all love you and miss you."

"He whispers, "I love you, Mandy!" He tries to smile but it hurts too much. "I missed you a lot! Thank you for visiting with me today."

"She smiles at him and says, "Aw, Jonny! So good to see you awake, how are you feeling?"

"The pain is bad. Fortunately, the pain medicine is helping me to sleep. The doctor said I need to stay overnight again. He doesn't think it's a good idea for me to take a trip in the car with my ankle and knee so swollen."

"I know and agree with your doctor. Glad you're getting good nursing care here. I won't stay too long. I don't want to overtire you. Maybe we can talk on the phone for a few minutes tonight. I'll give you a call, okay?"

"Yes, I would love that. Dad is going to bring my phone from the lake house tonight. We'll talk just before bedtime so that we can say goodnight. I love you!"

"I love you! Please get the rest that you need. We'll talk soon and I'll visit with you again tomorrow. Is there anything that I can bring to the hospital for you?"

"Dad is going to bring my personal things for me. I don't think there's anything that you can do for me. Thank you!"

"My pleasure! I'll go for now." She walks over to kiss his forehead. He tries to reach up to touch the back of her head. He tries to kiss her on the lips. He doesn't quite make it. She leans down instead to give him a sweet gentle kiss on his lips. They gently laugh! They exchange goodbyes and she walks out the door with misty eyes.

Jonny has misty eyes as he watches her walk out the door. He settles in to rest until his nurse brings in his supper tray. He's hungry and thinks about Sadie's delicious Chicken Soup. He falls asleep again.

Back at home, Sadie asks if Jonny can eat food from outside the hospital. Gary calls to get an okay to bring the soup from home for Jonny. His nurse says that it's okay. Sadie packs up a little basket with a thermos of soup, crackers, bowl, spoon, napkin and placemat.

She says, "I'd really like to deliver this basket to Jonny's room and visit with him."

"He'd enjoy a visit with you, Sadie. I know that he'll be thrilled to see you. It'll be just the thing to give him a lift in his spirit. He loves your homemade soup and loves you like family."

"Is it okay if I go to the hospital now and visit with him? Are you going to be okay?"

"I believe this will be a perfect time. I'll write down his room number for you. Katherine and I are planning to visit with him around seven."

"I'm going to change clothes and leave here before seven. I'll see you later."

Sadie arrives at the hospital with her basket of goodies. He's awake and He's thrilled to see Sadie. She's been his friend through childhood. He's happy and feels comfort from her visit with him. His eyes widen when he sees the little basket.

"Sadie? Is that your homemade chicken soup? I fell asleep earlier wishing that I could eat your soup for supper. Thank you so very much! You're very thoughtful and I really appreciate you! I'm thankful for all that you do for my Dad and I."

She adjusts the bed and the pillows so that he can sit up ever so gently. She slides his bed table around and sets out the crackers, bowl, spoon and napkin on a little placemat. Now that he's settled at the table, she takes out the thermos of soup and pours it into the bowl. It's just the right temperature.

She sits in a chair close by in case he needs help. She encourages him to take his time. He usually eats crackers but the liquid is sufficient. He feels stronger physically. When Sadie serves him the homemade soup, he feels a lift in his spirit.

She tells him, "Your Dad will be here soon! I'll pack up the basket and leave now. Please get the rest you need, Jonny. We want you to come home tomorrow."

"I will Sadie. Your soup is at work strengthening me. I can feel the difference already. I wasn't able to eat all of the food they served here. Your soup is very nourishing. Thank you so much! I'll see you tomorrow!"

They exchange goodbyes. Just as Sadie is walking out of his room, Katherine and his Dad are walking in. Perfect timing! His Dad is amazed by the difference in his son from this morning. Sadie's homemade soup nourished him and her TLC lifted his spirit. He feels and looks stronger.

His Dad and Katherine visit with him for about a half an hour. His Dad hands him his cell phone which makes him happy. He likes staying connected with his family and friends. His Dad asks him for a list of items that he'll need for tomorrow. Jonny has high hopes of returning home. He asks for a change of clothes and his toiletry bag.

Before his Dad and Katherine leave him for the night, they share that the spare room downstairs is ready for his arrival. He's relieved that he won't have to climb the stairs to his room. He appreciates the TLC that everyone is giving him.

His cell phone rings. It's Mandy calling to say goodnight. They talk quietly about things for about a half hour. They share their goodbyes and exchange an "I love you!"

CHAPTER TWENTY
JONNY RETURNS HOME

Jonny rests through the night with the help of a low dose of pain medicine. The ice packs have decreased the swelling in his ankle and knee as well as the bump on his head. The nurses have taken good care of him.

The doctor visits him in his room at 10:30am. He examines him and notices that his ability to move has improved. He appears to be stronger and not in as much pain. The swelling is down. He still needs a lot of care. He believes that he can get the care he needs at home. The doctor signs the papers to release him. His Dad is waiting for him out in the waiting room.

The doctor explains to his Dad what he needs to know. Jonny needs aftercare to continue healing. The doctor recommends a Home Nursing Care. They can send a nurse over to visit Jonny daily. This care might improve his chances for healing quickly. He gives Gary a business card. Please call my office to schedule a follow-up appointment for next week.

His Dad takes care of the paperwork. He goes into Jonny's room and gives him the change of clothes and his toiletry bag. He goes out to the parking lot and drives the car up to the curb outside the hospital doors.

A nurse pushes a wheel chair into his room. She helps Jonny change into his street clothes. He has several bandages. A brace on his knee and on his ankle. She helps him with his toiletry bag so that he can freshen up.

She helps him sit securely in the wheel chair and pushes him into the hallway. His Dad comes back to Jon's room to carry his bags. They carefully help him into the passenger side of his Dad's Cadillac. He folds the wheel chair and places it in the trunk. His Dad drives home very carefully.

When they arrive home, he's able to assist Jonny to sit in the wheel chair without any problems. They have a ramp set up for him to enter through the front door. He's greeted by Sadie, Katherine and Mandy! They're excited Jonny is able to return home today.

His Dad parks his wheel chair in the living room to give everyone a chance to visit with him and welcome him home.

Jonny enjoys the visit but is very sleepy. He asks them, "Would it be okay if someone helps me settle in the spare room so that I can take a nap? I'm really sleepy."

"You're in luck, Jon, the four of us are all willing to help you in any way that we can."

"I don't want to put anyone out. I need help. Who is willing to volunteer?"

Katherine speaks up and says, "I'll help you, Jonny and then I can check your vital signs before you fall asleep."

Sadie offers to bring a glass of water with a bendable straw for his bed table.

His Dad says, "I can lift him out of the wheel chair."

Mandy pushes the wheel chair into the spare room. She folds back the covers and fluff the pillows. His Dad removes his shoes. Jonny is already wearing comfy clothing. His Dad lifts his son out of the wheel chair and places him on his bed. Katherine uses items from her nursing bag to take his vital signs. Sadie places the glass of water on his bedside table.

His Dad asks Jonny if he would like a visiting nurse to come in and help him in the morning? He said that he would give it some thought when he's not so sleepy. He falls asleep.

They leave his room and quietly close the door. The four of them go to the kitchen to sit at the table to discuss Jonny's care. Sadie makes lunch and iced tea for everyone.

Gary shares that his doctor recommends a nursing care for a daily visit. He thinks it might improve his chances for a shorter recovery time. I think it's a good idea for him to have a male nurse in the morning to help him shower, shave and change into clean clothes.

Katherine says, "I'll be happy to take an evening shift to check his vital signs and change a bandage or two. I'm willing to do whatever I can to help him get back on his feet."

"That would be great, Katherine. You're very generous. When Jonny is up to a chat, I'll share these ideas with him."

Mandy speaks up, "I'm also willing to help him in any way that I can."

Sadie says, "I'm here, too! If I can do anything for him, please let me know."

Gary says, "We'll need you to feed him at least. The schedule will be a little unusual since he sleeps through our usual meal time."

"That's okay! I'll be here to feed him whatever he wants to eat. We need to keep up his strength."

"He'll probably sleep for a couple of hours. I need to check in with the office. Afterwards, I'll come home to rest for a few minutes in my recliner. Katherine, will you be able to hang out here for a couple of hours until I return home? He might wake up with a need for more pain medicine."

"Yes, I can wait here and listen for him."

Sadie says, "I'll be here to assist her and prepare lunch for him."

"Great, thank you very much. I'll head out to the office now. What about you Mandy?"

"Yes, I have things to do back at the office, too. Is it okay if I return here after work to visit with him?"

"Yes, you're like family to us, Mandy dear!"

Everyone has my cell phone number so please don't hesitate to call me if you have a question or an update."

"Mandy, do you have the house phone number? Sadie will answer and you can speak to her about Jonny."

"Yes, thank you, Jonny gave me the number."

Mandy and Gary give Katherine goodbye hugs. Gary peeks in on Jonny and he's still sleeping. He quietly closes the door and doesn't disturb him.

He says goodbye to Sadie with a big smile. He says, "Thank you for everything, Sadie. See you later."

Mandy and Gary leave the house to drive to the office.

They arrive and have a meeting discussing the issues causing the most concern. They take care of business at the Agency for a couple of hours. They're at a stopping point and agree that they want to take the rest of the day off.

Gary tells Mandy, "I'll see you back at the house. Just make yourself at home."

She replies, "Thank you! See you there. Is there anything I can do for you? You're looking really tired."

"No, dear! I've been feeling tired and stressed over things a lot lately. I'll be okay. We'll get through it. I'll just be happy when Jon is up and about again and is able to be himself."

"I agree, it's hard to watch him suffer in so much pain. He's going to be okay. He's lucky to have so many caring for his needs." She gives him a quick comforting hug. "Goodbye, I'll see you later."

Gary takes time to contact his mechanic to tow Jonny's car from the lake house to their garage at home. *I hope to spend Memorial Day weekend out there but I don't like the idea of his car sitting unattended for that long."*

He's anxious to get home to his son. He calls Katherine to ask if everything is going okay. He wants to know if he needs to make any stops on the way. She assures him that Jonny is okay and there's no need to stop anywhere.

He arrives at home to find Katherine, Mandy, Sadie and Jonny sitting in the living room. Jonny is sitting in the wheel chair looking rested. He's holding Mandy's hand and smiling. Jonny is elated to be home again and awake. Gary is greeted by the four of them with smiles.

Gary sits in his recliner and joins the conversation. They're trying to decide what to make for supper. Jonny, of course, wants Sadie's homemade chicken soup but he's hungry for steak and potatoes as well.

His Dad says, "Well it's a really a good sign that you have your appetite back."

"You'll have to help me cut up my steak and potato in bite size pieces because I'm still very sore throughout my body. Using a knife and fork will be very painful."

"Okay, any one of us can do that for you. What do you say, Sadie? Do you think you can cook Jonny's favorite meal for all of us here?"

Katherine says, "Oh, no not for me, thank you. I'll be going and let you have some quiet time together. I'll call later to check in after the supper hour."

Mandy also says, "Not for me either, thank you. I agree with my Mom. You should enjoy this time in a quiet and peaceful way. I'm going to leave now and I'll check back later."

Katherine and Mandy stand up to leave. Gary gives them a hug to say goodbye. They say goodbye to Jonny without disturbing him in his chair. Mandy gives him a sweet kiss on his forehead and whispers sweetly in his ear. They walk out the front door and drive to their own homes.

Jonny says, "Can we go to the kitchen? I know it's late in the day, but I would love a cup of coffee."

His Dad says, "Sure, I need a chance to rest and relax, too. I'll pour your coffee and join you for a cup. I'll wheel you into the kitchen. You can sit at the end of the table."

Sadie is in the kitchen cooking the steak and potatoes for Jonny and his Dad. When she sees that Gary is preparing to brew a pot of coffee, she smiles and offers to do the job. He lets her because he loves the way she prepares it."

The three of them chat about this and that in a quiet and peaceful way. They're tired and taking it easy except for Sadie. But she's happy cooking Jonny's favorite meal and that he's home again.

Gary asks Jon, "Son, the doctor recommends a Home Nursing Care that can send a nurse out daily to check in on you. Are you interested in having a male nurse come out in the morning? He can give you a hand with your shower and morning routine."

"That would be helpful, Dad. It's still difficult to stand up with my knee and ankle injury. I would appreciate someone that is able to help me. What time will he be here?"

"I'll have to give them a call and get the details. He'll also check your vital signs and monitor your pain medicine. If your bandages need changing, he'll do that for you, too. I'll give them a call right after supper. Sadie is fixing your plate for you and heating up your soup, now."

"Thank you, Dad and Sadie. I really appreciate it."

"Please relax and take your time, son. We're here for you. You're doing just fine."

They finish eating supper and Jonny wants to return to his room to rest on the bed. His Dad helps him freshen up and securely places him in the bed. Jonny checks the table for his cell phone because Mandy is supposed to call.

Katherine calls Gary just as she said she would. Gary tells her, "Jonny is okay for now. He's back in bed resting after eating supper. I'm going to call to make an appointment for a nurse to care for Jonny in the morning." She's happy that things are working out.

Katherine says, "Please call me, if you need my help. I'll call again tomorrow. Goodnight."

Gary sits in his recliner resting while he calls the Home Nursing Care office. He makes arrangements for a male nurse to assist Jonny around 9:00am in the morning.

He goes to Jon's room and knocks on the door. He opens it to see if he's awake. He's awake but on the phone with Mandy. He slips back out and writes the time on a notepad. He'll be sure to give him the note. He doesn't want him to be surprised by the news when he wakes up in the morning.

Gary returns to his recliner and rests after a long day. He needs to unwind and assist Jonny at least one more time before he goes to bed.

CHAPTER TWENTY-ONE
ON THE ROAD TO RECOVERY

Blake Davis arrives at 9:00am and rings the doorbell. Sadie answers the door. He introduces himself and explains that he's looking for Jonny Young.

She says, "Come in, we've been expecting you. Please wait for just a minute while I check on him. I'll let him know that you're here."

His Dad told him last night that the nurse would be here at 9:00am. He set his alarm so that he would be awake. Sadie heard the alarm through the door and heard Jonny turn it off. She knows that he's awake. She knocks on the door and opens it slightly.

"Jonny? Blake Davis, your visiting nurse is here. Is it okay if he comes in?"

"Yes, please send him in."

Sadie shows Blake to Jonny's room. He goes into the room and closes the door behind him. Jonny and Blake greet each other.

"How are you doing this morning, Jonny?"

"I'm still very sore in some places. I'm still having pain in other areas. Can you help me get up and take a quick shower, please? I didn't take any pain medicine this morning. I want to be wide awake while you're here."

"I'm here to help you shower and dress according to your morning routine. I can change your bandages. I'll check your vital signs first.

We'll need to make sure that your ankle and knee brace remains clean and dry. How is your ankle and knee feeling? I don't see a lot of swelling right now."

"They're feeling better today. Do you think it's okay to take the braces off while I shower?"

"No, that'll be a decision for your doctor. I'll be taking notes about things and we'll give him a copy. If it's too painful for you to stand in the shower, I can help you get a sponge bath."

"I'd prefer taking a quick shower. I can sit down on a seat in the shower. How are we going to keep the braces dry?"

"I carry some plastic sheets in my bag just for this need. I'll help tape them on. Let's remove the old bandages."

"Okay, Thank you!"

"Let's get you into the chair and I'll wheel you in to the bathroom." He turns on the shower and makes sure it's the right temperature.

Jonny puts a hand under the shower to be sure. Jonny is able to shampoo his hair by himself which is an improvement since the accident. He's clean and Blake hands him a towel to dry off.

He wheels him back to the bedroom. His Dad set out a change of clothes for this morning. He's struggling to dress himself because of the pain. Blake helps only when necessary. He's careful to place the new bandages on a few spots where he was cut by the sharp rocks and twigs in the water.

Blake writes out his report and asks Jonny how he's feeling? He asks him if he still needs pain meds.

"I'm feeling much better after the shower. I think the warm water helped and it was good to be up moving around again. I think I'll only need one pill instead of two this morning. Thank you so much for assisting me. I think I'll be able to care for myself once my ankle and knee can hold my weight."

"Do you need help with anything else? I can ask Sadie to prepare ice packs for your knee and ankle if you're going to be awake. They're not very swollen but the ice packs will also ease the pain."

"I'll eat breakfast soon and I can ask her about the ice packs. Do you mind pushing the wheel chair to the kitchen?"

"Sure, I'll push the chair and set you in place at the table before I go."

He pushes the chair into the kitchen and parks it at the end of the table. Sadie is there waiting for him. She pours a cup of coffee for him. Jonny thanks and says goodbye to Blake. He says, "I'll see you tomorrow." Blake leaves the house after he picks up his nursing bag from Jonny's room.

Sadie asks Jonny what he would like to eat for brunch. He's worked up a big appetite. He asks her to cook bacon and eggs, toast and jelly. She cooks it for him and sets it on the table in front of him.

"Jonny, you are looking so good. I'm so glad you're home and able to move around better than yesterday. It's great to see you so wide awake."

"Thanks, Sadie. I'm feeling better today. I'm planning to take only a half dose of pain meds. Will you help me get back in bed for a nap after I'm finished eating please? Mandy plans to stop by after work for a visit today. Will you help me freshen up, too, please?"

"Sure thing!"

"Thank you for cooking my meal. It was delicious. I think I'm ready to go to my room now."

She pushes the chair back to the bathroom in his bedroom so that he can freshen up. She helps him fill a glass with water so that he can take his pill. Then, she helps him safely return to his bed for a nap. He drifts off to sleep in a short amount of time.

When Jonny wakes up, he's surprised to hear muffled voices in the living room. He calls out to Sadie because he's not able to get out of bed and his chair is out of reach. Sadie hears and rushes to his room. She taps on the door and opens it slightly. He invites her in to help him out of bed. He doesn't realize that his Dad is home.

He steps to the door and says, "How are you doing, son? So happy to see you awake again. Can I do anything to help you?"

"Hi Dad! I'm happy to see you, too. I think Sadie would appreciate your help. Can you help me sit in the chair and wheel me out to the kitchen? I'm hungry. I need a cold drink and a snack?"

Jonny asks Sadie, "Do you have any of your delicious apple pie leftover for me to eat today?" He smiles.

"Yes, I have a slice of pie with your name on it!" She laughs. "I'm excited that your appetite is improving. "Would you like some vanilla ice cream with it?"

"Yes, please, that sounds refreshing. Can we go to the kitchen now?" He smiles with gratitude.

The three of them make their way to the kitchen. Sadie serves the pie and pours iced tea for everyone. They sit at the table and discuss the events of the day.

"How did the visit from the nurse work out? Did he give you the proper care that you needed this morning?"

"Blake was right on time. I had the alarm set. I wanted to be awake when he arrived. He changed my bandages and put plastic wrap on my braces to protect them. He was very professional when he helped me shower and change. I was able to move around a lot better this morning. He assisted me only when necessary. It won't be long before I can take care of myself again."

"That's really good news, Son. Katherine offered to assist you in the evenings. Sounds like you're doing very well. It'll be up to you. Do you think you'll need her nursing experience to help you in the evening?"

"No, I don't think so. I have been taking less pain meds and feeling a lot stronger. If she stops by, maybe we can have a chat about it. You know, Dad, I think Mom is watching over me."

"Yes, Jon, I had the same thought!"

"Your apple pie is delicious as usual, Sadie! Thanks for adding the ice cream. It's a wonderful treat."

"You're welcome Jonny!"

"Dad, how's business going? I miss being in the office and working with you and Mandy. I'm anxious for you to share an update on what's happening there. I was thinking that maybe we can set up video chats in my home office. At least during my awake time, I can sit at my desk in this chair. I can listen in on business meetings especially with you and Mandy. I don't want to be too far behind in learning the ropes. I'm anxious to be physically able to take over for you as well."

"That might work out just fine. Well, how are you feeling son? Would you be up to sitting at your desk in your office now? We can take a look at what's available on your computer together."

"Sure, Dad! Is Mandy still at work? I haven't heard from her today. Maybe we can play with the software and try to find Mandy on her computer just for fun. Let's give her a call and see what she might know about it."

"Ok, Let's pick up your phone on the nightstand on the way to your home office."

"Thank you very much, Sadie, for taking good care of me! We'll see you a little later. Unless, you want to join us in the search for video chat software. I may need your help tomorrow in getting around and setting myself up in the office."

"You're welcome! I'll be here to help you when you need it. I have video chat on my personal computer and often chat with my family and friends. Go ahead and have your fun with your Dad and Mandy. If I can help with it tomorrow, I'll be happy to give you a hand."

His Dad pushes the chair up to his door. He finds the phone on the nightstand and places it in his son's hand. He calls Mandy and discovers that she's in her office at work. He shares his idea with her about conference calls with her and his Dad. He thinks this will be helpful while they're in business meetings and other discussions. She likes the idea and tells him that she has video chat software on her computer. She explains how he can locate her from his office computer at home.

His Dad sits with him in his home office. He assists with the computer software setup when necessary. Jonny chats with Mandy on the phone while she walks him through the setup. In a short time, they are connected and chatting via video. They're both very excited about this new plan.

Gary asks, "Can you set up my computer in my office, too for the three of us to connect?"

She says, "Yes, how about tomorrow? Is it okay, if I take the rest of the day off? I would really love to visit with Jonny soon."

She says to Jonny, "I miss you! I'm anxious to see you in person. You look like you're feeling better."

"Yes, tomorrow would be a great time for us to work on my computer. Of course, please feel free to take off and visit with him. Someone here is missing you, too."

They share smiles and say their goodbyes.

Jonny asks, "Dad would you like to set up the video software on your computer in your home office?"

"Yes, let's try to get that set up now if you're feeling up to it."

"Let's try it. Based on Mandy's instructions we should be able to set up your computer for video chatting. This form of communication can come in handy especially after you retire."

Gary maneuvers the wheel chair down the hall to his office. They're pleased with their success. This will certainly improve their ability to stay connected. They can keep in touch on a business and personal level from their home offices.

It's close to supper time. They decide to check in the kitchen to see what Sadie is planning to cook. Jonny is hungry and thirsty. He takes a soft drink from the refrigerator and the three of them chat while she's cooking a spaghetti dinner. She baked a loaf of Italian bread.

They are delighted and thank her. It really smells delicious. The doorbell rings. Gary answers the door and invites Mandy to come in. He escorts her to the kitchen where Jonny is sitting at the end of the table.

They're happy to see each other and exchange a gentle hug and kiss. He asks, "Would you like to stay for supper? Sadie cooked spaghetti and baked bread."

Sadie cheerfully says, "I can add a salad to the meal if you want one."

"Please don't go to that much trouble."

She replies, "I would love to stay for supper, Jonny. I appreciate the invitation. I've really missed you and I've been thinking about you all day. How are you feeling? You look great! Are you in pain? It's so good to see you up and awake again."

"I've missed you too. Thanks for staying for supper. It'll be fun to have you join us for a meal. It's our first home cooked meal together. Yes, I'm in pain but not as much. I've managed on less pain medicine today. I'm making progress."

Sadie says, "The meal is ready to eat. As soon as I set the table, we can gather around it and enjoy this meal together."

Gary says, "I should've invited Katherine over to join us for supper tonight. She's supposed to visit here but I'm not sure when she'll be free."

The doorbell rings. Gary answers the door and he's surprised to see Katherine. He invites her in. He asks, "Would you like to join us for dinner? We're just about to sit down to eat. Your daughter is here!"

Sadie overhears their conversation. She starts setting the dishes and serving bowls on the dining room table.

Jonny is able to wheel his chair by himself to the dining room table. He surprises everyone by the progress he's making. He's definitely on the road to a speedy recovery.

They all encourage her to join them. She says, "Okay, yes, this is wonderful. Thank you."

The five of them sit and enjoy this meal together as though they're celebrating a big win. A celebration for Jonny's recovery. Also, celebrating a time of feeling like a happy family again.

CHAPTER TWENTY-TWO
PLANS FOR THE FUTURE

They enjoy eating Sadie's homemade spaghetti dinner and home baked Italian bread. They all chat about what their future holds for them.

At the present, they all want Jonny to be well and healed from his injuries. Katherine says, "I brought my nursing bag but I left it in the car. I didn't want to presume anything. If you would like help, Jonny, please let me know. We can discuss it more after dinner if you'd like."

He said, "Okay. After dinner, we can go to my room and talk about any concerns regarding my recovery. Thank you!"

Jonny shares his excitement about returning to work. He tells Katherine, "Mandy assisted Dad and I with setting up the video chat software. I'll be able to take care of business issues from home. I should be up on my feet soon. Then, I'll return to the office downtown. I really like the idea of video chatting for business conferences from my home office."

Katherine and Sadie are both happy to hear this news. Sadie congratulated Jonny. She knows how important it is to him to take over for his Dad.

Katherine asks Gary, "Do you have an official date set for your retirement?"

"No, not yet. I hope to retire this summer before I take my dream cruise vacation." He smiles with glee. "We hired Mandy, with her excellent qualifications to sort through our business issues. As soon as the three of us are able to get a healthy perspective on all of the businesses, Jonny will take over my office and responsibilities. We want to make the transition smooth and as stress free as possible."

"I don't think it's my place to ask about your business but I do hope that everything goes well for you. I know how much you want to retire and travel the world. I hope that you'll be very happy."

Gary gently picks up her hand and kisses it. He says, "Thank you, my dear! You said that you and Paul used to travel. Will you consider taking a cruise vacation with me when the time comes?"

"I do miss traveling to new places. I never felt comfortable about traveling after Paul passed on. Being a single lady makes me feel less secure outside my home."

"I understand. I don't feel insecure traveling alone. It's more fun to share the joy of seeing beautiful sites with a companion. Please consider it? I can afford to book us separate rooms and all the fancy trimmings."

"Fancy trimmings are not necessary. I'll be happy to be your companion and share the tourist sites with you. Sounds like lots of fun for both of us. Have you decided on a destination?"

"No. I've been reading brochures from the travel agency. There are many places that I dream of seeing. I can't seem to make up my mind. If you want to take a look at them, maybe you can recommend one of your favorite places."

"Okay, we can take a look at them another day."

Sadie asks, "Does anyone want dessert? I baked fresh pies today. I baked apple pie and a peach cobbler. There's ice cream in the freezer."

Everyone is too full from the spaghetti dinner. Gary says, "Maybe in about an hour. I would love a slice of pie with a cup of coffee." Everyone nods in agreement.

Mandy asks, "Jonny, how are you feeling? Do you need to take a rest? Maybe this would be a good time to talk to Mom about things regarding your recovery process."

"Yes, this would be a good time to rest on my bed. Do you want to sit with me in my room, while I talk to your Mom? There are a couple of chairs in there for you two to sit on. I can prop up on pillows and rest while we chat."

Gary says, "You can rest propped up with pillows on the couch in the living room. That way you won't be too crowded in the bedroom. If you'd like, I can get you set up in there."

Gary goes to the bedroom for the pillows. Katherine goes out to her car and carries her nursing bag into the house just in case. Mandy pushes his wheel chair to the Living Room. She assists him in standing up long enough to scoot over to the couch where the pillows are in place.

Gary gives Sadie a hand clearing the table and placing dishes in the sink. She cleans up the kitchen and prepares the coffee pot for later.

It's been a long time since they've eaten a meal in the dining room. Last Christmas was probably the last time the dining room table was used for a family gathering.

Gary gives Jonny time to visit with Mandy while talking to Katherine about his recovery. He'll hear what he needs to know from his son. He goes to his office and locates a few of the traveling brochures. He picks out his favorite cruise options to share with Katherine. *Maybe there will be enough time this evening to share these options with her. It'll be fun for her to join me on my dream cruise. I love spending time with her. She's very caring and loves to laugh.*

He returns to the living room to see how things are going. They moved to Jonny's bedroom. He's lying on the bed and she's checking his vital signs. Mandy is removing a few old bandages. There are new ones and a tube of ointment set out on the bed before her. He has a few on his back that need to be changed as well. They're giving him the TLC that he needs to continue recovering from his injuries. He walks to the bedroom door.

"How are things going in here? Are you feeling okay, son?"

"I'm doing great. These ladies are doing a great job taking care of me. I'm very grateful."

"If there's anything that I can do, please let me know. I'm willing to help you in any way that I can."

"I think they're just about done here. Maybe you can change the two bandages on my back for me at bedtime, please? I seem to be healing a lot quicker than I expected."

His Dad says, "Sadie made a pot of coffee. We can drink a cup of coffee with a slice of pie. Whenever you're done here, we can either sit in the kitchen or the dining room. We can take a vote."

Jonny says, "It'll be quicker and easier to get cozy around the kitchen table."

They nod in agreement. Gary says, "I'll go to the kitchen and assist Sadie. Whenever you're ready for pie and coffee, just come on in and we can visit there."

"Dad, do you think it would be okay if I try to walk with the crutches? They're in the closet. Can you get them for me?"

"Yes, are you sure that you're feeling strong enough to walk with the crutches? The chair will be safer for you if your ankle and knee are still hurting."

"They're not hurting really bad but I haven't tried to put my full weight on them yet. I just want to try. I'm anxious to get out of the chair and walk on my own again."

"Here, let me help you up and balance yourself with them. Please take your time and don't rush it. If you fall, it will cause a serious setback for you."

"I know, Dad. I'll be careful. I'm not sure I can put my full weight on this leg but I'll take it easy and limp my way to the kitchen. I'm just excited to do this on my own."

His Dad helps him up off the bed with the crutches and he balances himself very well. He has his strength back. His Dad follows close behind just to be sure. He wants to be there if there's a problem. Mandy and Katherine are smiling and feeling relieved that he's recovering from the accident so quickly.

Katherine tells Gary, "His vital signs are good and his injuries are healing up better than expected. He's doing very well. He's determined to get up and go as quickly as possible. I'm very proud of him!"

"Yes, I'm proud of my son, too. Thank you for checking on him and giving me this good news."

Slowly but surely Jonny manages to walk with the crutches to the kitchen. He's not free from pain but he's able to move forward. He's happy and believes he prefers the crutches to the wheel chair.

They gather at the kitchen table. Sadie is serving the pie and ice cream while Gary pours the coffee. He sets the sugar and cream on the table for Mandy.

They enjoy this time together. They chat while they eat their dessert. Jonny is showing signs of exhaustion and needing sleep. Katherine and Mandy say that they need to leave for home.

They exchange their goodbyes. Katherine and Gary share a sweet and gentle hug. Mandy and Jonny share a gentle hug and kiss. Tomorrow is a work day.

Mandy and her Mom talk outside for a few minutes before getting in their cars. They talk about Jonny's progress briefly. Mandy says, "I'll try to call you tomorrow after work. Thank you for giving him your nursing care."

"You're welcome, sweetie. He's going to be okay soon. He's a fighter and has lots of determination. I hope to talk with you tomorrow. See you later."

Katherine drives to her house. Mandy drives to her apartment. They enjoyed their time feeling like a family again. They sleep well.

Gary changes the bandages on Jonny's back. He tells his son that the cuts are almost healed. He still has a couple of bruises where he landed on the stones at the edge of the lake. They're showing signs of improvement but he's still feeling sore. He takes a low dose of pain medicine to insure a good night's sleep. With a little assistance from his Dad, Jonny puts on his sleeping clothes. He sets his alarm for Blake's visit in the morning.

He says, "Good Night, Dad. It's been a great day. I'll see you tomorrow. I love you!"

"I have to go to the office but I'll see you tomorrow. I love you, too, Jon! Good Night!"

Gary goes to the kitchen to tell Sadie goodnight. She's putting away the last of the dishes that she washed and dried. He's so exhausted that he practically collapses in the chair at the table.

She looks concerned and asks, "Are you okay? Is there anything that I can do for you? You're looking very stressed. I'm here if you want to talk about anything. Sometimes it helps to share your feelings. It's not good to keep them bottled up inside."

"I know it helps to talk and share but I'm so exhausted. I hardly know where to begin. My mind is overflowing with thoughts regarding our future plans. My mind is constantly working trying to make the right decisions. There are both personal and business issues that will affect others that I care so much about. I've got to find time to go back to the lake house and clean up things there. I'm tired. I guess I should go up to bed. Thanks for listening.

"Thank you for sharing. Please try to get a good night's sleep. If I can give you a hand at the lake house, let me know. I love working there and seeing the beauty that surrounds it."

"Before Jon's accident, I thought about planning a cookout at the lake house over the Memorial Day weekend. It's a great place to relax and have a little fun again. Would you like to join us there? If the weather is warm enough, you can invite your family. I'll call Katherine and talk to Mandy about making plans tomorrow. Of course, we need to talk to Jonny to see if he's up to the drive and hanging out there."

"We can talk about it again tomorrow. Let's check the weather forecast. It sounds like a lot of fun. We can't make any final plans for the weekend tonight. I'll say goodnight so that you can get your rest. Sleep well!"

"True, we'll talk again about the weekend plans. Hope you sleep well, too. Good Night!"

Gary walks up the stairs to his bedroom. He freshens up and dresses in his sleeping clothes. He curls up under the covers on his bed. *So much to think about. I have lots of decisions to make concerning our future lives. It's difficult to let go and put the thoughts out of my mind.*

CHAPTER TWENTY-THREE
GOING OUT AND ABOUT

Jonny's alarm buzzes! It's a few minutes before 9:00am. Blake is scheduled to arrive for Jonny's morning routine and check on his recovery progress. He's sleepy but feeling a lot better than yesterday. He feels slight pain in his knee when he tries to move it. His ankle is a little sore. Overall, he's feeling stronger and has better mobility this morning.

Blake rings the doorbell. Sadie answers it and invites him in. When he goes to Jonny's room, the door is open. He's sitting on the edge of his bed.

Blake says, "Knock! Knock! Is it okay for me to come in?"

Smiling, he says, "Yes, I've been expecting you!"

"How are you doing this morning? You look like you're feeling well. I can see that you've made a lot of progress since yesterday morning."

"I've had a lot of TLC from my family and friends. Thank you for your help again this morning. I'm feeling pretty good. I'm not planning to take any pain medicine today. I have a low level of pain in my knee and ankle. I believe I can manage it without the meds. I'm using crutches now and will plan on taking my time."

"That's really great! Do you need help with your shower? I have the plastic sheets to cover your braces. Why don't we check your vital signs first? Then I'll remove your bandages."

Jonny sits patiently on the edge of the bed while Blake removes the necessary items from his Nursing Bag. His vital signs are normal. Blake removes the bandages and places the plastic sheets on the braces to keep them dry.

Jonny is able to walk to the shower stall with his crutches. He's feeling strong and doesn't really need Blake's help today. He's thankful that Blake is there just in case. He takes a shower and washes his hair by himself without any problems.

Blake offers to help but Jonny is determined to do it all if he can. He dresses carefully while sitting on the edge of his bed. Blake asks, "When is your follow-up appointment with your doctor?"

"Next week, I think. Dad made the appointment for me while I was out of it. I'm not really sure!"

While taking notes, Blake shares, "You're moving along very well with your ankle and knee. I'm wondering how long you'll have to wear the braces. Your cuts are healed to the point that you no longer need the bandages. Just a little dab of ointment will protect the areas. They are almost completely healed. You're recovering quickly! I'm very pleased for you. Do you think you'll need my assistance tomorrow?"

"Actually, I thought about that, too. I feel strong enough to care for myself as long as I take it slow and easy. I'm not taking pain meds which gives me better balance with the crutches. I can probably manage by myself tomorrow. Thank you for everything that you've done in my time of need."

"I'll turn in a report to your doctor. You're recovering from your injuries in a remarkable way. It's amazing. I'll see myself to the door. Have a good day and please be careful."

"I will. It's wonderful to be in control again. Life is good. Hope you have a good day, too!"

Blake leaves Jonny's room and walks out the front door. Sadie hears him leave. She walks toward Jonny's room concerned for him. He's walking out with his crutches and greets her. She's relieved to see him up and about.

"Good morning, Sadie. How are you?"

"Good morning, Jonny. It does my heart good to see you up and dressed. You're moving fast with those crutches."

"I feel strong today! Will you please feed me?" He laughs. "I'm hungry and ready for a cup of coffee."

She laughs, "Yes, come on, let's go to the kitchen. The coffee is ready. I'll pour you a cup. What would you like for your breakfast?"

"How about eggs, bacon, toast and juice?"

"You've got it! Make yourself comfortable at the table."

She pours him a cup of coffee. He checks the messages on his phone while she cooks his breakfast. He has a text message from Mandy with hearts and smiles.

He shares it with Sadie, "Hope you're feeling better today. I'd like to stop by after work for a quick visit. I'll call or text first. I don't want to disturb you if you're napping. I love and miss you!"

"That's sweet! Thanks for sharing. I really like her. I suppose you do, too?"

"Yes, I like her a lot. I'm in love with her."

Sadie sets his glass of orange juice on the table. She serves the bacon and eggs with toast. She pours a cup of coffee for herself and refills his cup. She sits down with him and they have a friendly chat.

Jonny says, "I'm going to check in with Mandy and Dad via the video chat on my computer in my office. Just for fun, I'm going to try to contact them on a personal level. I want to learn how to use it properly for future business needs."

"Good luck with it, Jonny. Have fun! I'll be here if you need anything. I'll check in on you to make sure you're holding up okay."

"Thanks, Sadie!" He makes his way to his office and sits in his chair at the desk. He's not feeling very comfortable there. He removes a couple of cushions from the sofa in his office. He props up his leg with the cushions on an ottoman.

He wakes up his computer with a shake of the mouse. He notices messages on the screen. His Dad and Mandy were trying to connect with him. It was just a test run for fun with them, too. He's not sure what to do because this is new to him.

He reads the messages and clicks on one to try to reply. He connects with his Dad. They're elated. His Dad explains that he was able to set up the video software without Mandy's help.

Mandy is in his Dad's office and steps in front of the camera. She blows him a kiss. He pretends to catch it in the air. *I'll wait until I can give her a real kiss this evening.*

"Good morning, Mandy! I look forward to visiting with you later today!" He smiles and waves at her.

"Dad? When is my follow-up appointment with the doctor?"

"Next week, I wrote it on the calendar at home. Why? Are you having a problem?"

"No, Blake asked me about it but I didn't know the date. Thank you for taking good care of me. He believes as I do that my recovery is going very well. I feel strong today. I took a shower and dressed without his help. We agreed that I don't need him to visit tomorrow."

"That's great news, Son! We can talk more about it when I return home tonight, Ok?"

"Yes, I'm tired and sleepy now. I've been hobbling around the house. I think I'll cut this short for now. I'll see you both later tonight. Thank you for everything. Have a good day!"

He closes the video screen and puts the computer to sleep. He slowly and carefully makes his way to the kitchen. He pours another cup of coffee. Sadie is not around to help him. He can't carry a cup of coffee while walking with crutches.

He sits at the kitchen table and drinks his coffee. He uses the time to reply to Mandy's text.

He's got cabin fever. He walks to the back door and looks out. It's a beautiful spring day. He sees Sadie on the terrace watering a few of the flowers in hanging baskets. He calls out to her. She hurries over to see if he's okay.

"Sadie, can you please help me through this door so that I can sit outside in the sun. I want to breathe the fresh air."

"Wonderful idea, Jonny! Be careful. Slow and easy." She helps him settle in on a padded lounge chair. She grabs a cushion from another chair to elevate his leg.

"Are you comfortable there, Jonny?"

"Yes, this is perfect. Are you going to stay here with me Sadie? Let me know when you're ready to go in. I'll need your help walking up the step when it's time. Thanks so much!"

"I just have a couple of plants left to water. Then I will take a rest out here with you. I'll be happy to help you up the steps to the house."

"I miss swimming in the pool. Doesn't Dad usually call the Pool Service before the Memorial Day weekend. It should be warm enough to swim this weekend."

"Yes, I believe your Dad plans to have the pool cleaned and ready by this weekend. I'll check the calendar later to see if he has an appointment for them to come out and service it."

"I look forward to having the freedom to swim and do other outdoor activities. I'll see the doctor next week and hopefully he'll say it's okay to remove the braces. Then I'll be free to do the things that I love again."

"You're recovering very well. It'll be great when you have your freedom again. Is there any chance you can check in with your doctor before this big weekend?"

"I'll check with Dad tonight. He made my appointment for me while I was out of it."

"Speaking of being out of it, Jonny, you look relaxed like you might fall asleep any minute. Are you ready to return to the house? I don't want you to get a sunburn."

"Yes, I was telling Dad that I was tired and sleepy when we were video chatting. I'm glad I had this opportunity to sit outside and experience the beauty, feel the sunshine and breathe the sweet fresh air. Seeing Mom's flowers gave me a lift, too. Thank you, Sadie, for helping me to sit out here."

He stands up and hobbles to the door. She helps him on the step and through the door back to the kitchen. He's able to walk with the crutches to his bedroom. He stretches out on his bed and rests for a couple of hours.

When he wakes up, it's lunchtime. He gets up and thinks about what he wants to eat. He's hungry for a sandwich from the Deli. He walks to the garage and notices that his car is there. He remembers driving it to the lake house and his ambulance ride to the hospital. *Thank you, Dad, for taking good care of me and my car. I want to drive my car to the Deli and stop in to see Dad and Mandy. I know that's not a good idea yet.*

He finds Sadie and tells her that he's hungry for lunch. When she asks what he would like, he replies a sandwich from the Deli.

"It's been a long since I've eaten there. Angela used to invite me to eat lunch with her there. Are you sure that you're up to taking the trip, Jonny?"

"Yes, will you drive me there? It'll be my treat. Maybe we can invite Dad and Mandy to join us for lunch, too. It's still early yet."

"Yes, I'll drive you there. I'm excited to get out and about on this beautiful spring day, too. I'll call your Dad and you can call Mandy."

Sadie calls Gary and he's happy to hear the good news. If his son feels up to the trip, he'll enjoy eating lunch with him and Sadie.

"Jonny is hungry and ready to eat lunch now. I'll drive him out there as soon as he's ready to go. He's inviting Mandy to meet us for lunch there, too."

Jonny says, "Mandy said that she'll meet us for lunch at the Deli. I'm ready to go when you are, Sadie."

She tells his Dad, "Mandy will meet us for lunch, too. We're ready to leave here. We'll let you know when we arrive at the Deli. See you soon."

She helps Jonny into her car and places his crutches in the back seat. They arrive downtown and walk in the front door of the building. Mandy and his Dad are overjoyed to meet him and Sadie for lunch. They're waiting for them at the front door.

They greet each other with gentle hugs and big smiles.

"Let's find a comfortable table for you, okay, Son?"

They find a table in a quiet corner. He makes himself comfortable. They ask him what he wants to eat so that they can place the order for him.

"I'd like a Ham and Swiss Cheese on Rye, please. Oh, and a soft drink. It'll be my treat for lunch today. I'm celebrating my quick recovery."

Mandy says, "Thanks, Jonny! We're all celebrating with you! I'm relieved to see you out and about again. This is just wonderful."

Sadie says, "Yes, Jonny, thank you for letting me drive you here and celebrate with you, too."

He hands his personal credit card over to his Dad. He tells them to order anything that they want. "It's my treat!"

They leave him long enough to place their orders. He sits waiting for them to return. He feels grateful to celebrate his ability to go out and about again.

CHAPTER TWENTY-FOUR
LOVEBIRDS

Gary, Sadie and Mandy return to the table in the café where Jonny is waiting. They chat about a variety of things while waiting for their food to be prepared. Jonny shares his experience about Sadie helping him to sit outside on the terrace. He told them how he enjoyed his visit with her. Sitting by his Mom's garden gave him a lift in his spirit.

"Dad, I miss swimming in our pool. Do you plan to have the pool cleaned before the weekend? You usually have it serviced before Memorial Day weekend. Will we have a cookout on the backyard patio again this year? I look forward to swimming again."

"I guess with everything that's happened, I neglected to schedule an appointment with them. I'll make a note to do that. I doubt that they'll have time to service it before the weekend. I've been thinking about having a cookout at the lake house this weekend. Are you up for the drive out to the lake?"

Their food and drinks are being served at their table. They start eating their sandwiches but continue to chat amongst themselves.

"I'm not sure. I hope that I'll feel up to it by the weekend. I enjoy spending time out there. I don't think I'll be able to go swimming in the lake or other activities."

"As soon as I have a date and time, I'll invite Katherine. You can invite Mandy. I invited Sadie and her family to our cookout, too. We'll check the forecast and make final plans based on that."

Mandy laughs and says, "I look forward to an invitation. Sounds like fun. I hope you won't push yourself too hard, Jonny."

Sadie adds, "I look forward to a cookout with the family at the lake house. Getting together over the long weekend is relaxing and fun for the kids."

Jonny's ankle and knee are throbbing and he feels discomfort. He has been sitting in the chair for an hour or more.

"Sadie, when you're ready to return home, please let me know. I'm feeling discomfort in my knee and ankle. I'm ready to go when you are. I need to stretch out on my bed and rest again."

"I'm ready. I'm glad we had a chance to get together and visit here at the café. Thank you! We'll leave now. Let's take you home where you can stretch out."

They all stand and exchange hugs and goodbyes. They follow close to Jonny as he walks to the car. He's moving a little slower due to the discomfort. His Dad helps Jonny into the passenger seat of Sadie's car. She puts the crutches in the back seat. Mandy leans in to the window to say goodbye and I love you to Jonny. They share a quick kiss.

"I'll see you later after work at your house. I hope you feel better and will rest well."

"I look forward to seeing you then. Have a good afternoon."

Mandy and his Dad return to their offices and go back to work.

Sadie drives Jonny home. He tells Sadie, "Thank you for driving me to the Deli. It was fun."

"You're welcome! I thought it was fun, too! The food was delicious."

"I'm going to rest on my bed before I try to do anything else. I'll see you a little later."

He walks straight from the front door to his bedroom. He stretches out on his bed with a couple of pillows under his knee to help ease the discomfort.

Sadie asks, "Would you like an ice pack or two?"

"Yes, please that would be great for easing the pain."

She goes to the freezer and takes out a couple of plastic bags with ice cubes. She wraps a towel around each one and gives them to Jonny. She helps him place them on his knee and ankle. He sets a timer so that he doesn't fall asleep with them.

Sadie hears his alarm and takes the ice packs and disposes of them in the sink. He's asleep. He's worn out from the walk outside and trip downtown.

Katherine calls the house phone to ask Sadie about Jonny's recovery. They talk for several minutes while Sadie updates her on the events of the day. Katherine is surprised at how well he's doing in such a short period of time.

She tells Sadie, "I would like to drop by and check on him. I'll call Gary after work and see if it'll be okay for me to visit tonight."

"That sounds fine. Hope you have a good afternoon. Maybe I'll see you later."

Mandy and Gary were busy all afternoon. They're ready to call it a day. When he arrives home, Jonny is awake and sitting in the living room.

He says, "Hi, Dad! I'm waiting for Mandy to call me. She wants to stop by for a visit after work."

"Hi, Son! I'm going to sit in my recliner for a quick rest before dinner. I had a busy day. Eating lunch with you at the deli was the best part of my day."

Gary's cell phone rings. He answers and hears Katherine say, "Hello, Gary! How are you doing?"

"I'm fine but tired from a long day."

"I called Sadie today about Jonny's recovery. He seems to be doing very well. I told Sadie that I would like to stop by for a visit. But since he's doing so well, he doesn't need a nurse to check on him."

"That's true. He's recovering so well that he doesn't need the visiting nurse in the morning."

"I have another idea. I'm feeling a little shy. I'd like to invite you to dinner with me at my house tonight? I haven't prepared a big home cooked meal in a long time. I'm a little rusty."

"That sounds wonderful and very generous. Thank you. We can cook a meal together! Sounds like fun!"

"Would you like to bring your travel brochures? We can relax after we eat. There should be enough time this evening to look over them. We can have fun discussing the options for your dream cruise."

Gary's eyes light up. He says in an excited tone, "Oh, yes, I really look forward to talking about the dream cruise with you. Is there anything that I can bring for our dinner?"

"I can't think of anything. Is 6:00pm a good time for you to arrive?"

"It's perfect! I'll see you then!"

"Great! Bye for now!"

Gary shares his plans with Jonny. He's very happy for his Dad and very excited about the plans they're making for his dream cruise.

"I don't dream about traveling on a cruise ship but maybe we can take a cruise vacation together."

"You know that I'll really enjoy that, Jon! Would you like to travel with me this summer? Every time that I share my dream to travel, I get the impression it's not something that you want to do."

"That's true, I don't dream of traveling like you do. Maybe I'll feel different about it when I'm at retirement age. Anything that we do together is fun and memorable. I'll travel with you anytime you want me to. Of course, coordinating the time for a vacation will be the hard part."

"Yes, that's why I haven't taken a vacation in a long while. Vacations are not only time consuming but often exhausting."

Jonny's phone rings. He answers it and hears, "Hello, Jonny! How are you doing?" He asks her to please hold on for a second and covers the phone with his hand.

Gary stands up and says quietly, "I'll see you later. I'm going to talk to Sadie and update her on my plans. Then, I'll change my clothes and leave for my dinner date."

"Mandy will be visiting with me here tonight. I'll see you later."

He returns to his phone conversation with Mandy. He invites her to eat dinner with him.

He shares, "My Dad is eating dinner with your Mom at her house, tonight. They're going to talk about travel plans."

"That's exciting. When is a good time for me to arrive at your house for dinner? Can I bring anything?"

"I don't think so. You're welcome to come over anytime. I don't think Sadie is preparing our meal, yet. I'll go check with her. Hold on for another second."

He walks slowly into the kitchen, "Sadie is pulling out a skillet from the cabinet. I guess she's starting to prepare our meal."

Jonny says, "Sadie, Mandy is going to join us for supper. Is there anything that she can bring for our dinner?"

"I can't think of anything. I have everything I need right here."

Jonny tells Mandy, "She can't think of anything that you can bring. I hope that you'll come over soon. I miss you. I look forward to holding you in my arms."

"Oh, Jonny! I miss you, too. I'll be there soon. I just need time to change my clothes and freshen up."

Gary is ready to leave for his dinner date. He's dressed and looking handsome. He stops at the floral shop for a bouquet of spring flowers in a crystal vase for Katherine. He drives over to her house and walks up the sidewalk. He rings the doorbell. She answers it. She's dressed up and looks beautiful. She's wearing her new pearl necklace and matching earrings.

She opens the door and invites him in. He hands her the spring flowers and gives her a sweet kiss on her cheek.

He says, "Thanks for the invitation. What can I do to help you?"

She leads him to the kitchen where she has a roast cooking in the oven. She places the beautiful vase with flowers in the center of the table that is set for two.

"I hope you like roast beef? We can make mashed potatoes and gravy. I have fresh mushrooms that I'm going to bake with garlic and butter as soon as the roast is done. How about a tossed salad? I have several dressings to choose from."

He walks up to her and places his hand on the middle of her back. He says, "Katherine, the food smells delicious! The meal is perfect. I'll make the salad for you."

"How about dessert?"

Gary asks, "What do you like?"

"I don't usually eat dessert. I'm not talented at cooking and baking like Sadie. You're lucky to have her around to cook meals at your house."

"Yes, I'm really spoiled by her talents and her loving care. I don't need a dessert. It's up to you. A cup of coffee while we talk about travel plans will be good enough. Are you okay with that?"

"Yes! I bought a bottle of wine to drink with dinner. Do you like wine?"

"No, I'm sorry, I don't drink anything with alcohol. You can drink it with your meal though."

"I bought it because I thought you might like it. It's okay, I have sweet tea made for us, too."

"Iced tea with our meal sounds good."

"I think the potatoes are done and ready to be mashed. It's going to be loud with this old mixer." She smiles!

Gary removes the roasting pan from the oven at her request and places the prepared mushroom dish in the oven. He sets the timer at the time she suggests.

"Will you please take the roast out of the pan and place it on the platter? I appreciate it. There's a knife beside it that you can use to slice a few pieces for us."

"WOW! Katherine, this roast is tender and the spices are a perfect blend. I don't think you're rusty at all."

They both laugh and smile with loving eyes. She says, "Thank you! I really appreciate that you accepted my invitation and that you're willing to give me a hand."

Gary says, "Why don't you let me run the mixer and whip the potatoes while you make the gravy? I've never had success at making gravy."

"Ok, here you go!"

They work together to complete the meal. She serves the hot food in decorative bowls and places them in the center of the table.

They happily sit down and enjoy their meal. When they're finished, she clears the table and loads the dishwasher. It doesn't take a lot of time to clean up after two people. He offers to help but she declines.

She brews a fresh pot of coffee and sets out two mugs. He waits at the table for her return. He remembers the travel brochures are in the car. He slips out and brings them in. He places them on the table. She also has a few brochures that they can look over.

She pours the coffee into the mugs and sets them on the table. They sit beside each other on the long side of the table. They have a fun time sharing and laughing about places where they want to go and sites they want to see.

They make plans to visit a travel agent together once they decide on their dream destination.

Back at home, Jonny and Mandy enjoy the meal that Sadie prepared. They're eating blueberry cobbler with vanilla ice cream. They're snuggling together, laughing and talking.

Sadie served the meal that she prepared and slipped out quietly. She wanted to give the lovebirds a chance to freely enjoy their time together.

CHAPTER TWENTY-FIVE
SADIE'S EXTENDED FAMILY

Sadie has known the Young Family for well over a decade. She became close friends with Angela while Jonny was a young boy. Their kids played sports together at the park as well as other activities.

Sadie has a grown son and a grown daughter. Her son, Michael is the oldest of the two children. He's married and has two children. He has a little girl, Marie and a little boy, Mike Jr. Marie is five years old and Mike is seven. Her daughter, Amelia, is married and has a little girl, Tanya, three years old. Sadie loves being a Grandmother or Nana as the kids call her.

Angela offered tremendous comfort to Sadie when her husband, Tony, was killed on his motorcycle. He was driving on the highway when he skidded out of control on an icy patch. His accident left her to raise their two children alone.

Angela knew that it would be difficult for Sadie to find a good paying job with benefits. She needed to support her children but didn't have a college education. It would be a major challenge for her to find a long term career.

The Young family lived in a luxurious house. Angela was working at the modelling agency part time assisting her husband, Gary. She would come home after work and take care of her family. She loved her family very much. Taking care of them was NOT a chore. She felt like she needed assistance with the never ending household chores.

She had a passion for growing flowers and vegetable gardens. It was hard work but it was worth it to her. The beautiful pink sweetheart roses fed her soul. They made her feel energized and full of life when she worked with them.

She always put her family's needs first. She had great compassion for Sadie. When Sadie was unable to find a job that would meet her needs, Angela offered her a job to assist her with the household chores.

Sadie said yes without any hesitation. She felt that working for the Young family would truly make her happy as well as her kids. She would be able to afford the mortgage. She didn't have to uproot her kids. She worked only during the time her kids were in school. She felt very fortunate and grateful.

Angela and Gary were wealthy and could afford to pay her well. They were very generous to her especially at Christmas. Sadie and her kids always felt like extended family. There's lots of love and respect to go around even today.

When Angela became ill, Sadie was there taking care of the house and caring for Angela's needs. When Angela passed two years ago, it was devastating to Jonny and Gary.

Since Sadie's children were grown and living away from home, she had extra time on her hands. She could see a need to prepare meals and do other things to help them through their grief process.

Gary and Angela bought this big house on a large lot. They were thrilled more than words can say. They liked the size of the house but they were excited about the extra bonuses. There was enough space for Angela's greenhouse and gardens. Jonny loved the backyard pool. He loved inviting his friends for pool parties and cookouts on their large patio. There's a large multi-car garage which Gary appreciates. He managed to collect a few sport cars over the years.

Another bonus is a beautiful two bedrooms and two bath house built on the left side of the lot. It has an attached garage and a driveway leading to it. It was built as private quarters by the previous owner for their housekeeper. Gary had it remodeled for Sadie to meet her needs. She was told to feel free to redecorate it to please her tastes.

They never considered Sadie to be a servant because she's more like extended family. Gary offered her a chance to live in that house. Her family is also welcome to visit at any time. Sadie is very happy with this arrangement. She didn't like living alone in her old house.

Her grandchildren have overnight visits on the weekends. Sadie truly enjoys living there and considers it to be her home. But now, there are a lot of questions on her mind. She's struggling to find the answers.

Gary is retiring and wants to travel. He won't be around as much for me to cook and care for him. Jonny is no longer a child that needs my help. I'm wondering if my assistance will be needed after Gary retires and travels the world. The house is really too big for just one person. That's the one reason why Gary encouraged Jonny not to move out. Jonny stayed to help his father through his grief, too. I'll ask Gary to sit down with me and have a serious talk. I need to know what my future will hold, too. There are lots of changes ahead for the Young Family.

Today is Friday. It's Memorial Day weekend. Gary invited her and her family to have a cookout with them. No final plans have been made. Sadie thinks, *I'll have a talk with Gary this evening if there's free time available. I need to know what my family role will be. Time passes by too fast and our lives are changing.*

It's in the middle of the afternoon. Gary is working in his office downtown. Jonny has been resting and working in his home office.

The doorbell rings. Sadie answers it. She sees a very tall, rugged, heavily suntanned man standing on the porch. He's so tall that she has to tilt her head back and look up to see his face.

She asks, "Yes, may I help you?"

He says in a very deep masculine voice, "Hello, my name is Charles Roberts. I'm looking for the Young residence."

"This is the Young residence."

"I'm the owner of the Pristine Pool Service. My crew and I have an appointment to clean and service your backyard pool today."

"Oh, we weren't expecting you. I didn't see an appointment on the calendar. I know that Gary and Jonny have been talking about having the pool serviced."

Jonny heard the doorbell and hobbled out of his office. He's excited to hear that the pool service is here. He tells Sadie that his Dad must have scheduled the appointment as he routinely does. Evidently, with all the confusion of my accident he forgot to write it on the calendar.

Jonny asks Sadie, "Do you have time to help me go in and out of the back door? I'd like to be out there while they clean the pool. I can sit on the terrace and watch."

"Yes, I have time. We can sit outside with a glass of iced tea and enjoy the afternoon as well.

Jonny tells Charles, "Please, ask your crew to meet us in the backyard."

Sadie closes the front door. She asks Jonny, "Would you like something to eat with your iced tea? You've been working most of the day."

He checks his watch. He says, "Oh, no, it looks like I missed the lunch time meal. I'm sorry Sadie if that caused you an inconvenience. I'd appreciate a sandwich. Will you join me for lunch on the terrace?"

"Let me help you out to the terrace first. I'll get you settled and return to the kitchen for the iced tea and sandwiches. I'd love to join you for a picnic out there once again. We should be able to watch the pool cleaners work while we eat."

"That would be great, Sadie, thank you."

She helps him out the door and he sits down in a chair on the terrace. They watch as the crew sets up their equipment by the pool. Charles of course is supervising his crew while smiling in the direction of Jonny and Sadie.

Sadie returns to the kitchen and prepares two sandwiches. She places them on plates on a serving tray with two glasses of iced tea.

Charles and Jonny are chatting on the terrace. Charles sees Sadie struggling slightly to carry the tray out the back door. He walks over to her.

"Here, may I help you, Ma'am? I can carry the tray for you."

She's taken by surprise but lets him take the tray. After she steps down off the step, she reaches over and retrieves the tray from his large strong hands. She sets the tray down on the table. Jonny takes his plate and glass of tea. She places her plate and tea on the table.

"Thank you, Sir. That was very kind of you to offer your help with the tray. Would you like a glass of sweet iced tea, too?"

"That sounds really great but I don't think it would be fair to my crew. When we're done with our work, we will drink some cool water."

Sadie sits down and takes a bite of her sandwich. Jonny ate half of his sandwich while Charles and Sadie were talking.

Charles says to Jonny, "You probably don't remember me, but I've been here before. I remember meeting your Mom a few years back when I came out to clean the pool. I remember seeing you play in the backyard while I was here."

"Yes, I do recall seeing you here before."

"I used to be an employee that cleaned and serviced your pool. Now, I'm the owner of the company. It's good to see you again. Hope your injuries will heal soon so that you can enjoy your pool this summer."

"Thank you, Charles. That's great news. I'm glad that you own the company now. Mom and Dad were always happy with the work that you did for them. I'm pretty sure Dad will be happy again this year. Your crew is working hard and it looks like they're doing a great job."

"I better get back to them and make sure everything is going well. I'll be back after we're done for you to sign off on the work order. Thank you, Jonny and Ma'am."

Sadie laughs, "My name is Sadie. You don't have to call me Ma'am."

He smiles and says, "Nice to meet you, Sadie. Thank you very much for your hospitality. I'll be back when we're finished servicing the pool."

"Thank you! Jonny and my grandchildren love swimming in that pool. We appreciate you doing a good job for us."

"I'll make sure that everything is done right." He walks back to the pool. They see that he's talking with his crew but can't hear what they're saying.

Sadie and Jonny enjoyed their sandwiches but they're ready for another glass of iced tea. It's a bright and sunny spring day.

Sadie places the empty glasses and plates on the tray and carries it to the kitchen. She sets the tray on the counter while she moves the plates to the sink. She pours two fresh glasses of sweet iced tea.

She hears a voice behind her asking, "May I have one of those glasses of tea?" It startled her but when she turned around she saw that it was Gary smiling big.

"Oh, Gary, I didn't realize you were home. I can pour a new glass of tea for you."

"I was just kidding you. I noticed you and Jon sitting out on the terrace when I first arrived home. I wanted to change into more comfortable clothes before joining you two outside. I noticed the pool company's van parked outside."

"I'll take this tea out to Jonny and for myself then. Please let me know if you change your mind."

"I'm going out to talk to Charlie first. Then I might sit down to rest with a glass of tea and visit with you and Jon."

He holds the door open for her.

"Hello, Son! How are you feeling today?"

"Hello, Dad! I'm feeling a lot better. I worked in my home office today. It's good to sit outdoors and rest. Are you going to join us?"

"Yes, but I want to check on the pool and the crew first. I must have made the appointment but neglected to write it down on the calendar. My mind has been busy with too many other important things lately. Thank you Sadie and Jon for being here and allowing them to do the job for us today."

He goes out to the pool and shakes Charlie's hand. He's happy to see him again. They talk for several minutes. He returns to the kitchen and pours a glass of tea. He takes it outside and sits with Sadie and Jon on the terrace in a lounge chair. There's a nice cool breeze adding to the lovely evening. It's a great time to sit outside.

He says to both Jon and Sadie, "We really need to get together and talk about making weekend plans. There are lots of topics open for discussion. Let's try to enjoy the Memorial Day Weekend. We can use this time to relax and reenergize for the weeks ahead."

Sadie says, "I have a lot of questions on my mind that I need to ask you. I don't have the answers that I need to make decisions about my future life. I agree that we should enjoy the weekend. I look forward to fun family time together."

"I think it'll be great to have a cookout here on the patio now that the pool is ready to use. The kids will have fun in it. I can lay around on a float in the pool. I will enjoy the sun and water. Those plastic sheets I use in the shower should work well to cover my braces."

"Now, you're talking, Son. Having a cookout here instead of the lake house is an excellent idea."

Charlie walks over to the terrace with a pen and a clipboard. The work is done and he needs someone to sign the worksheet.

"He hands it to Gary. While he's signing it, he says, "Charlie did you meet Sadie? I'd like to introduce you two. Charlie please meet a very sweet lady, Sadie. Sadie, I'd like for you to meet an old family friend, Charlie."

Charlie extends his hand to Sadie and says, "It's really nice to meet you Sadie. I don't believe that we've had the pleasure of meeting cordially before. How are you?"

Sadie lifts her hand to meet his. They shake hands gently. She says, "I don't believe that we officially met before."

Charlie says to her, "Perhaps I'll see you again. Have a great day!"

He tells Gary, "You'll need to test the water again tomorrow morning to make sure the chemicals are balanced. You'll want to be sure the water is safe before your first dive. You can give me a call if there are any problems. Here's my business card."

"Since you don't have any family living here in town, would you like to join us for a cookout this weekend? We haven't decided which day yet. We are thinking of relaxing and enjoying the cookout right here in my backyard. Jon is still recovering from an accident."

"Oh, that's very thoughtful of you, Gary. Will you give me a call and let me know the date and time? I would appreciate a chance to relax and enjoy a cookout with you and your family.

You can reach me at the phone number on my business card."

"Sadie, Jonny and I will make final plans tonight. I'll give you a call tomorrow."

Charlie looks at Sadie, smiles and tips his hat. He asks Gary, "Will this pretty little lady be joining us here for the cookout, too?"

Sadie blushes. Gary replies, "Yes, of course, she's part of our family. We've invited her family to join us, too!"

Charlie takes the pen and clipboard from Gary and gathers his crew together to leave. They're loading up the last of the equipment into the van. *I'm excited about receiving an invitation to the Young family's cookout. I wonder how Sadie is related to the family.*

CHAPTER TWENTY-SIX
ONE BIG HAPPY FAMILY

Sadie ponders, *Saturdays often feel confusing with all the busyness. Most people think that a weekend is time to play after a long work week. Truth is, some people work harder over a weekend than they do all week on their job.*

Sadie was up early brewing coffee and cooking breakfast for Jonny and Gary. While they drank coffee and ate, they discussed the events of the day.

What they need to do today hinges on their plans for the weekend. If they decide to celebrate with a cookout, Sadie will go shopping to buy items that are needed. Gary will need to clean the grill and prepare it for cooking their meal. The food will need to be prepped. Outside furniture will need to be cleaned, patio swept off and tablecloths put in place.

Jonny is walking with one crutch but only when necessary. He's slightly limping but moves along very well. He plans to locate all the pool toys that have been stored away. He wants to clean them. He'll try to blow up the beach balls and inflatable rafts as well as rings. He knows that Sadie's grandchildren will have a good time playing with him and with the pool toys. Swimming and playing in the pool was one of his favorite childhood activities. There's a volley (beach) ball game that he might be able to play in the pool with Mandy. He looks forward to the fun time that they can have this summer.

Gary tests the pool water to be sure that the chemicals are balanced. They're okay according to Charlie's instructions. The pool is ready for swimming and/or playing. *I'll call Charlie as soon we have the plans for our family get-together finalized.*

He gives Katherine a call to check when she'll be available. Katherine doesn't answer her phone. She's outside working with her flowers while the lawn service is mowing and cleaning up her yard.

Jonny calls Mandy to invite her over for a visit. He hopes that she'll help make the plans for the cookout. He really just wants to spend as much time as he can with her. He doesn't feel confident enough to drive with his knee injury.

Mandy doesn't answer her phone because the noise of the vacuum cleaner drowns out the ringtone. After she cleans her apartment, she sits down to rest on her couch. While she sips a cold soft drink, she checks her phone messages. She returns his call and replies to his invitation.

"I've been busy cleaning my apartment this morning. I felt that it's time for spring cleaning. I'm done cleaning for the day but now I'm really exhausted."

"You can rest with me here at my house. I look forward to seeing you."

"I need to rest before I take a shower and dress. Then, I'll give you a call when I'm on my way to your house."

"That sounds great, Babe! Hope to see you soon! I love you and miss you!"

"I love you, too!"

Katherine returns Gary's call. She agrees to drive over to his house for a visit. She wants to rest before she takes a shower and gets dressed. Working outside was exhausting but she'll be ready to leave there soon.

Sadie, Gary and Jonny take a break outside while sitting on the lounge chairs. Sadie made delicious lemonade and served Gary and Jonny a glass with ice. They're relaxed and appear to be lost in thought.

Sadie says, "Have you decided when you'll have your backyard cookout? My family and I are free on Sunday. I'm planning on driving to the cemetery on Monday. I want to visit with Tony and honor him on Memorial Day. He was a military veteran!"

"Even though Angela wasn't in the military, Jonny and I have talked about taking flowers to her in loving memory. We'll need to prepare in advance for a cookout. Sunday will be the best day to relax and have fun. I just hope that Katherine, Mandy and Charlie will be free to join us. Let's say around 3:00pm. That'll give everyone a chance to play in the pool before we sit down to eat our meal."

Jonny adds, "I agree that Sunday afternoon will be the best time for a family get-together. I'll check with Mandy soon because she's planning to visit with me, today. Oh, I should call and remind her to bring her swimsuit, today. When our work is done, we can play and splash around in the pool."

Jonny calls Mandy and she answers, "Hi Jonny, I'm on my way out the door. I'll be there soon."

"I'm calling to let you know that the pool is ready for us to swim and play in today. If you'd like to bring a swimsuit with you, we can have fun after the work is done. Dad has decided on 3:00pm tomorrow afternoon for our cookout. Does that time work for you? Can you join us?"

"Okay, sounds like the perfect time for the cookout. I'll be there! Playing in the pool, today, sounds like fun. I'll go pack my swimsuit and sunscreen. Oh, I guess, I'll pack my sun hat and a change of clothes, too. Thanks, Jonny, for the call. I'll see you soon. Love you!"

"I'm waiting and I love you! 'Bye!"

Katherine arrives at the house and rings the doorbell. Since everyone is sitting around in the backyard, they can't hear it. She walks around the side of the house and sees them sitting there.

She calls out, "Hello! I'm here!"

Gary stands up and walks to the gate and opens it for her. She's dressed in a spring outfit with a sun hat. Gary gives her a welcoming hug and they share a kiss. They're happy to see each other again.

He escorts her to the patio and pulls up another lawn chair for her to join them. Sadie offers her a glass of lemonade. She says that sounds refreshing. Thank you, Sadie!"

"My pleasure. Enjoy your visit with Gary. I'll be right back."

"How are you doing, Gary? You've been on my mind all day. How's your day going?"

"Actually we've all been busy and trying to make plans for a family cookout tomorrow. It seems to be the best day to relax and have fun. Monday, Sadie wants to visit Tony at the cemetery. Jonny and I will visit Angela in loving memory, too."

Yes, I visit with Paul as often as I can. Memorial Day is a good day to do that since he was enlisted in the military when we first met."

"How does 3:00pm tomorrow afternoon sound for our family cookout?"

"Sounds fine to me. I'll be here! You said Sadie and her family will be here, right? That'll be the perfect time to let the kids play before the meal is prepared and ready to eat. I'll do whatever I can to help prepare the food."

Sadie steps outside with a glass of lemonade and hands it to Katherine. She laughs and says, "If you want, we can sit down and make a list of items we need to buy at the store. If you want to shop with me, I could use your help. If not, that's okay, you can stay and visit with Gary. I just thought it was fair to offer you a chance to buy the food as well as prepare it." They smile at each other as though they were the best of friends.

Gary enthusiastically says, "Please don't forget that I'm paying for the food to feed all of us at our cookout. I'll make a list of items that I need to grill the steak, burgers and hot dogs. I really appreciate having a variety of food to choose from. Maybe corn on the cob and potatoes. Mmmm!! Please add my favorites to your list?"

"Sounds like a lot of good food. Leftovers are good but are you sure that we'll need that much for tomorrow?" Sadie laughs.

"It's a lot of food but I'm not sure. Last night I invited an old family friend, Charlie, to join us for our family cookout. I'm not sure what or how much he'll eat. He's a big man and I know that he works hard. I'm not sure if he'll be free to join us. I need to call him to share our final plans."

Jonny says, "OH and yes, Mandy says that 3:00pm is a good time for her. She'll join us tomorrow for the family cookout. I'm really excited to have the families together again. If only, I didn't have to wear these braces. Everything else is perfect."

"I'm glad Mandy will join us tomorrow. We can talk to Katherine and get her expert opinion as a Nurse. Right now, I'm going inside to find Charlie's business card and give him a call. I'll be right back!"

Mandy rings the doorbell while Gary is inside the house. He answers the door and invites her in. He explains, "Jonny is in the backyard sitting on the patio with your Mom and Sadie. Sadie made a pitcher of fresh squeezed lemonade. We're drinking it outside on the patio. Would you like a glass with ice?"

"That sounds delicious. I can pour it myself, if that's alright?"

"Sure, help yourself, dear! I'm going to make a quick phone call. I'll return to the patio soon."

"Ok, see you later then!"

She pours a glass of lemonade with ice and carries it out to the patio. Jonny stands and makes room for her to sit next to him. They say hello and share a warm hug and a kiss as well as big smiles. They cuddle in together after she greets her Mom. The four of them chat amongst themselves while Gary is inside making his call.

Gary calls Charlie's number which is listed on his business card. He answers but it's noisy. They can barely hear each other.

"Hello, Gary! I'm outside on a call right now. The pool cleaning equipment is running. Is everything okay with the service we did on your pool yesterday?"

"Yes, Charlie, everything is fine! Looks like the pool is safe and ready for the family to have fun tomorrow. That's why I'm calling. We set a 3:00pm start time for our cookout tomorrow. Will that time work for you? Will you have time to drive out and join us?"

"Thank you for the invitation. That time will work out just fine. Is there anything that I can bring with me to add to the cookout?"

"We've got everything covered. I can't think of anything. I want you to just come over and relax with us. I remember that you once served in the military. We honor and thank you for your service."

"Thanks, Gary, I feel honored that you remembered my time spent serving our Country."

"Besides, I think Sadie got a kick out of meeting you yesterday. She asked about you this morning."

"She came to my mind a few times today, too. Maybe we can become friends after all."

"Maybe, both of you are single. You're both free to pursue a friendship."

"True. Hey, Gary, I've got to go help my crew. I'll see you tomorrow as close to 3:00 as possible. Thanks!"

They exchange goodbyes. Gary returns to the patio and sits down close to Katherine. They chat and laugh about life in general. They relax and have a good time. They're confident that their work will be finished in time for their cookout.

Sadie stands up and asks, "Is anyone ready for lunch? I can make sandwiches and bring them out for us to eat on the table here."

Katherine and Mandy stand up joyfully and say that they'll help make the sandwiches. Katherine offers to make Gary a sandwich. She asks him what kind he would like and he replies. Mandy offers to fix a sandwich for Jonny and it's the same order. The three of them go to work in the kitchen. In a short time, they have the prepared sandwiches placed on plates and on a serving tray ready to go out the door. Sadie carries a full pitcher of lemonade and another pitcher filled with sweet iced tea. They settle around the picnic table on the patio. It's a beautiful spring day. They enjoy their Saturday afternoon together.

The table is cleared and the kitchen is clean. The two ladies sit down with Gary and write the cookout shopping list.

Mandy helps Jonny with locating the pool toys and prepares them for the pool party tomorrow. She sweeps the patio and washes the tables and chairs.

Jonny is unable to keep up with her because of his knee injury. She reassures him that it's okay. She's excited about the get-together tomorrow. She wants everything to be perfect. She doesn't want him to overdo. She wants to relax and have fun with him at the cookout.

After the shopping list is complete, Katherine and Sadie go to the grocery store. Gary returns to the patio and thanks Mandy for her help. He goes to work cleaning the grill. He's excited about all the activity going on in his backyard. *I'm overjoyed at the thought of our families blending and feeling like "one big happy family".*

CHAPTER TWENTY-SEVEN
BACKYARD COOKOUT

Memorial Day Weekend, Sunday. Gary and Jonny made plans for a family get-together today. At 3:00pm this afternoon they'll gather for a pool party and backyard cookout. They invited Katherine, Mandy, Charlie, Sadie and Sadie's family.

When Sadie and Katherine drove to the grocery store yesterday to buy items for the cookout, they talked about their personal lives. They've become good friends as they discover they have a lot in common.

They learned that their deceased husbands were military veterans. They put their heads together and bought decorations at the party store for the backyard.

Katherine arrives around noon to help Sadie and Gary prepare the food for the cookout. The three of them decorate the backyard before the party guests arrive.

They strategically plant the small flags on sticks in the ground. They drape a banner, '*Happy Memorial Day*' on the patio wall. They place the strings of red, white and blue twinkle lights on bushes and trees around the patio area. They'll look beautiful when the sun starts to set.

Stars and stripes party plates, napkins and cups were purchased to use for the outdoor meal. Decorating with red, white and blue as well as stars and stripes will be a joy to the kids. This is one way of celebrating life and honoring the veterans who fought for our freedom. They miss and love their husbands. *Gone but never forgotten.*

When Gary sees the decorations, he fights back tears. He knows exactly why the ladies decided to decorate in this way. He says, "Thank you! You've touched my heart deeply with an act of loving memory and honor to your husbands. Decorating with red, white and blue colors as well as stars and stripes is patriotic."

Gary says, "Charlie is a military veteran. He'll certainly feel touched by the way you decorated for our cookout. I'm really happy that you two chose to do this."

Sadie says, "Oh, I didn't know that Charlie is a veteran, too! That's nice to know. I'll thank him for his service in the military when I see him this afternoon."

Katherine says, "Me too. I haven't met Charlie, yet. I'll be sure to thank him for his service to our Country as well. I look forward to meeting him. You told me that he's a family friend, right?"

"Right. Angela and I met him many years ago. We used to chat with him while he cleaned the pool. We enjoyed our visits with him. He's a hard worker and trustworthy with the pool service. When I saw him yesterday, I discovered that he owns and operates the pool service now."

Sadie asks, "Would anyone like a sandwich to eat? I have a pitcher of sweet iced tea in the refrigerator to drink. Where is Mandy and Jonny?

I haven't seen or heard from them since Mandy arrived."

Gary answers, "I heard them talking and laughing in the living room earlier. Jonny was telling her about our pool table in the basement. Maybe they wandered down there to play a game. I recall hearing Mandy put out a challenge for him to play a game with her."

Sadie says, "I'll ask them on the intercom if they're hungry for lunch." She goes to the intercom and presses the button for the basement. "Hello, anyone hungry for a sandwich?"

Jonny presses the button to reply, and she hears them laughing. "Yes, we'll be right up. We're hungry and thirsty."

Katherine, Gary and Sadie laugh as they recall memories of "young love".

Sadie asks, "Katherine and Gary if they would like a sandwich and tea?"

They agree that it's a good time to eat lunch. Katherine offers to help in the kitchen. She prepares the sandwiches for Gary and herself. Sadie prepares sandwiches for Jonny, Mandy and one for herself. They all eat at the kitchen table. It's a little too warm outside at this hour.

After they're finished eating, Sadie clears the table and washes the dishes. She's ready to walk back to her house. She wants to freshen up and change into a springtime outfit. Her children and grandchildren are due to arrive there soon.

Katherine and Gary retire to the living room to rest for an hour or so. They'll need energy to prepare and cook the food for their big meal. There are two recliners. Gary sits in his favorite and invites Katherine to relax in the other.

Jonny and Mandy return to the basement to finish their game of pool. Mandy won the game! She wants a chance to freshen up before she changes into her swimsuit. She needs to apply sunscreen and wear a sun hat. They walk upstairs to find her bag. She set it down in the living room when she first arrived.

Mandy asks, "Where is the best place for me to change into my swimsuit and freshen up?"

Jonny replies, "I'm not using the spare room anymore. It's clean if you want to use the rooms for changing and refreshing."

Mandy says, "That's perfect Jonny. Thank you!"

Katherine asks Gary, "Is it okay if I use the spare room to change and freshen up while I'm here?"

"Yes, of course, Katherine. Please make yourself at home."

Jonny changes into his swim clothes, too. He's not sure yet if he'll play in the pool but he'll play with the little kids and Mandy. There are kid games he can play with them. He can play a type of volley ball game using a beach ball. He dresses in his swim trunks as well as a t-shirt and applies sunscreen.

Mandy comes out of the spare room wearing her swimsuit set. She's wearing a spring mini-dress over the top of it. She's also wearing a floppy sun hat and designer sunglasses. She seriously looks like a model. Jonny is blown away by her beauty.

Gary and Katherine are pleased to see their kids so happy and so much in love. They won't change into swimsuits because they'll be busy prepping and grilling the food.

Sadie changes into a modest swimsuit set and applies sunscreen. She loves playing around the pool with her little grandchildren. Yesterday, she purchased a new life jacket for her three-year-old granddaughter. She wants her to be safe around and in the pool. She also wants everyone at the party to relax without the worry. She's sure her parents will watch her every second. Everyone will keep an eye on her.

It's a few minutes before 3:00pm. Two cars pull up into Sadie's private driveway. Her son and daughter arrive on time Sadie opens her front door to invite them in and the kids run up to her. You can hear their sweet little voices, "Nana! Nana! Nana! We're so happy to see you." They throw their little arms around her waist and knees trying to give her hugs. She bends down to pick up the little one. They plant sweet kisses on her cheeks.

She escorts them all into her house. Her son and his wife greet her lovingly. Her daughter and her husband do the same.

She tells them, "Please come on in and make yourselves at home. You can take turns using my spare room and bathroom to change and freshen up. If you forgot the sunscreen, I have extra. Are you all ready to go next door? The pool is ready for you to have a fun time. Gary will start cooking the food on the grill and then we can all sit down and eat together."

The three-year-old responds, "Yes, Nana! I want to play in the pool. I want to eat and I'm thirsty."

"Look at the new life jacket. I bought it for you to wear in the pool. Isn't it pretty?"

"Yes, Nana. Let's go!" Everyone laughs at her sweetness and eagerness.

After everyone in Sadie's house is settled and ready to join the party, the kids hold Nana's hand and they walk over to Papa Gary's house together.

Gary and Katherine are sitting next to each other on lounge chairs drinking iced tea. Mandy and Jonny are sitting in chairs by the pool waiting for the kids to arrive. They're also drinking their iced tea in the stars and stripes cups.

The kids run the last few feet to Papa Gary and greet him lovingly. He's happy to see them, too. He introduces Sadie's family to Katherine and vice versa. They all greet her with smiles. The kids see Jonny and Mandy by the pool. They run over to greet them with hugs and smiles, too.

The parents of the kids are following behind them. They're dressed in swimsuits and ready to have fun with their kids in the large pool.

Sadie offers to serve them glasses of iced tea. There's a variety of beverages to choose from. There's a large ice chest on the patio filled with soft drinks. In the kitchen, there are pitchers of tea, lemonade and fruity drinks for the kids as well as milk.

They accept her offer of iced tea. They use the stars and stripes party cups. Her daughter and daughter-in-law offer to help and carry out the drinks for their kids and husbands. Sadie is happy to have their help.

While Sadie is in the house, she hears the doorbell ring. It's shortly after 3:00pm. She opens the door to see a tall and very handsome looking Charlie!

He smiles, "Good afternoon, Sadie! How are you doing today? Gary invited me to a backyard cookout this afternoon. I hope that I'm not too late."

She smiles at him and says, "No, not too late at all. Come on in. We're all expecting you. First of all, I want to thank you for your service. It's an honor to have you here."

"Thank you, Ma'am, um, I mean Sadie."

"I was in the kitchen pouring cold drinks for my family. Would you like a cold drink before we go out to the patio?"

"Yes, I would. I'll follow you to the kitchen and pour it. No need to wait on me."

"You can use these party cups. What would you like to drink? There's a variety to choose from in the refrigerator and a cooler outside with soft drinks."

"I'll have a glass of iced tea. I'll serve myself and carry my glass out. Is there anything that I can do for you? Do you need help carrying a tray to serve your family?"

"No, my daughter and daughter-in-law already carried their drinks out. My cold drink is still outside. We can go out to the patio now if you're ready? Gary has already fired up the grill. The kids are playing and having a fun time in the pool. What about you, do you swim?"

"Sometimes, but as tall as I am, I feel really awkward."

"As you already know, Gary's pool is large. Maybe you'll find it enjoyable today. I'm ready to go out to the patio now."

She opens the back door and walks down the first step. He holds the door open so that she's secure on the steps. He sees Gary at the grill and walks out to greet him. They shake hands and Gary welcomes him to the family party.

Charlie asks, "Is there anything that I can do to help you grill the food? I have lots of experience."

Gary says, "Not at the moment. I just started the fire. It needs to heat up a little more. Sadie and Katherine have already wrapped the food in foil to be grilled. They'll bring the food out for me soon."

"I'm impressed by the decorations that you have in your backyard. I really enjoy seeing the flags. All the red, white and blue lights as well as the festive picnic supplies add a nice touch."

"We owe Sadie and Katherine thanks for the decorations. Sadie's and Katherine's deceased husbands were military veterans. They decorated with flags, stars and stripes in honor of their loved ones. They didn't know until this morning that you're also a veteran."

"I must thank them for being so thoughtful. I'm deeply touched by their impressive decorations. They add a special touch to your backyard party."

Katherine walks over to Gary and hands him a gift. She bought him a stars and stripes apron, heat resistant mitts and pot holders. Also a cute little chef hat that is all part of a matching set. He smiles, thanks her and gives her a hug. He puts on the apron and hat.

She turns to Charlie with a smile and says, "Thank you for your military service, Charlie. Gary told me that you're a veteran."

Charlie says, "I'm sorry for your loss. Gary told me about your husband. He was a military veteran, too. Thank you for the way you decorated here with stars and stripes. I appreciate the Memorial Day decorations."

"Yes, thank you Charlie. Sadie and I planned the decorations together. It turned out better than we expected."

Katherine turns to Gary and says, "Do you want me to carry out the platters with the food for the grill? Is it time yet?"

"Yes, I'll help you in the kitchen and you can help me place the food on the grill. Thank you."

Gary says, "Charlie? Sadie is playing over at the pool with the kids. Maybe you'd like to join her or at least sit in a chair by the pool. They're playing a game that you can watch."

"Sure, good idea. Let me know if I can help with anything. I'm not used to standing or sitting idly."

"OK, but I hope that you'll relax and enjoy your time out here with us."

Gary and Katherine walk toward the house to the kitchen. Katherine whispers, "You don't have to wear the hat. I gave it to you to share a smile. I thought it was a cute matching set. You look cute in it!"

They carry out platters and start placing the food on the grill. There are potatoes and corn on the cob wrapped in foil. He grills the steaks, hamburgers and hot dogs. Cheese slices are placed on a few burgers for anyone that prefers cheeseburgers.

They look around and hear Charlie and Sadie laughing. She introduced him to her family and now the kids are tossing the ball to him. He enjoys Sadie's company and her family.

The red, white and blue twinkle lights add ambience and brings joy to the little ones. The weather is perfect with a soft gentle breeze.

Jonny walks out of the house with his camera in hand. He takes a lot of random shots as well as asking people to SMILE. He takes a lot of fun photos by the pool. He sets up the camera to take pics of Mandy and her Mom. Pictures of his Dad at the grill are a delight. Mandy takes the camera and asks Jonny and his Dad to smile. He also takes family photos of Sadie with her children and grandchildren. Charlie gets in on the fun and poses with Sadie for a memento. Jonny still has a strong passion for photography.

Everyone is hungry and thirsty. They're all getting out of the pool. They wrap up in beach towels and dry off. They wear t-shirts and mini-dresses to cover their swimsuits.

Gary announces that the grilled food is done and ready to eat. Katherine places buns, condiments and chips on a separate table. The festive paper plates, napkins and cutlery are in place. They work together to set all the food on serving platters and in dishes on the same table, buffet-style.

They all gather around and seat themselves at the outdoor picnic tables. Sadie's children are filling her grandchildren's plates first. Sadie pours the beverages and takes care of anyone that needs help. There's plenty of elbow room at the tables for everyone to sit together.

After they finish eating, Sadie's children and grandchildren are ready to return to their homes. The kids give lots of hugs and kisses goodbye. They leave feeling very happy and sleepy.

The three couples take a late evening dip in the pool. They play volley (beach) ball. The three men team up against the three women.

Jonny takes a chance and removes the braces while he's in the pool. He's not feeling any pain nor resistance. He believes this is a very good sign.

They're all having a fun time. There's lots of laughter. Playing like kids proves to be refreshing and energizing. The fun activity is a great stress and tension reliever. The backyard cookout and pool party is a great success. They enjoy their time together until late at night.

CHAPTER TWENTY-EIGHT
MEMORIAL DAY

Everyone had a busy weekend. Sadie is in the kitchen brewing the morning coffee. Gary and Jonny are sleeping in. They're thankful for a chance to rest for the week ahead. The aroma of the fresh coffee awakens them. They take their time getting out of bed and getting dressed.

Sadie sips her first cup of coffee while sitting out on the terrace. It's another beautiful spring day. She enjoys the Memorial decorations that are still on the patio. She's reminiscing about the party last night with her family. Last night, Charlie asked her out for a dinner date. She's trying to decide whether she should say yes or not. It's been too many years since she went out with anyone. She's devoted her life to her children, grandchildren and the Young family. *I plan to visit Tony at the cemetery today. I'll share my thoughts with him as well.*

Gary and Jonny walk downstairs to the kitchen. They notice Sadie sitting out on the terrace looking like she's lost in thought. They each pour a cup of coffee and sit down at the kitchen table. They don't want to disturb her. They want to give her time to enjoy the beautiful morning.

They chat about their plans for the day. Jonny says, "I'll pick up the pool toys and store them away. I was too tired last night to do it. We'll want them to be in good shape the next time we have a pool party. The party was lots of fun. Thank you, Dad!"

"My pleasure, Jon! I had a wonderful time! It was a lot of fun for me, too. I think everyone had a good time. One of the things I want to do is visit with Angela today. Do you want to visit with your Mom today, too?"

"Yes, Dad! There will be lots of people out visiting their loved ones on Memorial Day. We can stop at our usual florist and pick up something special for her. I believe that she's watching over us and smiling."

"I believe that, too, Jon! Yes, I want to bring flowers to the cemetery, also."

Sadie hears their voices and returns to the kitchen. She says, "Good Morning, are you two ready for breakfast?'

Jonny asks, "Are you up to cooking for us, Sadie? You appear to be lost in thought this morning."

"Sure, I'm thinking about what I want to do with my time, today. First of all, I'll cook your breakfast. Then I want to leave for the cemetery to visit with Tony. I'll stop for a special arrangement at the floral shop on the way there."

Gary says, "Jonny and I plan to visit with his Mom today, too. We could plan on driving out their together if you want company."

"If I thought my visit would be short, I would say yes. I have lots I want to share with Tony. It does me good believing that he's watching over me still."

Gary says, "I understand. If you need someone to talk to, I'm a good listener." Jonny nods in agreement and says, "I'm here for you, too, Sadie! It seems like something is troubling you."

"If I can't work it out, I'll share my problem and ask for a little advice. Thank you both for caring."

Sadie asks them what they want to eat for breakfast. They ask her to cook their favorite food. They pour a second cup of coffee and chat while Sadie prepares their meal. She fries bacon and eggs. She also makes Texas Toast.

Jonny stands up and sets the table for three. He pours the orange juice in glasses. He finds jelly for their toast and places it on the table. They sit down together and chat while they enjoy eating their breakfast.

Sadie walks back to her house. She freshens up and changes her clothes for the drive out to the cemetery. She stops at the floral shop. She buys a wreath that is designed with red, white and blue ribbon. Fabric with stars and stripes is entwined with the ribbon and flowers. The flowers are red, white and blue carnations. It's a Memorial Day wreath that she believes will honor Tony.

Jonny hasn't driven his car since the accident. Gary drives the two of them to the floral shop and then to the cemetery. They purchase two special flower arrangements. One from Gary to Angela and the other from Jonny to his Mom.

They arrive at the cemetery noting that it's a busy place. There are Memorial Day decorations as well as flags by the headstones. It's a sight to behold. They both have tears in their eyes. The tears are not only for Angela and his Mom but for all the loved ones that are being honored there.

They take time to sit on the bench and reflect on the love they shared as well as saying their prayers for her. Gary is also thinking how Angela might feel about him and Katherine. He believes that he'll never stop loving Angela. If he were the one that passed on first, he believes that he would want Angela to move on and be happy with a new love. Their love will never die. Life is too short!

They return home and decide to clean up the backyard. They plan to leave the Memorial Day decorations up throughout the day.

Jonny picks up the clutter by the pool. He deflates the rafts, rings and the beach ball. He folds them and places everything in a storage bin. He wheels it back to the storage area until the next pool party. He lines up the chairs by the pool making the area appear neat and clean. He gathers up a few beach towels that were left behind and takes them inside to the laundry room. *I'm happy the pool is ready to use again. I'd like to go for a swim today but I want to invite Mandy to join me.*

Gary is busy cleaning the grate on the grill. Gathering up the utensils from last night and washing them as well. All the trash from the picnic was collected in trash bags last night. He carries the bags to the front yard to be picked up tomorrow morning. He rearranges the tables and lines up the chairs on the patio. Well, I think that the patio and pool area look neat again. Maybe Katherine would like to visit today.

Sadie is home after her visit with Tony. She's feeling down and struggling with mixed emotions. She knows that life must go on. She's been doing that for years now. She still misses him and remembers the love that they shared. Sharing her thoughts and feelings with Tony cleared her mind.

She's still not sure what to do with the invitation from Charlie. She walks up to the house where she sees Gary and Jonny resting on the patio. She asks Gary, "Is it okay with you, if I invite Charlie to have lunch with us?"

"Sure, is everything okay, Sadie? Do you want to talk about it? You really look stressed and I'm concerned."

"Yes, Gary, Charlie asked me to go out with him for dinner. I shared my feelings with Tony and thought about it a lot. I'm just not sure what's the right thing to do. We laughed and talked a lot last night. We had fun together visiting with my children and grandchildren. He seems like a really nice man. I haven't been out on a date in many years. I've devoted my life to my children, grandchildren and to the Young family."

"From what I know about Charlie, he's a good man. He's hard working and trustworthy."

"If I invite him to lunch today, I'll have a chance to talk to him more about it. We can get to know each other a little better."

"Sounds like a good idea to me. I might not be around for lunch today. I thought about inviting

Katherine over but I recalled her plan to visit Paul at the cemetery. I'll call her now and make a plan for us to get-together. Maybe we can spend a little time out at the lake house."

"The lake house is a great place to spend a warm spring day. Hope your plans work out to be fun for the two of you."

Jonny says, "I'm planning to call Mandy to invite her to swim with me today. If you're busy with Charlie, we can prepare our own lunches. Hope you have fun on your lunch date."

"I thought about inviting him to my house but I don't feel like I know him well enough to do that. I appreciate that you're okay with us having lunch here. The day is beautiful. We can visit here on the terrace while we eat lunch. Thank you! Hope you two have a fun and happy day, too."

Jonny pulls out his cell phone and calls Mandy. Gary moves to the living room to sit in his recliner. He calls Katherine on her cell phone. Sadie uses her cell phone to call Charlie while sitting at the kitchen table.

Jonny is elated that Mandy agrees to swim with him in the pool. She plans to go with her Mom to visit her Dad at the cemetery first.

Gary makes plans to visit with Katherine after she visits with Paul at the cemetery. They haven't decided yet where they'll meet.

Sadie calls Charlie and invites him over for lunch. He accepts the invitation. He'll arrive there within a half an hour.

Mandy arrives at her Mom's house. Mandy drives her Mom first to a local florist to buy a Memorial Day wreath and then to the cemetery. Katherine takes several minutes drying away tears and closing her eyes to pray and reflect. Mandy does the same. Paul died last year so the heartache and the memories are still fresh. They love him and miss him very much. Keeping her thoughts from Mandy, Katherine wonders about Paul. What if she wants to move on with someone like Gary? Life is short! She cares about Gary and his family. She's lonely without Paul but has found happiness feeling like she's part of the Young family.

Mandy and Katherine comfort each other with warm hugs. They silently say their goodbyes to him in their own loving way. They go back to the car and Mandy drives them home.

Mandy tells her, "Mom, Jonny invited me to swim with him in the pool today. I'm going to do that while the weather is still warm. It'll be chilly again once the sun starts to go down."

"Gary called and asked me to meet with him today. We haven't decided where, yet. I guess Sadie is having lunch with Charlie at his house on the patio. He wants to give her space to chat with him."

"Jonny mentioned something about that, too. We won't bother them. We'll play in the pool and take care of ourselves. We'll give her the freedom to spend time with Charlie."

"Have fun with Jonny at the pool. I'll keep in touch and let you know what's happening today with Gary and I."

Katherine calls Gary to let him know that she's free to meet with him. He suggests that he pick her up to drive out to the lake house for a little quiet time. They can sit at the gazebo for a picnic lunch. If she's up for it, they can eat dinner at Ted's Steakhouse where they first met.

She thinks it's a great idea. If he's paying for dinner, she wants to provide the picnic lunch. He agrees. He tells her that I'll drive out to pick you up as soon as possible. It's lunchtime and he's hungry.

Sadie waits for Charlie before she prepares lunch. She doesn't know what he likes to eat. The doorbell rings. She walks to the door and opens it. It's Charlie looking tall and handsome. She invites him in. He hands her a bouquet of springtime flowers in a vase.

They walk together to the kitchen and she places the vase on the kitchen table. She says, "Thank you for the beautiful flowers. You didn't have to do that."

"You're right but I want to thank you for your invitation for lunch."

"I invited you over here so that we can have a talk about your dinner invitation. I'm not sure how to answer you. I would like to get to know you better before we go out on a dinner date. I haven't been out with anyone in a very long time."

"I understand. This is a good way for us to learn more about each other. I appreciate your willingness to give me a chance. I really enjoyed visiting with you and your family last night. I hope that we can at least be friends and have fun spending more time together."

"Thank you, Charlie. I don't know what kind of lunch you would like to eat. I can make sandwiches or something else that you might suggest. What would you like to eat?"

"A sandwich is great. I usually like cheeseburgers with all the trimmings but I also like cold cuts. What do you have to offer?"

"We can eat cheeseburgers with all the trimmings. I have hamburger patties in the freezer. How do you like it cooked? I like mine medium rare."

"Medium is my favorite with cheese, lettuce, tomato, pickles, onion and mustard."

"I like all of that except for mustard. I prefer mayo. I have hamburger buns in the bread box. I guess we're in luck. We can use leftovers from the cookout last night. Would you like a glass of iced tea while you wait?"

"Yes, thank you. I can help you prepare the lettuce, tomatoes and onions while you fry the patties on the griddle. You'll have to find the things that I need."

"Thank you for being so thoughtful."

She locates the cutting board and a sharp knife and sets them out on the counter. He finds slices of cheese in the refrigerator. He rinses a couple of lettuce leaves and slices a tomato as well as the onion. He places them on a serving platter including the sliced pickles.

She sets two plates on a tray to carry outside to the patio. They assemble their cheeseburger sandwiches just the way that they like them. The tray is ready to carry outside. Charlie is quick to pick it up and carry it for her. She pours a glass of iced tea for herself and picks up his glass from the table. They both carefully make it out the door to the patio. They sit at the picnic table to eat and to talk.

Sadie says, "Thank you for your help. We make a good team." She smiles sweetly. "I hope you enjoy your meal."

Charlie says, "How nice that the Memorial Day decorations are still up and the flags are waving in the breeze. Very nice!"

They notice Mandy and Jonny playing with the beach ball in the pool. They're laughing and batting the ball across the net. Stealing a kiss or two when they're close enough to do so.

Sadie and Charlie laugh and try to avoid looking in their direction. They have their own memories of young love. They ask and answer several personal questions trying to learn more about each other.

Gary and Katherine enjoy their lunch in the gazebo at the lake house. The day is still young. No one is really sure what the evening will hold. There are lots of mixed emotions to deal with.

On this Memorial Day everyone is trying to live their life to the fullest. Lots of love, honor and respect are powerful feelings between the members of these families. They're trying to make new and happy memories in the present. They won't forget their loved ones or their memories from the past.

CHAPTER TWENTY-NINE
GOOD OLD SUMMERTIME

It's the first week of June. Just to play it safe, his Dad drives Jon to his follow-up appointment. He hasn't been behind the wheel of his car since his accident. They're surprised that he's pain free even after playing in the pool yesterday.

His doctor sends him to radiology for X-rays to double check his ankle and knee. The doctor examines all of the injuries and reads the X-rays. He's absolutely surprised by how quickly Jonny has healed. All of the injuries from his accident are totally healed. The doctor gives him a clean bill of health.

Jonny is really strong and healthy. He had a lot of determination and fought hard during his recovery to be whole. His Dad and Mandy were his inspiration. He was determined to be there for his Dad and the love of his life, Mandy. He feels like his Mom is watching over him which also contributes to his frame of mind. Sadie has been like a second Mom. She's taken really good care of him over the years and while he was in bed recovering from this accident. He has a lot of positive reasons why his recovery was fast.

Jonny is anxious to return to work and other activities. He's looking forward to playing golf with his Dad on Father's Day. That's one of his favorite family traditions.

He looks forward to taking Mandy over to the lake house. He still dreams of them playing at the lake. He wants to relive the fun childhood memory of swinging out over the lake on a rope and splashing down into the water. He wants to share this fun with Mandy.

He longs to do all of his favorite family traditions that are a special part of his life. His favorite season of the year is Summer! Boating, skiing, fishing and hiking are activities that he longs to do with his Dad. He's hoping that Mandy will enjoy doing these things with him, too.

Jonny says, "Thank you, Doctor. I'm grateful that your examination proves that I'm healed. I can do the things that I love to do again."

Jonny asks his Dad, "Please can you drive us to the office now? I'm anxious to go back to work. I'd like to stop at the Deli first to eat a sandwich. I'm feeling nervous and didn't eat very much for breakfast."

"I was nervous for you, too. It's amazing to me how fast you have healed. I've watched you exhibit lots of strength and determination. If you're up to going to the office, I'll drive us there. I'll enjoy eating lunch at the deli with you."

"I'll call Mandy and ask her to meet us. I can share the good news with her. Oh, on second thought, would it be an inconvenience for you to drive me home first? I'd like to drive my car again. That will give you the freedom to leave the office early if you want."

"Not a problem. I'm happy that you're able to drive again. You'll have the freedom to enjoy the evening out with Mandy after work."

Gary drives Jon home. Sadie is working in the kitchen. She asks if the doctor appointment went well. They give her an update that he's healed. He's able to return to work and other activities.

They could see the look of relief on her face. She hugs Jonny and feels grateful that he's doing what he loves to do again.

She offers to prepare their lunch. They tell her that they need to go back to work. Gary explains that he drove Jon home to pick up his car.

"If you're not busy, Sadie, you can drive out with me and join us for lunch at the deli again. Jonny is going to call Mandy to meet us there. We'll update her on his recovery at that time."

"I have previous plans." She blushes and smiles. "Maybe next time. I agreed to meet Charlie for lunch mid-afternoon today. His favorite sandwich is a cheeseburger. He invited me to his favorite fast food restaurant. He assures me that we'll be able to relax and chat during our time together."

Gary says, "Sounds like fun for you Sadie. I'll have to check out that restaurant sometime. I enjoy eating cheeseburgers, too. Hope you have lots of fun with Charlie." Jonny smiles and nods in agreement.

"I'll call Mandy before I leave here. If you want to call Katherine and invite her, please do."

"No, Katherine has plans for today, too. I'm going to leave here now. I'll meet you at the deli."

Jonny takes out his cell phone and calls Mandy at work. When she answers the phone, he asks her if she would like to join him and his Dad for lunch at the Deli. She agrees to meet them. She's anxious to know how the doctor's visit turned out. He tells her that it's all good news.

Gary and Jonny end up in the garage at the same time. Jonny pulls out in his car and Gary is following close behind. Gary is feeling a bit nervous about Jonny driving again.

Jonny and Gary drive the same route to the downtown office. They arrive at the building parking lot and park close by. Gary is relieved to see that Jonny is able to drive without any problems. Jonny is also relieved and very happy to drive without pain.

When they walk in the building, they see Mandy waiting by the door of the Deli. They greet each other but resist sharing affection in a business setting.

They order their sandwiches and sit at a quiet table in the corner. Gary orders tea while Jonny and Mandy order soft drinks. While they wait for their sandwiches to be served, they chat about the appointment with the doctor. Jonny updates Mandy on the results by telling her that he's totally healed.

Gary tells her, "I'm thankful that Jon is eager to return to work."

Mandy says, "Jonny, your Dad and I have worked long hours together while you were away. I've prepared a PowerPoint presentation to share with you. Your Dad and I met with administrative staff and other top executives. We all worked together to see the big picture of where the businesses stand today."

"When will you share the PowerPoint presentation with me?"

"We can do that today in your Dad's office at the conference table. Is that okay with you, Gary?"

"Yes, that should work out perfectly fine. It's a great way to update Jon on what happened while he was away. He's anxious to get back on track. Viewing your presentation together in my office is perfect."

Mandy continues to explain to Jonny, "The businesses are strong. We've all come to the conclusion that you'll do a great job. Are you ready to take over your Dad's responsibilities and go to work in his office?"

Jonny says, "Well, not today, not right this minute. I'd at least like to view your presentation first." They all laugh.

They eat their sandwiches and continue to chat. Gary is sharing about an appointment he has with his attorney this week. Mandy is rejoicing over Jonny being well enough to return to work. She missed him a lot. Jonny is feeling nervous about the takeover but he feels confident that his Dad and Mandy will be there to support him.

Mandy shares that she's making plans to enroll in night classes in the fall to receive her master's degree in business. Jonny confesses that he took a few online classes at night. When his Dad first asked him to take over the business, he took a few classes to work toward a business degree. He's planning to work on it again in the fall. He really has a strong desire to enjoy the family fun this summer.

Gary shares with Jon, "After the appointment with the attorney, the paperwork will be in place for you to own half of the businesses. I'll still own a half and will be around to help out when needed. We can text, call or video chat to troubleshoot a problem. I'll give you the power to make the major decisions and oversee the operation of our businesses. I have lots of faith and confidence in you, Son."

Mandy says, "I really appreciate all the hard work that goes into your businesses and I'll be here to support both of you for as long as I'm needed. I'm totally in favor of your businesses being successful and prosperous. I'm willing to do what I can to help make that happen."

Both Gary and Jonny say, "Thank you!"

Gary tells Jonny and Mandy, "After the appointment with the attorney, we should sit down together to determine a final retirement date. We'll need to put out memos to everyone down the line to keep them in the loop. It'll be the same day that Jonny will officially take over my office, too. It'll be a day to celebrate!"

They're finished eating. They agree that this would be a good time for Mandy to share her presentation. They go upstairs and settle in at the conference table in Gary's office.

Her presentation is very impressive and filled with lots of valuable information that Jonny needs to know. If it wasn't for his accident, he would have been present in the meetings. He's very thankful for the outstanding work that went into the presentation by his Dad and Mandy.

Mandy has spent lots of hours putting forth effort to learn the businesses inside and out. She loves her job and of course Jonny. The future is looking bright for his Dad to retire happily. *I want to talk to Jonny about planning a big retirement celebration for his Dad. It would be fun to rent one of the party rooms at the Imperial Inn. Their restaurant can cater the food for a big party. We can invite his friend Ted Harris and family. I'll need Jonny's help to make a list.*

After the presentation, they sit at the conference table and talk about this and that. It's a chance to make other future plans as well. Gary wants to make plans for his dream vacation but doesn't want to leave Jonny feeling abandoned. He hopes that Jonny will be comfortable in his office before he leaves on a vacation halfway around the world. They discuss this amongst themselves.

Gary brings his calendar over to the table. They take a look at it together. Jonny shares that he wants to have a Father's Day celebration before he plans his escape. His Dad agrees that he'll enjoy spending that special day with his son. He'll plan a vacation after that date. He explains that Katherine will go with him to a travel agency and they'll obtain more information about dream cruises. He'll let them know what they decide.

Jonny and Mandy are both happy for their Dad and Mom. They're glad that they'll travel together and share the fun. They know that their Mom and Dad dream of seeing the world.

Gary is ready to leave for home. Mandy and Jonny agree that they'd like to leave, too. It's been a long day for Jonny.

Jonny says, "I'll see you later, Dad. I want to spend a few minutes with Mandy to talk about plans for tonight. I'm not planning to be home for supper. Will you please tell Sadie for me?"

"See you later, Jon. I'm not sure what my plans are for tonight. Sadie had lunch plans with Charlie. I don't know if she'll be home to cook supper tonight."

Mandy says, "Mom is playing cards with a group of ladies at her friend's house tonight. I'll see you later, Gary. I hope you have a good evening."

Gary goes down to his car and drives home. When he arrives, he realizes that Sadie is not in the kitchen. He sees her sitting outside on the terrace.

He steps out the door and quietly asks, "Is it okay if I join you, Sadie?"

She replies cheerfully, "Sure! If you're up for a chat, I would really like to speak with you about a few things."

"Yes. Is it okay if I take a few minutes to catch my breath and switch gears?" He chuckles. "It's been a long stressful day! I'm interested in what you have to say but I need to clear my mind a little first. There are things that I'd like to share with you, too. How did your lunch date work out with Charlie?"

"We enjoyed the cheeseburgers. We talked and laughed a lot. He's got a great sense of humor. I like him more each time I see him."

"That's great Sadie! I'm happy that you and Charlie are friends. Do you have plans for dinner tonight?"

"No, not tonight. Would you like for me to start preparing a meal for you and Jonny?"

"No, Jonny asked me to tell you that he won't be home for dinner tonight. Would you like to eat out for dinner tonight? Katherine is busy playing cards with her friends. We both have a lot to talk about. We can go to Ted's Steakhouse and talk about things over dinner."

"That sounds wonderful. I haven't eaten out in a steakhouse in a long time. Thank you so much for inviting me. Should I change into something fancier?"

"No, I'm going to change into something more comfortable. We can just relax out on the patio at the restaurant and enjoy the beautiful night. The garden there is lovely. I think you'll like it."

"Okay, I'll go home and freshen up a bit. I'll be back in about twenty minutes or so."

"I'll be ready to go when you return. Would you like to ride in the convertible?"

"Sure, I'll pin my hair up and wear a hat." They laugh.

She walks to her house. He walks upstairs to change into a sporty outfit. Sadie is already dressed in a casual spring time outfit. They're dressed perfectly for a dinner meal on the patio.

She returns to the terrace where he's waiting for her. He escorts her to the garage. He opens the passenger door for her. Once they're settled, he drives to the Agency's parking lot. He loves walking through the gardens. Sadie enjoys walking through Angela's garden, too. She hasn't seen the garden since last year. They walk to the patio just outside the restaurant where they find a table in a quiet area. They sit down on padded chairs by a table covered with a white linen tablecloth.

The waiter brings out two glasses of water along with two menus and sets them down on the table in front of them. They say thank you with a smile.

Gary encourages her, "Please order whatever you want to eat. It'll be my treat. I'm going to order a steak with potatoes. Their food is delicious here, Sadie, but not as good as your cooking."

"Mm! I had beef today already. I'm going to try their boneless BBQ Chicken with a baked potato. Thank you so much! This is a special treat for me. This atmosphere is a great place for us to talk about important issues."

The waiter returns to take their orders. While they're waiting for their food to be prepared, they sit silently for a few minutes. They relax while breathing in the fresh air. The air is sweet with the fragrance of flowers. The gentle breeze adds to a very pleasant summertime atmosphere.

CHAPTER THIRTY
EBB AND FLOW OF LIFE

The waiter serves Gary and Sadie their meals on the patio at Ted's Steakhouse. The food looks delicious. They're hungry but they're anxious to talk about future plans.

Gary starts the conversation by sharing about the lunch at the deli with Jonny and Mandy. He updates Sadie about their conversations. He tells her about the time they spent in his office. How they looked at the calendar trying to set up an official retirement date. He wants her to know that Mandy showed Jonny her impressive PowerPoint presentation. He tells her about the appointment with the attorney that will officially make Jonny a business partner.

"Jonny asked me to wait until after Father's Day before I leave on my vacation. We both enjoy spending time together celebrating that special day. Maybe we'll play a game of golf together. That's been a family tradition since he was in high school."

"Have you and Katherine decided on a destination and timeline for your cruise? I know that you're anxious to take a vacation after you officially retire."

"We have plans to visit a travel agency together. The agent can help us figure out a timeline once we decide on a destination."

Sadie asks, "Can I take this time to share with you what's on my mind, Gary? I've had a few sleepless nights worrying about what my role will be with your family once you've retired. I'm concerned about where I'll live once you no longer need me to work at your residence."

Gary replies, "I'm so glad we're having this conversation, Sadie. I've also thought about you and your welfare. You've been a big part of my family and we all love and care about you. First of all, I hope that I can set your mind at ease by telling you that you'll always be welcome in our family. I have enough funds set aside that I can pay you to work for us for as long as you want to."

Sadie smiles and looks very relieved. She says, "Thank you, Gary. That was a big concern of mine. I know that you'll be traveling and away from home. When you're not there, there's not a lot for me to do. I can still care for Jonny but he's not at home as much now that he's spending more time with Mandy."

Gary says, "Your job might change from day to day but it's financially secure. I really can't predict how things will change. We still need your assistance with housekeeping. We'll always appreciate your hard work in that area."

"Housekeeping is not as easy as it used to be. It's probably a good thing that I'll have less to do. Getting old makes it harder to climb the stairs especially with a full laundry basket. But I'll always do my best work for you."

Gary says, "As long as you want to work for us, we'll appreciate your ability to do so. Thank you very much for everything that you've done for us in the past."

Sadie says, "It's been my pleasure. I really care about you and Jonny, too. I'm happy to do whatever I can to make your lives easier."

Gary says, "I hope that you'll continue to live in your house. It's paid for and we like having you around. We appreciate your loving kindness. Please feel free to invite your family and Charlie over to use the pool and have fun in the backyard. I trust your judgement. You can feed and entertain them in my house."

Sadie says, "I will love living in my beautiful house as long as you want me to be there. Thank you for your generosity. It gives me great pleasure to be around and cook your meals. I'm happy to do family things with all of you. Another concern is whether you remarry or Jonny brings in a wife. Will I still have my place there? Two women in the kitchen usually doesn't work out very well."

Gary says, "I don't think that'll be happening anytime soon, Sadie. I'm just not sure what to say about that. I know that in my mind, you'll still be welcome as part of our family. If I were to marry Katherine, it won't be a problem at all. You two are friends and have had a good time in the kitchen together."

Sadie says, "That's true. As long as it's okay with you, I'll continue on as I have been. I'll just play it by ear one day at a time. Thank you very much for the delicious dinner. I appreciate the update on your future plans."

She wipes tears from her eyes as she says, "Thank you for relieving my fears. I don't have the proper words to express how grateful I am. I'm happy knowing that I can continue working for you. I'm overjoyed knowing that I can continue to live in my house. I'll always be grateful that you accept me as part of your family."

Gary says, "I'll always be grateful, too, that you've become part of our family." He also dries tears from his eyes.

He asks, "Would you like dessert, Sadie? They have tiramisu and great coffee. It's not as good as yours but I think you'll enjoy it. If you would like dessert, I'll have a cup of coffee with you. Otherwise, I can pay the bill and we can leave."

Sadie giggles softly, "I'm full from my meal. I had lots of butterflies fluttering around, too. I'll pass on your offer to eat a dessert. If you still want coffee, I'll join you in drinking a cup. There's a cool breeze blowing through here."

"Yes, we can take time to relax over a cup of coffee. I'll order it when the waiter comes back to check on us. I'm really enjoying the cool evening breeze out here in the garden. The twinkle lights will be on soon. They change the whole atmosphere of the patio."

The waiter returns to their table. He asks if they want dessert. Gary says, "No, thank you but I want to order two cups of coffee." The waiter serves the coffee with the bill.

They sip their coffee and enjoy a relaxed conversation. There are moments of silence as they appear to be lost in thought. When they're finished drinking their coffee, they agree to take a stroll through Angela's garden. They walk back to the convertible and drive home.

Sadie says, "If it's okay with you, I'd like to relax out on the terrace after I remove the decorations from the backyard."

Gary says, "I can help pick up the decorations. We can both sit and relax on the terrace. It's a beautiful night. I'm going to wait up for Jonny for a few minutes longer."

They sit down on lounge chairs after they pack up and store the decorations. The chilly evening breeze spoils their chance to relax. She says goodnight to Gary. They wish each other "sweet dreams". Sadie walks over to her house. Gary walks to the living room to rest in his recliner. He waits for Jon to return home.

Jonny and Mandy drove out to the lake house after work. He wanted to talk to her about personal things. He really felt that the lake was a beautiful setting for them to enjoy the evening. They stopped along the way to buy picnic food, supplies and swimming suits. He finally had a chance to play on the rope swing with Mandy. They laughed and played in the lake before eating their picnic at the table by the lake.

Now, they're sitting on the two-seater swing and sway while they talk. Jonny feels nervous about being here again and reliving the sad memory of his accident. He tries to put that out of his mind and focus on Mandy. They hold hands and cuddle while they sway in the swing.

Jonny says, "Mandy, there's a lot on my mind that I want to talk about. It has to do with our future plans. Would you be willing to hear me out and give me feedback?"

"Yes, of course, there's a lot on my mind, too. Lots of emotions are stirred up inside after our visit at the office today."

Jonny says, "I hope you know that I'm in love with you. I don't want to cause you to feel any pressure about us. I want you to know that I think a lot about our future. Where our personal lives are concerned, how will working close with you every day affect our relationship? I often think about this but I don't want to live without you. That's how much I love you."

Mandy says, "We don't want to rush things in our relationship. Are you thinking that if we were to marry, that working together all day might affect our home life? That question has crossed my mind a few times, too. I don't have an answer for it."

Jonny says, "We spent time at the office together and then we came out here after work to spend time together. I think about how that might be when we start working full time together. I hope that you'll be okay with our personal relationship apart from the office. I'd like to make it work. I really do love you and hope that I can make you happy."

Mandy says, "I'm happy so far. I enjoy working with you. I always feel happy to be around you at the office. I'm happy sitting here with you right now."

Jonny pulls a small box from his pocket. He hands it to Mandy and says, "I want you to be my beautiful lady always. Will you accept this friendship ring from me to show the world that you're MY sweet love?"

Her face lights up and with great joy she says, "Yes, Jonny, I'm very much in love with you. I'm thrilled to show the world that I'm taken by you." She leans in to kiss him. They share several sweet loving kisses.

He removes the ring from the box and slips it on her ring finger. She holds her hand out to admire it. She says, "Thank you, Jonny I love it! I'll always cherish it."

"I'm glad that we were able to have this special moment while sitting on our swing. It's where we first declared our love for each other."

Mandy says, "There's something else that I want to ask you. When we were talking about your Dad's retirement date today, I thought maybe we should plan a celebration for him. Can we talk about planning it soon? We need to make reservations and put an invitation list together."

"Sure that's a wonderful idea. I'm glad you thought about that. Yes, let's talk about it real soon. I'd like to just focus on my time here with you right now."

He leans in to kiss her and they kiss again. The temperature has cooled down a lot because of the breeze off the water. They agree that they should leave there. They came from downtown in their own cars. They kiss goodnight and hug each other tight. He asks her to call him when she arrives at her apartment. She agrees! They get into their cars and drive their separate ways.

Jonny drives to his house and Mandy drives to her apartment.

He barely walks inside the front door when his cell phone rings. He answers it and hears Mandy's voice, "Hello, Jonny! I'm home safe."

"Hello, Mandy! I'm relieved to hear from you. I had a wonderful time with you today."

"Thank you again for my beautiful ring. I'm really tired. I'll say goodnight and sweet dreams. I love you! See you tomorrow."

"I'm really tired, too. Goodnight and sweet dreams. I love you! See you in the morning!"

His Dad is sitting in his recliner half asleep. Jonny quietly says, "Dad, I'm home. You look tired and sleepy. Do you want to go to bed now? It's been a long day and I'm ready for bed."

His Dad replies in a sleepy voice, "Yes, I was waiting up for you. I want to be sure that you're doing okay. Even though I know that your injuries are healed, I'm still a bit nervous about you driving tonight. I love and care for you very much! I'm glad you're home safe. Hope you had a good evening with Mandy. We can talk tomorrow at breakfast, okay?"

"Yes, I have good news to share with you. I'm going upstairs to my bedroom. I'll say goodnight to you. I love you, Dad! Sweet dreams."

"Yes, goodnight. I love you, too, Son! Sweet dreams to you, too. I'll be right up as soon as I turn off the lights."

EPILOGUE

The attorney arrived at Gary's office with the contracts and new will. The meeting was held at the conference table in Gary's office. This was a big important day. Jonny and Mandy were present and sat at the table while the papers were signed. Mandy was included because she's Jonny's assistant extraordinaire. Jonny hopes that Mandy will agree to marry him in the near future.

Gary has changed his will for Jonny to inherit full ownership of all of the businesses. His Dad officially turned over half of the businesses to Jonny. The moment that they signed the contracts, they officially became business partners. Jonny has the power to oversee and make major business decisions for his Dad. His Dad officially retired on June 23rd. Jonny moved into his Dad's office and took over his Dad's responsibilities. The transition is complete!

Jonny celebrated Father's Day with his Dad. He gave him a brand new king size set of luggage for his dream cruise. They traditionally play golf together on Father's Day. This time, they invited Katherine, Mandy, Sadie and Charlie to play golf with them. Afterward, they all enjoyed a Father's Day celebration at the lake house including Sadie's family.

Mandy and Jonny planned a big retirement celebration in the party room at the Imperial Inn. The restaurant catered delicious party food. Invitations were sent to a long list of family and friends. The list included both personal and business friends. Ted Harris and his family were at the top of the list. They all had a wonderful time.

Katherine and Gary visited with the travel agency. They were excited to learn about a cruise to Australia. They decided to wait until later in the year. They want to wait for the summer season there. Their first cruise destination was to Hawaii. They watched the 4th of July fireworks on the beach. They want to see the world but only one cruise at a time. They don't want to be away from their children for too long. They love them and want to maintain close relationships.

Katherine and Gary really care about each other. They enjoy a lot of fun family activities together. Katherine is still grieving the loss of Paul. Gary hopes in time that she'll be able to move on. He has tried to express his love and admiration to her. She's just not ready to make a commitment.

Sadie is happy with her living and work arrangement. She continues to work at the Young residence. She doesn't see them as often as she used to. When they meet at the big house for a meal or holiday, it's still a joyful time of family togetherness. She's happy to be there assisting Gary and Jonny when they return home. She likes taking care of them.

Charlie still comes around often to visit with Sadie. He keeps busy with his Pool Service business. They go out on dates on the weekends and talk on the phone. They really like each other. They enjoy spending time together. Time will tell.

Jonny and Mandy are deeply in love with each other. Their love grows more each day. When they're not at work, they make plans to do fun activities together. They love the lake house and enjoy outdoor activities at the lake. They spend a lot of time cuddling together on the swing. They talk about future plans every chance they get.

They're talking about setting up a foundation in Angela's name. They want to establish educational programs that teach kids about flowers and gardening in the community. There will be pink sweetheart roses growing on the property as soon as they find and purchase the perfect acreage.

In August, Jonny proposed to Mandy. He gave her a beautiful engagement ring. He was down on one knee while she sat in their swing at the lake house. She said, "YES!" She wants to wait for a spring time wedding. She suggested a date in May when the pink sweetheart roses bloom again. She wants to have an outdoor garden wedding. He's totally in agreement with her. He suggested Angela's pink rose garden in his Dad's huge backyard. They believe it'll be a perfect place for their wedding and reception. They have sufficient time to make plans before May of next year. There's time for their love to grow!

Like most Fairy Tales, they all live happily ever after... They all live where their Love Grows in Omaha!

ABOUT THE AUTHOR

I'm a wife, Mom of 3, Mom-in-law, Gramma to 7, sister, aunt, with cousins by the dozens. I love spending quality time with my family, friends & extended family. We currently reside in Nebraska.

My pen name, Lola, was created by merging the first two letters (LO) of my name with the first two letters (LA) of my husband's name. He is my proofreader, encouragement and support.

I've always loved WORDS! I appreciate puns, word games & creative writing. I've enjoyed writing original music with Christian lyrics, Christian poems and other poems in the past. This year, I felt overwhelmed with passion to write my first novel, 'Love Grows in Omaha'. I have hopes of writing sequels about the Young Family. My favorite stories are about love, family and commitment. I enjoy watching movies and reading books that are romantic comedies. I'm currently in the process of writing my 2nd novel which is also a love story.

My hobbies/interests include creating fun videos while singing Karaoke as a member of an online community, camping in our RV, picnics by the lake, baking, photography, creating art, listening to relaxation music and lots more. These hobbies help me cope with multiple health challenges on a daily basis. I'm also hearing and vision impaired.

My favorite flowers are pink sweetheart roses. I wish you all love, peace and joy!

Lola aka Lois

www.ingramcontent.com/pod-product-compliance
Lightning Source LLC
Chambersburg PA
CBHW061544170626
46811CB00001B/82